Other People's Pets

OTHER TITLES BY R.L. MAIZES

We Love Anderson Cooper: Short Stories

Other People's Pets

R.L. MAIZES

CELADON
BOOKS
NEW YORK

OTHER PEOPLE'S PETS. Copyright © 2020 by R.L. Maizes. All rights reserved. Printed in the United States of America. For information, address Celadon Books, a Division of Macmillan Publishers, 120 Broadway, New York, NY 10271.

www.celadonbooks.com

Library of Congress Cataloging-in-Publication Data

Names: Maizes, R.L., author.
Title: Other people's pets / R.L. Maizes.
Description: First edition. | New York, NY: Celadon Books, 2020.
Identifiers: LCCN 2020002701 | ISBN 9781250304131 (hardcover) |
    ISBN 9781250304124 (ebook)
Classification: LCC PS3613.A3527 O84 2020 | DDC 813/.6—dc23
LC record available at https://lccn.loc.gov/2020002701

Our books may be purchased in bulk for promotional, educational, or business use. Please contact your local bookseller or the Macmillan Corporate and Premium Sales Department at 1-800-221-7945, extension 5442, or by email at MacmillanSpecialMarkets@macmillan.com.

First Edition: 2020

10 9 8 7 6 5 4 3 2 1

For Steve
and
For All the Rescued Animals Who Rescue Us

Other People's Pets

Prologue

One minute, La La joins a flock of geese, skating across the lake as they fly overhead, and the next, *squeak, crack,* she plunges into darkness. Her snowsuit inhales icy water and clings to her, weighing her down and threatening to pull her under. Though she tries to tread water, her skates are too heavy. She opens her mouth to scream, and the lake rushes down her throat. Just when she thinks she'll drown, she sees her mother. "Mama," she gurgles. But the woman who calls herself Mother turns and skates away. Frigid black water tugs at La La's ankles, pours concrete into her muscles. She goes under.

Still and cold, it's the loneliest place she's ever been. Too dark to see anything that might thrive there. Perfectly silent until the sharp bark of a dog cuts through the water, summoning her back. Maybe help has arrived. Remembering swim lessons her father gave her, La La gathers her strength and frog-kicks to the surface. Ten feet away, a black dog awaits her. She swims toward him, reaching the edge of the hole in the ice. Hands on the white mass, she pushes as hard as she can but can't raise herself. She frog-kicks again, desperate to stay above water. The dog howls. Urged on by the animal and no longer alone, she presses her arms against the surface of the ice but lacks the strength to lift herself out.

Exhausted, the cold stiffening her muscles, she waits to sink again. But this time, she doesn't go under. The arms of her jacket have frozen to the ice. That's all she remembers.

Later she learns: a man and woman arrived to skate. They found the dog keeping watch, La La unconscious, attached to the ice. On her cell phone, the woman called emergency services, who rescued La La. The dog bounded into the woods before anyone could reward him. No one knew whose dog he was or where he had come from. It wasn't until La La was being loaded into an ambulance that her mother returned. She had gone to get help, she said.

From under warm covers the next morning, La La hears a dove coo-coo to its mate. The bird's heart thrums with excitement. When her own pulse takes up the beat, La La doesn't know what to make of it.

1

In Exam Room 4, La La rubs the silky muzzle of a Labrador retriever named Duck. A woman who looks to be in her thirties pales as she points out a lump on the Labrador's side, but focusing on the dog, La La barely notices the owner's anxiety. She takes a history and performs an exam. Soft and moveable, the growth is probably a harmless lipoma.

"What do you think?" the woman says.

La La knows better than to offer a diagnosis before the resident has seen the patient. "I'll get the doctor."

With a twenty-two-gauge hypodermic needle, Dr. Mun extracts cells from the lump. Though nowhere near the tip, La La feels the prick as it goes in. The doctor shows her the cells under a microscope, then gives the owner the good news. It's a benign fatty tumor, just as La La suspected.

Pleased to give the dog a reprieve, La La remembers why she loves her work, even the general practice rotation, which others find dull. Her exhaustion from working twelve-hour days fades.

Color returns to the owner's face. "I don't know how to thank you both."

"We're glad to help," Dr. Mun says. When La La is silent, the doctor clears her throat. She turns to La La expectantly.

"Glad to help," La La parrots, already thinking about her next patient.

An hour later, La La prepares to place an IV in a border collie's cephalic vein. The dog must have eaten peanut butter biscuits in the waiting room. They make La La's tongue feel sticky and thick. She shaves a spot on the dog's front leg and scrubs the site with alcohol and chlorhexidine before inserting the needle. She can hardly believe in less than a year she'll be graduating and seeing patients of her own. When the phone in her pocket goes off, it isn't the ringtone for her fiancé, Clem ("Doctor, Doctor, Give Me the News"), or her father, Zev ("Run, Daddy, Run"), so she puts it out of her mind.

Treating a nervous, aging poodle, La La scratches above the dog's heart and feels a pleasurable ache in her own chest. "You're a champ, Gordie," she says, after drawing his blood, but the dog doesn't look at her or otherwise seem to hear.

She walks the poodle to the waiting room, where a man in a navy suit reaches for the leash. "He never greets me at the door anymore," he says, his voice quavering.

"He's not a butler," La La mutters.

"Excuse me?"

"Could be his hearing. He is an older dog."

In the break room, a tofu and avocado sandwich in one hand, La La finally taps the phone message. Hearing John O'Bannon's voice, she stops chewing. O'Bannon is an attorney who represented Zev and La La in a burglary case when she was a teenager.

"Sorry to tell you this," he says. "Your dad was arrested. Bail hearing is tomorrow at ten. Why don't you stop by this afternoon? I'm still at 329 Carson, second floor."

La La's throat tightens around a lump of bread. She taps the message again. At the word "arrested," she squeezes the sandwich, her fingers punching through the whole-grain bread. Zev can't go to prison. He's the only parent she has left; she can't afford to lose him. The sandwich falls apart, avocado streaking the industrial tabletop. Gathering the pieces, she stumbles to the trash and drops them in. She e-mails Dr. Mun that a family emergency has come up and she'll be out that afternoon. She would tell the resident in person but doesn't trust herself to speak.

"They're charging him with burglary," O'Bannon says. The lawyer has aged. His cheeks sag. The pores on his nose are big enough to house a fly. "I'll need a ten-thousand-dollar retainer. But it's going to cost a lot more than that before it's over." Sloppy piles of official-looking papers rise on his desktop. Crime is as popular as ever.

La La's knee bounces. She wishes O'Bannon brought a dog to work, the kind to lay its muzzle in your lap. "What did Zev say he could give you?"

"When he heard the DA was asking to set bail at fifty thousand dollars because a victim was in the hospital, Zev said he'd have to rely on a public defender. He can barely scrape together the seventy-five-hundred-dollar fee for the bail bondsman."

La La isn't surprised. What little extra money Zev had, he gave her to help with veterinary school tuition. Though she can't afford to pay O'Bannon, either, she hates to turn the case over to a public defender. As a teenager, she watched them in the court-room while she waited for her own burglary case to be called. They leafed through client files as though they'd never seen them before.

She would ask Clem for the money, but he disapproves of Zev's occupation, and besides, what he earns as a chiropractor barely covers their bills. There was a time she would have raised the money herself, breaking into the homes of the wealthy—some people have more than they need, more than anyone should—but she promised Clem she was finished with that. La La thinks briefly of her mother. She has no idea where Elissa is or if she'd be willing to help. "Give us a few days to figure something out."

The lawyer drums his fingers on his lips. "I suppose that would be okay."

As La La gets up to leave, she sees, on O'Bannon's desk, a studio photograph of a harried woman and three robust boys. It's a different family than the one he used to have. Round two, she presumes. Or perhaps the boys are his stepchildren, cared for by a host of mothers and fathers.

Growing up, La La had only Zev. Her mother disappeared when La La was eight. Four years later, La La buried a pair of white cotton underwear at the bottom of the hamper because a constellation of mysterious brown stains convinced her she had an accident. Discovering the panties, Zev said, "You're a woman now. No need to be ashamed." Though it was ten at night, he drove to a supermarket and bought sanitary pads. Returning home, he bleached the underwear.

The next day, Zev arranged fruit—two lemons, an avocado, and loose purple grapes—on a table and demonstrated how a woman's reproductive system worked. "Pretty clever design," he said. He told La La it was one of the few things his mother had taught him in case he had a daughter. After Zev walked La La through two monthly cycles, they ate the grapes, and Zev made guacamole. "If you have cramps we can warm up a hot water bottle," he said, while he mixed the garlic and avocado.

La La scooped a dollop of guacamole onto a chip and opened her mouth. "Delicious uterus," she said, after she swallowed.

"Gourmet," Zev said.

When La La was thirteen, Zev accompanied her to a department store to buy her first bra. "Treat her nice," he said to a salesclerk, slipping the woman a twenty.

"That's my job, sir," the clerk said, but she stuck the folded bill down the front of her shirt and brought half a dozen bras to La La in a communal dressing room. La La faced a corner while taking off her shirt. She slipped her arms through a bra and struggled to hook the back.

"Here, let me do that for you," the woman said. She yanked the clasp closed, then turned La La around and tugged on the bra straps to adjust them. Her fingers were clammy. La La selected two bras just so she wouldn't have to feel the woman's hands on her again.

As she rode home with her father, she kept her eyes on the department store bag in her lap. She wondered what it would have been like to shop with Elissa, instead. Her mother's absence, familiar and heavy, squeezed the air from her lungs.

Zev caressed the back of her head with his hand. As if reading her mind, he said, "Not many fathers get to help their girls buy their first bras."

La La clutched the top of the bag, trying to keep from crying. "You didn't help me. That woman did."

"I guess she wasn't your first choice."

"No."

"Sorry about that."

"It doesn't matter," La La said.

"It matters."

The bag slid off her lap. Zev took her hand, and she let him, just that once.

Years afterward, when La La was in high school, Zev pleaded guilty to a burglary they committed together, so that the charges against La La would be dropped. Never mind that it had been La La's fault they were caught.

He was never exactly a candidate for father of the year, raising her to be a burglar, homeschooling her, and isolating her from other kids, but she can't afford to think about all that now.

The next morning, Friday, La La e-mails Dr. Mun that she'll be out again. By mid-afternoon, a bail bondsman has pledged to pay Zev's bail if he fails to appear in court, and Zev is back in his house. La La pulls up in her Honda and pauses before exiting the car, collecting herself. A dinged-up van with the equipment Zev needs for household rekeys and installations parks in front of the house, HONESTY LOCKSMITH splashed across the side. Between that and his illegal work, Zev eked out a living, though they had never had the kinds of possessions they saw in homes they robbed, designer goods that didn't come from discount stores.

Topped with a coating of Colorado snow, rosebushes line the flagstone path to the front door of the three-bedroom ranch house. Elissa had cultivated and pruned the flowers every spring, but now they grow wild. Long, barbed branches shoot out in every direction, taller than La La or her father. No longer fertilized, they nevertheless remain hardy. La La has begged Zev to trim them, has even offered to do it herself, but he won't hear of it. What she really wants is to dig them up, fill the holes with fresh earth, and forget about them, though she knows that would be impossible. If they were gone, she would search for traces of them, stubborn tendrils winding out of the earth.

A fresh scratch from the thorns always marks Zev's face. In the summer, deep cuts fester yellow and green on his exposed arms and legs. He isn't lazy. He paints the house every five years, dragging out ladder and drop cloths, mixing the same colors, maroon with white trim. But the bushes are a monument to his wife's treachery, never to be tampered with. Like the flower box that dangles vertically from a single nail. Zev stuffed it with geraniums every Mother's Day, when they still observed the holiday instead of ignoring it, boycotting TV and radio with their endless barrage of ads. The soil in the box has hardened to chalk.

La La circles around to the back door, avoiding the bushes. Her childhood dog, Tiny, died seven years ago, but La La still remembers how he'd come bounding toward her. He escaped from the house and was struck by a car while she was in college in Wisconsin. As La La sat in a biology lecture, pain jabbed her spine, so sharp she passed out. She woke on the floor minutes later, her body numb. When Zev called, she was in student health services. "I got him to Dr. Bergman as fast as I could," he said, adding after a while, "I'm sorry." La La wouldn't ordinarily experience the trauma of a creature a thousand miles away, but she wasn't as attached to other animals.

Oiled and polished, her father's collection of locks shines on the fireplace mantel and dozens of curio shelves. Antique and state-of-the-art padlocks, dead bolts—single cylinder and double cylinder—knob locks, lever-handle locks, cam locks, mortise locks, wall-mounted locks, furniture locks, vending machine locks, jimmy-proof dead bolts, rim-latch locks, key-in-knob cylinders, Berlin-key locks, disc-tumbler locks, combination locks, and more. Zev has disassembled the locks and reassembled them. When La La was ten, he began teaching her to pick them. It was a skill they practiced infrequently when they robbed homes. Usually it was faster to pry open a door or smash a window.

Mo, a seventeen-year-old cat with brindle fur and a flat, round face, curls up on the back of the sofa. When La La rubs the underside of the animal's chin, her own skin tingles and her throat hums. But as Mo adjusts herself, La La's elbows and shoulders begin to throb. "Are you giving her the tramadol?" she asks her father as he enters the room.

Zev resents the question. He's taken care of La La, after all. "You think I'd let her suffer?" His daughter's stubby, efficient fingers work Mo's joints. Her spruce-colored eyes shine, though they often seem dull when she regards people.

He takes her puffy coat, a chill clinging to the outside and La La's industrious scent—salty and medicinal—emanating from the inside, and he hangs it in the closet. Father and daughter settle on the couch, the beige cotton fabric pilled and threadbare. When she sits back, La La's sneaker-clad feet barely brush the carpet.

A fat ankle monitor pushes up the bottom of Zev's clean blue sweatpants. The DA successfully argued for home confinement as a condition of bail. Zev stabs a padlock with a slender pick, his fingers moving nimbly over the metal.

"What happened?" La La asks.

"Started like a thousand other jobs," Zev says. The lock pops open with a *click*, a sound that gives him pleasure and satisfaction even in the midst of his troubles. "Big house. Fresh paint. They take care of the outside, there's good stuff on the inside. I'd seen an RV there, but it was gone, so I figured they were on vacation. But I was still careful. I rang the bell a million times." Zev squeezes the shackle closed and goes to work on the lock again, telling La La how he jimmied the back door. "It was quiet inside. First thing I see is a painting of an old lady. She's giving me the evil eye. Should've known then the place was trouble. But I was sure I was gonna get a good haul. I grabbed the silver. A block of cash from the back of the freezer. Might as well tie a bow around it, but I'm not complaining. I thought about leaving then, but your tuition was due. I hate for you to take out all those loans."

"It's what everyone does," La La says, but Zev ignores her.

"I started up the stairs. Next thing I know, an old man is at the top. Guy's yelling. He sounds drunk. Must have been hard of hearing or something to miss the bell. Something's wrong with him. His face droops. He tries to grab the banister and falls halfway down the stairs." Zev's hands freeze. He stares at the lock, which remains closed, then looks up at La La, as if she can explain how things went so terribly wrong in the house.

She would give anything to change the end of the story, which O'Bannon told her, but all she can do is listen until he comes to it.

"I knew I should get out of there. But I couldn't. Not without calling nine-one-one. I'm not a murderer. I just wanted to rob the guy." He describes how he pulled out his cell phone, then remembered he removes the battery when he's working to prevent the police from tracking him. "I called from the guy's phone in the kitchen. Just dialed and left the phone off the hook so they wouldn't get a recording of my voice. Then I ran.

"Driving home, I felt good. I was glad I called. I figured the dispatcher would see the address of the house on his screen. He'd send someone and the old man would be okay."

Zev rests the lock and pick on the polished coffee table. "Didn't realize until I got home that I left my phone on the guy's counter." He takes his head in his hands, clutching the short, gray hair.

According to O'Bannon, the police traced the phone to Zev. Claude Thomas, the old man, had a stroke. The EMTs got him to the hospital in time to save his life, but he was in a coma, on life support. The DA was threatening to charge Zev with murder if he died.

"I got rid of the crowbar and the silver before the police searched the house."

Pinching her worn cotton shirt—an old one of Clem's that swallows her—away from her chest, La La fans herself with it. She should have stopped taking Zev's money a long time ago. But until yesterday, she believed he owed it to her. "I could pay O'Bannon."

Zev disappears into the kitchen. "Oh, yeah. How would you manage that?" he calls. Cabinets open and close, and he returns with a jar of metal polish, a rag, and a newspaper.

"The same way you would, if you weren't stuck in the house."

He spreads the newspaper on the coffee table. "Nope. No way. You have to finish school." Dipping the rag into the polish, he goes to work on the lock though the steel already gleams.

La La lifts Mo onto her lap and strokes the cat's belly. "If a public defender represents you, you'll end up in prison."

"I'll end up in prison no matter what."

"You saved the guy's life. O'Bannon will make the DA see that. He'll get you probation."

Zev lifts the rag from the metal. "He said that?"

"No."

He polishes the shackle. "I'm your father. I take care of you. You don't take care of me." He rubs the lock so hard, La La expects the rag to tear. "I'll see if I can get a loan on the house," Zev says.

La La sinks back into the cushions, relieved to keep her own ambitions alive, so close to fulfillment she smells sterile wipes when she breathes. She'll return to the veterinary hospital on Monday as if no call ever came from O'Bannon.

As Zev pads into the kitchen, one white tube sock bunched below the ankle monitor, the other pulled taut, La La eases Mo from her lap and follows. She heads for the chair that has always been hers, the one pressed against the far wall and too close to the table. Its rubber-tipped metal legs have erased the star pattern in the linoleum. The vinyl seat cover is cracked. She sucks in her abdomen and slides in.

On the side of the yellowing refrigerator, below photos of her college graduation, hangs a castle La La drew in first grade. Gray crayon for the stones; blue for the moat; her mother looming over the turrets, a giant stick figure with brown hair; her father holding La La's hand. She wonders for the hundredth time why Zev never packed it away.

Zev stores the polish and scrubs his hands. A pot of coffee is warming, and he pours a cup, sprinkling cinnamon on top. He adds a spoonful of Nestlé's, stirs, and hands the cup to La La. Inhaling the rich smell, she takes a sip. "Little-known fact," Zev says, "I invented the mocha latte. Starbucks stole it from me."

"Maybe we ought to report the theft."

Zev smiles, and La La is glad that despite everything, he still has a sense of humor.

"All I had to do to get a visit from you was to get arrested," he says. "If I had known that, I would have walked into the precinct years ago."

It's been weeks since she's seen him. Veterinary school keeps her busy. She warms her hands on the ceramic mug, whose fading decal reads WORLD'S BEST DAD. When she was ten, he suggested she buy it for him at a mall, and she did, though she was already becoming skeptical, wondering what her life would have been like if he'd just stuck to locksmithing.

His sweatshirt smells of laundry detergent. The floor reflects a muted shine. "Stay for dinner," he says, as he wipes the counter.

"Sorry, I can't." She's looking forward to eating with Clem and to pretending for a few hours that her life is normal.

"I guess the quack expects you."

"Don't call him that."

"Why not? He pretends to be a doctor."

"People choose to see him. They're not always as happy to get a visit from you." La La stands up and sets her cup in the sink.

"Even the people I rob need me," Zev says, washing the mug. "I teach them about impermanence."

"Where'd you pick that up? Some new-age magazine?"

"Maybe." He dries the cup.

"I'm sure whatever you read didn't suggest stealing other people's stuff."

Taking out a broom, Zev sweeps the pristine floor. "Not exactly."

He hands La La a dustpan. She lowers it, catching the invisible dirt Zev pushes into it, going through the motions of emptying it into the trash. "I have to get home."

"You used to call this home."

She buttons her coat.

"You're always welcome back. If it doesn't work out with the quack."

Annoyed, she embraces him loosely and returns to her car.

When his daughter is gone, Zev sits on the couch and lifts his right foot onto his left knee to get a better look at the monitor that transmits GPS data so the authorities can tell if he's left the house. A fiberoptic beam runs through the length of the strap that secures it to his ankle. Cutting the strap would sever the beam, setting off an alarm at the monitoring company. The device makes his skin itch. He pushes his fingers beneath the too-tight band, trying to scratch. The officer at the jail, sadistic son of a bitch, laughed as he fastened it.

As he lowers his foot to the floor, Zev says to Mo, "We got ourselves into a mess this time." The cat is asleep on the back of the couch. She blinks, then throws a paw over her face. "Believe me, I'd rather ignore the whole disaster, too."

Mo whistles in her sleep, the only sound in the too-quiet house. Grabbing the remote control, Zev flips to a *Sopranos* rerun, one of the early episodes, where Tony's on his way up.

In the car, La La's cell phone plays "Honky Cat," the ringtone for Dr. Bergman. She lets it go to voice mail. As their family vet, Dr. Bergman taught La La how to care for Tiny and Mo. He was the first to recognize her empathic connection to animals, even before she understood it herself. Without his encouragement, she might not have gone to veterinary school. Now and then he checks to see how she's doing and to ask about interesting cases she's following. She doesn't know how to tell him about Zev.

Ash trees with grim, leafless crowns, and tent-like blue spruce line roads streaked with tar, temporary fixes for cracks that constantly widen. In the west, the Rocky Mountains jab the sky. East the land is flat for hundreds of miles, to the Colorado border and beyond to Kansas. Longview is a town in transition. Cows feed in the shadows of packed residential developments. It takes La La ten minutes to reach the one-bedroom bungalow she shares with Clem.

When she opens the door, Blue, a cattle dog mix with one cerulean eye and one brown, clambers up her side. Trampled by a horse, he lost a hind leg and the ability to herd sheep, and the farmer who raised him abandoned him. *As if he were a broken tiller or a worn-out plow,* La La thought when she learned what happened. Blue steals—socks, belts, keys, Clem's wallet, untended food—burying the items under piles of snow in the yard or beneath sofa cushions. Her other dog, Black, is so excited to see her, he spins. Feeling dizzy, La La reaches a hand to the wall to steady herself. Black is part Labrador retriever with a short snout that turns up like a pig's.

Three and a half years earlier, right after La La and Clem moved into the house with a yard, they visited the shelter. In the crowded facility, barks ricocheted off gray cinder-block walls. La La stiffened. Growls rumbled in her throat. Longing for families who deserted them, the dogs whined, and La La's eyes burned.

She imagined locking their former owners in the kennels to show them what it was like.

Black and Blue were caged together, their water dish upended, soaking a frayed orange blanket. Blue gnawed Black's neck, the two as comfortable as littermates. La La wouldn't be the one to separate them. Paperwork showed how long they'd been waiting for homes: Blue seven months and Black, a stray whose muzzle had whitened with age, an astonishing three years. La La wasn't blind. With his square head, patches of fur lost to mange, and pig-like snout, Black was ugly. He also seemed familiar, an older version of the dog that had called her back from the lake. Yet dogs his size generally didn't live that long. If she felt drawn to him, it was probably only because she viewed herself as a kind of stray.

"He'd frighten children. Don't you think?" Clem said.

"Then I guess it's a good thing we don't have any." From the start, La La had told Clem she didn't want kids. Elissa had demonstrated that parenting could be a form of cruelty. Zev had done the best he could but still put her in harm's way. When La La imagined her future with Clem, which she often did, it was in a house overrun with animals. As she kneeled and reached through the bars, something in Black stirred, and he inched toward her, reinforcing a decision La La had already made.

"If we don't take him, who will?" La La said, looking up at Clem. "They're good dogs." He knew about her connection to animals.

Clem reached into a basket of treats kept next to the kennel and fed one to each of the dogs. "She rescued me, too," he said to them.

In the shelter's store, they spent more than they could afford on food, leashes, and toys. The shelter manager was so delighted that Black had found a home, he offered to forgo the dog's adoption fee. La La waved aside the suggestion, never wanting Black to feel any less valuable than Blue, or that he'd been obtained at a discount.

As she contemplates Zev's predicament, La La sits on her living room floor and buries her face in Black's neck, savoring the smells of dust and fur and the oils that waterproof his coat. Blue is on to his next adventure, restless energy driving him from one end of the house to the other. She loves them both, but Black is the one she turns to for comfort. With his heart beating alongside hers, she briefly forgets the upheaval of the last twenty-four hours. When she kisses his ear, he gives his head a vigorous shake.

On her way into the kitchen to prepare dinner, she passes a photograph of the Sangre de Cristo Mountains, hanging above the dogs' toy basket. When Elissa used to describe traveling through the Southwest after college, her voice floated up and her eyes lifted toward the ceiling. The only other time her mother seemed that happy was talking about her work as a behaviorist with shelter animals. Instructing La La to get ready for school or to take a bath, her speech was clipped and low.

La La tosses each dog a toy and pours herself a glass of red wine. She sautés mushrooms and chops salad.

When Clem gets home, dinner is ready. Distracted, La La overcooked the spaghetti and burned the roasted garlic and mushroom sauce. Hearing him take off his boots in the entryway, she rolls her shoulders, trying to release some of the day's tension.

In the kitchen, he leans over and kisses her. Wraps her feathery brown hair around her ears. La La drops her forehead to his chest and closes her eyes.

"Everything okay?" he says. "You're home early."

"Clinic was slow." She's not sure why she's lying. She isn't the one who got arrested. When Clem plucks a piece of cucumber from the salad, La La slides the bowl beyond his reach.

"Rosalyn Baylor stopped in," he says. "Brought me a piece of pecan pie. Nice of her, wasn't it?" He has a habit of turning statements into questions, a quality La La finds endearing because its effect is to include her in even the most mundane matters. "And Judge Macy had an appointment. I'm always afraid he'll find a reason to sue me."

I know a good lawyer, La La thinks.

While La La tosses the spaghetti, Clem massages her shoulders. "Let's go to Florida for Christmas," he says. "Surprise my parents. What do you think?"

"I'm helping Dr. Roeder with clinical trials." La La's face is hot, and not from the steaming pasta. She finished her work with Dr. Roeder. But she can't leave town as long as Zev is trapped in his house.

"Too bad. My mom is always saying how she'd like to get to know you better."

"I'm your elusive fiancée."

He brushes aside her hair and nuzzles her neck. "You don't feel elusive."

La La met Clem when she was a junior at the University of Wisconsin, and he was starting out as a chiropractor. His office was in an old Victorian next to the clinic where she worked part time as a veterinary technician. As she left after her shift one day, he was outside the house, a tall man with cropped, curly brown hair and a beard. He dug into the pockets of his overcoat and pants, patted his shirt, then tried the door, rattling the knob without success. He reminded her of a bear that had tried to break into a locked dumpster behind a restaurant back home.

"Problem?" she asked, approaching him. She wasn't in the habit of talking to strangers, but she was pretty sure she could help.

"Can't find my keys. Thought I had them. Pretty lame, right?" He raked his fingers through his beard. Then tried his pockets again.

"I might be able to open it, but you'll have to show me your license."

"Why's that?"

"I want to make sure that's your name on the sign." La La looked back toward the clinic, concerned she was revealing too much.

"Are you a vet? The clinic seems to get quieter when you go in."

"I haven't noticed. And I'm just a vet tech."

"I don't know why I said that about the clinic. Crazy." He pulled out his wallet and flashed his license. Satisfied, she slipped her plastic student ID between the door and the frame, and jiggled it. The door swung open.

Clem raised his eyebrows.

"Party trick," she said. "You're welcome. You should think about installing a dead bolt."

"What's your name?"

"Louise, but people call me La La." She was six when she overheard Zev tell someone on the phone the story behind her nickname. "When La La was a baby, she would lie in her crib singing 'La La La, La La La,' a fat smile on her face. One afternoon, Elissa complained, 'Miss La La won't shut up.' The name stuck."

La La found it hard to believe she had ever been that happy, and the frivolous name didn't suit her. She was reluctant to change it, though, because it was one of the few things her mother had given her.

"I'm Clement, but I guess you already know that. Call me Clem." He dropped his ear to his shoulder, stretching his neck, before putting away his wallet. "Can I take you out to dinner tonight? You saved me. I have a client coming in five minutes."

La La had never been on a date. Her first two years of college, she hadn't made a single friend. Her classmates spoke a foreign language of small talk and teasing, bands and books La La had never heard of. What would she talk about on a date? Her father's work? Her mother's absence? "I have to study."

"How about tomorrow night?"

"I don't think so."

His fingers combed through his beard again. "I get it. No date. That's too bad. There's a new organic steak house we could have gone to."

La La cringed. "I don't eat animal flesh," she said, and then wished she'd used the word "meat" instead. She didn't want to alienate Clem, who was attractive in a scruffy sort of way. She might enjoy sharing a meal with another person sometime.

He looked down at his Rockports. "This isn't going very well. Is it?"

La La changed her mind, perhaps because he reminded her of the bear. "We could go to Serendipity." A dog awash in relief padded away from the veterinary clinic with its owner. "It's an organic vegetarian place."

"Great. Pick you up at seven?"

"I'll meet you there." If the date went badly, La La didn't want him to know where she lived.

Back in her dorm room, she realized she had nothing to wear. Her clothes were worn and practical, ragged jeans and scrubs, clogs and sneakers. When she told her roommate, Althea, that she had a date, the girl let her borrow a black velvet dress and stilettos. She even offered to do La La's makeup.

"This shadow brings out the ocean colors in your eyes," the art major said, stepping back to admire her work. "The liner," she explained, as she held up the pencil, "will give your mouth shape." Looking in the mirror, La La compared her own lips, which were the color of earthworms and only slightly thicker, to her roommate's red, heart-shaped mouth.

La La's loose clothes hid her small breasts, but the dress showed them off. She couldn't walk in the three-inch spikes, so Althea found her a pair of wedge heels. When La La was ready for her date, she glanced in the mirror again and blanched. She looked like Elissa.

"Wow," Clem said, when La La took off her coat in the restaurant.

She looked down, as if she'd forgotten the effort she'd gone to. "These clothes wouldn't cut it in the clinic. I'd get blood on the dress when I assisted in surgery and trip over Simon, the cat who runs the place."

"You look nice in your scrubs, too. You seem happy in them."

"I'm happy around animals."

"Just animals?"

"Let's grab a table," she said.

Artsy photographs of vegetables—a giant radish, a wet head of romaine, chopped peppers—brightened the walls. Their table wobbled. A waiter took Clem's order for a bottle of imported beer. La La said she'd have the same. At the salad bar, they filled their plates.

Clem spilled dressing on his shirt and dropped his knife. La La didn't know what to make of his sudden clumsiness. Searching for something to talk about, she discovered they shared an interest in anatomy.

"A dog has one-third more bones than a human," La La said, drawing a cartoon skeleton in the condensation on her glass. "Isn't that surprising? Humans have two hundred six bones, while dogs have approximately three hundred twenty. Just one way dogs are more complicated."

Using both hands, Clem manipulated his neck, releasing a loud crack. "I wouldn't want to work on a dog. It's challenging enough to adjust humans."

"And most people are clueless about how dogs feel."

"Most people?"

Revealing her empathic abilities had caused trouble for La La in the past. She'd been fired from her job at a clinic when a veterinarian heard her mention that a drug he prescribed was making a dog paranoid. College classmates demanded to know what she had smoked when she argued the solitary rabbit one of them kept was lonely. To protect herself, she'd learned to refer to how animals feel only in the most general way. "A dog's pain threshold is very high. Unless you're used to treating them, it can be hard to read. Their genetic makeup," she said, changing the subject, "is more complicated, too. Humans have twenty-three pairs of chromosomes to a dog's thirty-nine. People think humans are number one at everything. It's ridiculous, because dogs have us beat in so many ways. I'd like to see a person sniff a jacket and track

its owner. Or predict that a person is about to have a seizure."
The family at the next table had fallen silent and glanced at the
young woman making a speech, but La La wasn't finished. "Not
to mention how loyal dogs are, which is more than I can say for
some people."

When Clem put a finger to his lips, shushing her, La La wanted
to slug him.

"You're pretty passionate about animals, aren't you?" he said,
smoothing the tablecloth.

La La sipped her beer, smudging the images on the glass. If he
wanted quiet, he could have it.

"You have a calling. I envy you." He pushed a piece of lettuce
around on his plate.

"Don't you feel that way about being a chiropractor?"

"My dad's a surgeon. Both of my brothers are doctors. My
parents expected me to be one, too, but I flunked out of organic
chemistry. Twice. People think what I do is bogus, don't they?"
He tore a roll in half, then seemed to lose interest and dropped
both pieces on his plate. "Technically, I'm a doctor, you know."

"I don't think what you do is bogus," La La said.

"Well, it isn't."

After the waiter cleared the table, Clem took La La's hand.
Warmth rolled through her fingers into the crook of her arm,
traveled from there like a small brush fire to her belly.

Examining a long scar above her knuckles, he asked, "How'd
you get that?"

She rubbed the skin as if she could erase the jagged mark. "I
wasn't careful with a surgical instrument." She remembered the
first time Zev had let her break a window, glass shattering and
blood pooling on a veneer floor.

After Clem paid the bill, they walked around the college town, his long arm around her small, square waist. La La leaned into him, surprised at how good it felt to be held, even by someone she hardly knew. Outside a falafel joint, she nodded to students she recognized from class, and they looked Clem over and smiled, as though at unexpected good news. Though she didn't let on, no one was more shocked to find her on a date than La La herself.

When they got back to his car, Clem pressed her against the metal door and brushed his lips against hers, his breath coming in warm, doughy puffs. His beard was infused with the bright smell of a citrus styling cream. He towered over her, and even through his coat, she could feel how strong he was. She liked the sensation of being trapped. Others in her life had held her too loosely or not at all. His heat contrasted with the frigid door, and she pulled him closer, his beard chafing her chin. Desire raised a tumult in her body. His tongue swept her lips, her teeth. La La pressed hard against his mouth.

After a while they separated, the force of her desire rattling La La. Clem reached for his car keys, but they weren't in his pocket. "Maybe I left them on the table."

"What's with you and keys?"

"I wanted to see if you had a trick for opening car doors, too."

"I don't," she said, though she could use a wedge, a wire hanger, and a slim jim, and could sometimes break in through the trunk.

Clem washes the spaghetti pot, and La La dries. Preparing to take the dogs out, Clem dresses Black in a sweater because lately the dog gets cold. He helps La La on with her coat, then wraps his arms around her. She leans into him, feeling his rib cage and the tendons in his arms, and they remain that way until Blue begins to whine. Outside, the dogs race from one scent to another—coyote scat, a field mouse burrowing under the snow, a yellow hamburger wrapper—pulling the humans along. The air is crisp and fresh, and La La imagines it washing away the day's corruption. If she focuses on the dogs more than she does on Clem, he doesn't seem to notice.

She and Clem have a good life. They rarely fight, and when they do, the sex is rough and inspired after, and lasts till nearly morning. They like the same TV shows—reruns of *Grey's Anatomy* and *House*—and the same classic country music. Clem has agreed not to eat meat in the house and La La looks the other way in restaurants. He listens when she talks about her work in the clinic, and if it bothers him that she never asks about his clients, he doesn't mention it.

They furnished their house with a castoff sofa; an overstuffed chair, velvet worn in the center of the cushion; bookshelves and a desk they found on Freecycle; a scratched oak kitchen table from the Salvation Army. The used items gave the place a lived-in feel and a bedbug problem. La La hated to call an exterminator—insect life was life, too—but Clem pleaded with her and she gave in. She'd had the same problem deworming puppies, but in the end, she couldn't avoid it if she wanted to be a vet. "Try to live a perfect life, you'll live no life at all," Dr. Bergman had counseled.

How far, La La wonders, can you stretch that logic before it breaks?

Clem clasps her gloved hand in his. "Thinking about school?"

"Something like that."

Black lies in the snow. Older than Blue, he tires faster, despite having a complete set of limbs. Lifting the fifty-pound dog to his chest, Clem carries him back to the bungalow.

When they get home, Clem reads the new post on his *One of a Kind* blog to La La. The blog is supposed to be for unusual acts of kindness. Clem started it months before, telling La La he wanted to do something about the decline in civility he had noticed and how quick people were to anger. He hoped the posts would remind people of their better nature. Like the one from last May about a woman who sacrificed her chance to win a marathon, carrying her exhausted friend across the finish line. And the story a month later about a man who intervened in an assault, though he made himself a target. He's looking for heroes. But today's post is more like what he usually gets and not what he wants to highlight: a teenager in Denver helped a man carry groceries to his car. "With all these posts about groceries, a supermarket chain should sponsor me," he says. La La knows that despite Clem's disappointment, he'll reply, thanking the visitor for his inspiring message, though it will just give others the wrong idea about what the blog is for. He has only ninety-five followers. Often the same people write in. "I should shut the thing down. Don't you think?" he says, but he won't. He'll keep it up, hoping for more posts like those early ones.

On the bed later that night, television playing in the background, Clem unbuttons La La's shirt. She's as attracted to him as ever: his arms ripped from working on patients; the single crystal earring he never removes, a gift to himself—the only gift he received—upon graduating from chiropractic school. His chin sticks out like a fuzzy shelf. In her more devilish moments, La La wants to balance a biscuit there, the way she does on Black's snout, the dog waiting for the command to eat it. Clem knows her the way few others do, from her connection to animals to what her life was like growing up. Knows her and loves her anyway. And she doesn't have to worry about him getting picked up by the police.

He kisses a spot between her breasts. La La buries her fingers in his hair, but she's preoccupied. She slips off her clothes. Goose bumps rise on her skin, not from cold but apprehension. Though Clem prefers to see her face, La La turns toward the wall. She bends over the bed and guides him from behind.

"Hey, slow down." He kneels and grasps her thighs, turns her around, and presses his mouth to her. Desire wracks her body, but her mind is elsewhere, until he pierces her with his tongue and she gasps, forgetting about attorneys and prisons. He draws from her guttural sounds and shudders. When he rises from his knees, she lies back on the bed, and he lifts her legs and enters her. She rocks into him, her hands grasping his forearms.

Later, he falls asleep, one arm around her. As he snores, La La nestles closer. The thought of losing him makes her feel as frightened as she did the morning she awoke to find her mother had disappeared without giving a hint of her intentions or bothering to say good-bye.

It was a school day. Elissa always roused La La, shouting from the bedroom doorway, "I don't want to have to explain why you're late." But on that day, Zev shook her shoulder. "Hurry up. I'm taking you."

"Where's Mom?" La La asked, still half asleep.

"She went away."

The words jolted La La. "Where?"

"I'm sure she'll call and tell us," he said, the uncertainty in his eyes more frightening than Elissa's mysterious absence.

La La stayed under the covers where it was warm, refusing to accept her father's news. Zev parted the shades, letting in weak light that illuminated a small bookcase filled with puzzles and next to it a wicker chair on which La La had arranged stuffed animals. At one end was a lion Elissa had brought home from a thrift store, fur matted and eyes hanging from fuzzy sockets. Her mother washed and sewed it, and it became La La's favorite. La La held out her arms toward the lion, and Zev delivered it.

"I'll help you get dressed," Zev said.

"I don't feel well."

Zev sat at the edge of the bed. He touched her forehead. "You're not hot."

"I'm waiting for Mom to come home," she said.

"You can't stay here alone."

La La buried her face in the lion's neck. "Stay with me."

"Just today."

They remained at home the next day, too, and the day after that. One by one, Zev took apart the locks in his collection and showed La La how they worked. He sprayed the moving parts with powdered lubricant before putting them back together, wiping his hands with rags he changed frequently. He contacted La La's school and said she was sick. Still, Elissa didn't return.

Each time the phone rang, La La was sure it was her mother. "I can't make it today," Zev said to one caller, and La La squeezed the lion so hard a seam popped. "Yes, sir. In half an hour," Zev said to another. "Get dressed," he said to La La when he hung up. She rode in the van with Zev, as she occasionally did on weekends, to a home where a man had locked himself out.

When a full week had gone by, Zev told La La she had to go back to school.

La La began to tremble. "What if you disappear, too?"

"I'll be here when you get home."

She clutched his arm. "What if you're not?"

"I have to work."

"I'll go with you." She liked how customers thanked him when he unlocked their doors.

"You can't."

"Don't you want me to come along? I can help." La La thought about things she had done for Elissa: setting the table for dinner, pairing warm socks out of the dryer, not crying when her mother combed her hair no matter how hard Elissa yanked. The memories hardened inside La La like clay after it was fired; they were heavy and impossible to set down. "I can hold your tools," she said, barely loud enough for her father to hear.

Zev smoothed a wrinkle from his sleeve where she had gripped it. "Okay. But never, ever talk about what we do. Okay?"

La La didn't understand—what was so secret about being a locksmith?—but she agreed.

Later that morning, Zev had her get into his car. "Why aren't we taking the van?" La La asked, but he didn't answer. In a strange neighborhood, he handed her a clipboard with a yellow form. "If anyone answers the door, we're selling magazines."

Over the years, La La would sell hundreds of subscriptions. They received dozens of complimentary issues at the house, from *Time* to *Southern Cooking* to the *Journal of Criminal Justice,* magazines Zev read and quoted freely. Zev made her put part of her earnings aside for college, though she complained. "You don't want to end up like me. Do you?" he said. La La didn't argue about the money after that.

"Magazines," Zev whispered, tapping the clipboard, as they stood in front of a stranger's door. Inside, a dog began to bark. "Let's go," he said. "You never want to mess with Fido."

"Wait," La La said. Since she'd been pulled from the lake, dogs were always happy to see her. All animals were. "It's okay, boy. We won't hurt you." The dog quieted.

Zev glanced up and down the street. "You're a goddamn secret weapon."

La La squeezed the clipboard to her chest. It was the nicest thing anyone had ever said to her.

2

On Saturday, while Clem lifts weights at the gym, La La calls Zev and catches him while he's cleaning drapes. She pictures him on the stepstool, unclipping the sailcloth fabric. He's barely taller than she is, wiry and pale, and no match for the people he'd meet in prison. "After you left yesterday, I called the bank," he says. "They won't give me a loan against the house because it's already pledged for bail." His voice cracks, and she wonders how much coffee he's had, whether he's eaten anything. Zev's mother died when he was in his teens. He and his father don't speak, and he has no brothers or sisters. No one willing to put up the kind of money he's going to need for O'Bannon. When she hangs up, La La throws on a jacket and yanks on boots. She thinks about leaving Clem a note, but what would it say? It's rare for her to visit Zev this often. Yet she doesn't know what else to do. Maybe together she and her father can figure out a way to pay the lawyer.

Fresh snow coats the street, bends evergreen branches under its weight. Driving toward a property surrounded by thick hedges, La La senses distress inside. It's not unusual for animals to suffer behind locked doors. She can't imagine what their owners are thinking. She hates to pass such pets by with merely the hope their ailments will heal or their owners will become more observant. But she can't treat every one, least of all the ones on private property.

The house is large, two stories topped by a fancy tile roof. Reached by a long circular drive. A rich family's home. The kind where she and her father did well. But all of that is in her past. If she stops now, she tells herself, it will be only to make sure the animal is okay.

She brakes, swerving left and right, her Honda pinballing off the curb before she manages to park and walk up to a window. A yellow Labradoodle lies on a rug, panting. When he scratches his ear, pain slices through La La. She shuts her eyes and waits for it to pass.

If she can't help Zev, perhaps she can assist some other creature. She'll advise the owners the dog needs a vet and be on her way. They might think she's crazy, or maybe they'll finally pay attention to his scratching and panting. When she rings the doorbell, no one answers. She presses the button a few more times and knocks on the storm door. Inside, the dog whines.

She looks around. The hedges provide good cover, but it's the weekend. No counting on people—the home's occupants or nosy neighbors—to be at work. At least for now, the street is empty, and the owners don't seem to have bothered with a security system. La La doesn't see any stickers on the windows or signs. If she were suffering as the dog is, she'd want someone to help. She'll be quick, she promises herself. From the trunk of her car, she grabs her veterinary bag.

She tries the front door. Though she and Zev got lucky sometimes, it's locked. Lifting a welcome mat sprayed with snow,

La La uncovers a thin layer of displaced earth, crumbling leaves that escaped a blower, but no key. She sifts through damp, brown mulch in a large planter sheltered under the eaves. Bingo.

Tires hiss through the snow. She wonders whether it's the homeowners returning. If you don't count the key in her hand, she hasn't done anything illegal—yet. A fire has lit beneath her wool coat. When the car passes, she reconsiders and starts back toward her Honda.

She's taken only two steps when pain shoots through her, and she clenches her jaw. He must be fussing with the ear. Her eyelids sweat. Opening her palm, she sees the key.

In the entryway, a sign above an oak bench reads KINDLY RE-MOVE YOUR SHOES. La La's boots drip onto the bamboo floor-ing. The sign isn't meant for her. The Labradoodle approaches and sniffs her, his collar embroidered with the name "Clyde." La La scratches his chin, her fingertips disappearing in soft curls, her pulse slowing. Animals are incapable of deceit. They don't say, "I'm making a run to the grocery store," while secretly planning to leave you. Crouching, La La offers the dog a biscuit and observes while he chews.

The house is quiet, except for a furnace that breathes like a dragon. Outside, the wind twists tree branches, brushing them against a window. A thump behind La La revs her heart. She wheels around, scrambling to her feet, but it's only a cat. He knocked her bag from the bench and scratches his claws against it. Reclaiming her property, La La pulls out an otoscope and examines the dog's ear. A foxtail is embedded in the canal. The barbed seed heads lodge there when people take their dogs hiking and can lead to serious infection. In rare cases, death. It's unusual for it to happen in the winter but not unheard of. Why didn't his owners—who must have heard him cry and seen him scratch—take him to the vet? She'd report them for animal cruelty if she weren't in the house illegally.

She wipes sweat from her forehead onto the sleeve of her coat. "I can't sedate you, but you'll have to hold still." The dog plants his paws as if he's appearing before a judge in the Westminster Show. With a pair of alligator forceps, La La removes the foxtail. "That'll be eighty-five dollars," she says, holding out her hand. The dog places his paw in her palm.

As she's about to leave, she notices a white envelope on a coffee table, *Donella* written on the outside. She picks it up and opens it, revealing a stack of twenties. Payment for a housekeeper? Without thinking, she stuffs the envelope down the front of her jeans and rushes to her car. It will make only a small dent in the payment for O'Bannon, yet she feels relief having taken it.

Anxious to get away, she drives too fast, her tires slipping on snow. As she pulls over in front of Zev's house, she has trouble stopping and nearly slides into his van.

Inside, Zev takes her coat.

"I would only do as many jobs as it took to pay O'Bannon. I'd finish school next year," La La says, as she sits on a kitchen chair.

Zev sets a mug before her. "What if you get caught?"

La La's chest tightens. "Only one out of every eight burglaries is solved. Aren't you the one who told me that? Sloppy jobs done by drug addicts and kids on crime sprees. Amateurs. You worked for years without getting caught."

"It's gotten trickier," he says. "People have doorbells that send video to their phones. Don't know why they have to make it so tough."

"Terribly unfair," La La says, laughing despite herself.

"It's not funny. We'll figure out something that doesn't involve you."

"Like what?"

"If I knew, we wouldn't have to figure it out." He sits opposite her. "Maybe my father will lend me the money."

It's been nearly two decades since La La saw her grandfather Sam, a man quick to anger, who'd broken two of their dining room chairs, raising them up and violently reintroducing them to the floor. Eventually, Elissa moved meals to the kitchen, where the chairs had metal legs, when he visited. He used to join them for Thanksgiving, complaining about the healthy side dishes she made—whole roasted yams, stir-fried string beans, and the tofu he called "soy paste."

Yet he always had a Hanukkah present for La La: a key-chain light, a notepad shaped like a duck, chocolates wrapped in foil and stamped with Jewish stars. Small things she kept on her nightstand, or in the case of the chocolate, devoured. But after Elissa left, he visited only once. When La La told him Zev was teaching her at home, he said to her father, "You? A teacher? Tell me another one."

"I'm not that bad," Zev said, without conviction.

"You'll ruin her life."

"Like you ruined mine?"

Their voices rose, and La La ran to her room and shut the door.

She can't imagine Sam giving Zev money, though there's no harm in asking. The cash meant for Donella presses against her stomach. She intended to tell Zev about it but changes her mind.

●　　●　　●

That afternoon, La La joins her friend Nat at a reservoir for their weekly hike. Fifteen years La La's senior, Nat enrolled in veterinary school after a career in finance, and La La was immediately drawn to her more mature classmate. They met in a large-animal anatomy lab their first year. Nat wore rubber boots, while La La, still trying to impress her classmates, sported new tennis shoes. Formaldehyde soaked the sneakers by the end of their first session dissecting a horse Nat named Secretariat. La La's favorite scrubs were ruined, too.

They share more than veterinary school. Once, after they drained a pitcher of beer at the Longview Tavern, Nat confided that her husband, Tank, had done time for drug possession. La La confessed her own criminal past and Zev's. She was tired of keeping secrets, and it felt good to return Nat's trust. Just as she hoped, Nat didn't judge her, just made a joke about Zev and Tank both having a thing for stripes.

Even now, when La La says, "Zev was arrested," and tells Nat the story, her friend frowns sympathetically. But La La doesn't really expect Nat to agree when she blurts out, "I'm considering doing a few jobs." Perhaps what La La actually wants is to be talked out of it.

A gray mist hovers beneath the sky. Nat pulls a bright wool cap over her ears, hiding her pixie cut. "Risky."

"I haven't told Clem." La La struggles to untangle the dogs' leashes, but they're pulling in opposite directions.

Nat grabs their collars. "Could be hard on the victims."

Freeing the leashes, La La hands Blue's to Nat. "It's just stuff. They have insurance."

"You could lose Clem and your career as a vet. And you still might not save Zev. Is your father worth it?"

"Impossible to say." Snow blankets a layer of ice above the water, and a child chases a silvery green duck until, annoyed, the bird takes flight. The scene excites Black, whose gaze follows the bird into the ether and then returns to La La. Remembering another frozen lake, La La tightens her scarf and looks for the child's parents. "At least Zev never abandoned me."

"That's a pretty low bar."

A spot of yellow peeks out from between Blue's lips, and La La reaches into his mouth and extracts wet keys on a damp fabric chain. "Yours?"

"Thought they were in my pocket."

La La drops them in her friend's palm.

"Seems to run in the family," Nat says.

She means it as a joke, but it's true. La La has crime in her blood as surely as the Flying Wallendas have acrobatics, and the Kennedys, politics. Maybe it's pointless to resist it. Especially now that Zev needs her. The mortgage on his house isn't going to pay itself while he's under house arrest.

The boy chases another duck. "Hey!" La La shouts, and waits for him to turn around. "Better watch out. A duck pecked a boy's eyes out on this lake. Might have been that very bird."

"I never heard of a duck doing that." The boy glances over his shoulder. The bird is getting away.

"They don't brag about it. They might honk now and then, but they're actually pretty shy." She's caught his parents' attention. Seeing a strange woman shouting at him, they corral him. "Anything interesting happen in the hospital on Friday?" La La asks Nat.

"Litter of pug puppies came in for their first checkup. It was all I could do not to slip one into my pocket."

La La removes a glove and feeds each dog a biscuit, uncertain if her friend is acknowledging the impulse to steal or simply filling her in on the happenings at school.

Back in her car, La La wonders what she'll do if her grandfather won't help.

After he rehangs the clean curtains, Zev takes out the smartphone La La bought for him to replace the phone the police kept as evidence. He reads everything he can find online about ankle monitors. He'll give O'Bannon a chance to keep him out of jail, but if it begins to look like the lawyer can't, he wants to be ready. He orders a duplicate of the monitor because he never really understands a device until he's taken it apart and put it back together. Approaching his foot, Mo twitches her nose. She rubs her cheek against the plastic edge of the apparatus, marking it. "Don't get used to it," Zev says. "I don't plan to wear it that long."

He photographs the device from above and below, front and back, only the side pressing his flesh still hidden. He zooms in to capture features he might otherwise miss. "Aren't many new locks," he says to Mo. "Haven't been for years. Just variations on old ones. This one's got high-tech features, which means they've been lazy about the physical ones. Better for us."

That night, he phones Sam and leaves a message. "It's been a long time. I'm in trouble and could use your help." Zev keeps his phone close for the rest of the weekend but doesn't hear back.

Monday morning, when Zev calls La La to report that he'll have to use a public defender, La La insists on taking a leave from school and paying O'Bannon herself.

"That's not what I want," he says.

"Then you shouldn't have taught me."

"If I could take it back, I would."

In the hall of the veterinary hospital, the flow of care all around her, La La types the name of the registrar into an e-mail on her phone. It's hard to believe she'll be leaving this place. Giving up, however temporarily, the life she's imagined for herself since she was a child. Leaving it forever if she's caught. Doctors and veterinary students stride past, bringing animals to and from examination rooms, their patients' needs elevated above everything else. The perfect environment for someone like La La, and the only place she's ever felt she belonged. Yet Zev has no one else.

My father's sick, she writes, and then pauses to reconsider. Accompanied by a nurse, a dog limps by. The animals need her, too. But the hospital is full of staff. The dog won't go untreated. None of the patients will. *I have to take a leave,* she types.

Leaning against a light blue wall, she doesn't know if she can continue. She highlights the message, intending to delete it. She should take more time to think about it. But she doesn't know how long O'Bannon will wait. And she's afraid if she doesn't do it now, she won't do it at all. That she'll choose herself over her father. *I'll be back next fall,* she writes. *I hope you understand.*

She reads the e-mail a dozen times before she can bring herself to send it.

3

Nine o'clock the next morning, La La drives sixty miles south to a town outside of Denver where she's a stranger. Aviator sunglasses conceal her eyes; a cap with a hardware store logo swallows her hair, which is pinned up. She wears a men's winter coat that she bought at a thrift store and loose jeans. Around her neck is an infinity scarf she'll pull over her nose and mouth as she enters the home in case there are cameras inside.

Reaching a neighborhood Zev suggested after realizing she wouldn't be deterred, she slows down and eases the Mercedes past houses with three- and four-car garages, sunlight reflecting off meandering snow-covered lawns. The day before, she traded in her Honda, hoping the fifteen-year-old luxury car she got in its place would blend into the upscale neighborhoods where she plans to work, as long as no one looks too close. Her eyes barely crest the steering wheel of the vehicle meant for someone larger.

At the end of the street, she identifies a potential target: a house where flyers flap on the door handle, and Saturday's snowfall still blankets the driveway. Five thousand square feet, she guesses, a size all but ensuring she'll find valuables inside. A blue-eyed Siamese cat, abandoned if only temporarily, keeps watch from a bay window. Feeling the animal's pinched heart, his confusion at having lost his family, La La says, "I'm coming, baby." But then she notices the red, white, and blue decal of a well-known security company stuck to a corner of a window.

Driving on, she feels relieved. Perhaps this isn't something she should do. But three blocks later, in front of a property surrounded by a privacy fence, La La's stomach cramps, the ache belonging to a creature inside. What if she stuck to robbing homes where animals need her? Sure, the owners would be upset, but she'd be keeping their animals out of pain. In exchange, they'd be helping her keep her father out of jail. They might not appreciate the good she's doing for them, but wouldn't it be there all the same?

The lattice-top fence, newly stained, shields the family from snooping neighbors and will allow La La to work unobserved, too. She parks around the corner. Taking off her small engagement ring, she slips it into the glove box and pretends she's someone other than Clem's fiancée, a woman he doesn't know and never will.

As she lowers her window, she listens. Trucks rumble and clank on a nearby highway, but the street is quiet. Snowblowers sleep, shovels rest, on the weekday morning. A gray squirrel burrows into a drift, recovering food he stashed or raiding another squirrel's store. La La reaches into her veterinary bag for a dog biscuit and tosses it. The squirrel stands, jerks his head, and darts toward the bounty. Surely her kindness toward the squirrel and the animal inside outweigh the material loss to the family. Even if they don't, there's Zev to think of.

Shutting the window, she pulls on clear medical exam gloves so she won't leave fingerprints. Many police agencies won't bother collecting prints from the scene of a burglary. They lack the resources to investigate nonviolent crimes and homes are full of fingerprints that need to be eliminated. But La La isn't taking any chances. Likewise, she wears oversize men's boots, toes stuffed with socks so she can walk, footwear meant to throw off the police in the unlikely event they photograph or cast an impression of the boot prints. She grabs a canvas duffel that conceals her tools: crowbar, wrench, dish towel, veterinary bag.

After determining the doorbell isn't one of those high-tech devices Zev warned her about, camera lens peering out above the button, she approaches the door and rings a dozen times. The sun shines like a spotlight on her. Though in movies burglars wear ski masks and climb through windows in the dark, most burglars actually work during the day when homes are more likely to be empty. La La waits, squeezing the handles of her bag. If someone comes to the door, she'll claim to be lost and ask for directions. The thing she fears most—more than being caught by the police—is surprising an owner who's armed.

When she was twelve, an associate of her father's lost his front teeth. "Did you have an accident?" she asked.

"Yeah, an accident with a baseball bat," he said. Now you'd be lucky if all an owner wielded was a bat.

When no one answers the door, La La walks to the side of the house and opens the sash lock on a sliding window by vigorously working the frame up and down. She climbs into a hallway. A grandfather clock ticks; fresh ice drops in a freezer. The floor creaks in another part of the house, and she stiffens. She waits but doesn't hear the sound again. Perhaps it was just the structure settling. Creeping toward the back of the house, she passes a display of family photographs on the wall: colorful present-day shots and sepia images of ancestors. In a modern one, a mother wraps a baby in her arms, touching her lips to his forehead. La La brushes the image with a finger, though part of her would rather smash it. She has no memory of a mother caressing her. She'd like to steal some of that affection, but since she can't, their possessions will have to do.

When the child gets older, the mother will greet him after school with a glass of milk and a plate of truffles that cost $5.50 each at Rocky Mountain Confectioners. Or at least that's how La La imagines it. Unlike her own childhood, Zev home with her, teaching her the differences between fine watches and fakes.

As La La steps into the dining room, a woman appears. La La panics, bumps into an ornate high-backed chair and then into a console table. She's about to flee when she realizes it's her own reflection in the glass door of a china cabinet. More than a decade has passed since she regularly entered strangers' homes, and she can't help but feel jumpy.

Reaching the back door, she unlatches it, giving herself a second escape route. She doesn't know whether the owner has stepped out for ten minutes or is gone for the day. Some people work at home, while others don't work at all. A woman might return from yoga or Pilates. A maid might show up to clean. Only the poor do everything for themselves.

Outside a bedroom, a cramp twists La La's gut. When it passes, she ducks inside. A cage monopolizes a child's desk, a tawny hamster lying against the bars. Carrots, lettuce, and turnip slices fill a bowl. Someone meant well, but the portion is far too large—it should equal, at most, a few raisins—and is making the animal sick, at risk of dehydration. La La dumps the vegetables into the trash and refills the animal's water. She cleans the heavily soiled wood shavings as best she can with the plastic scoop next to the cage, then gently strokes the animal's back.

In the master bedroom, she rummages among silk thongs in the top drawer of an antique dresser. A jade ring and diamond studs nestle in small velvet cases. La La drops the jewelry into her bag. Longines and TAG Heuer watches keep time on top of a polished men's bureau, and she slips them into her pocket. She pulls women's designer clothing from hangers in the closet. In an office, on a desk covered with files and a calendar turned to the wrong month, a laptop tempts her, but heeding Zev's warning about tracking devices, she leaves it behind.

A man's leather coat and a short mink jacket hang in a front closet. She thrusts the leather coat into her duffel and cringes as she takes the fur off the hanger, intending to wear it beneath her own coat. The fence will give her a good price for it. Why leave it behind for the owner to enjoy? But as soon as she slips her arm through a sleeve, her lungs slam shut and dozens of needles prick her chest. Gasping, she tears it off and drops to her knees, feeling the anguish of the dozens of animals gassed to make it. They deserve a burial, but there's no time. When she can breathe again, she folds the jacket and tucks it away on a shelf toward the back of the closet.

She checks the time on her phone. "In and out," Zev taught her. "Never more than seven minutes." She's been inside ten already, each passing minute increasing the likelihood an owner will return or the police will arrive after being called by a neighbor.

As she rushes out the back door, she slips on an icy step that leads down to the yard and falls hands-first into the snow. Her duffel sails away. Retrieving it, she plows through white drifts to her car.

She drives twenty miles on the highway and pulls over at a truck stop, trembling. An animal shakes after an encounter with a predator to clear the body of the stress hormones adrenaline and cortisol, a veterinary professor once explained. To calm herself, La La recites a dog's anatomic systems—cardiovascular, digestive, respiratory, urogenital, lymphatic, neurologic, and orthopedic— and the parts of each system.

It's not too late to toss everything into a dumpster. Maybe even get her Honda back. She could describe her father's miraculous recovery to the registrar and finish her final year. Her heart rate slows and she stops shaking. But then she pictures Zev in a stained orange jumpsuit, in a cell he can't clean. At the mercy of prisoners with shivs carved from toothbrush handles or fence wire. With his prior conviction—her fault—and without a good attorney, he could be locked up for years, especially if the old man dies. Zev needs her help until O'Bannon negotiates a plea or somehow manages to win at trial.

La La gets back on the road, plucking off her cap and releasing her hair while she drives. She finds the dollar store her father told her about and pulls in facing the dusty window, the Mercedes out of place next to a Chevy truck with mismatched replacement parts. Half of the storefronts on the street are dark. La La changes into old sneakers.

When she enters the shop, a buzzer sounds. Sponges, ammonia, and paper towel rolls line metal shelves. Scrub and toilet brushes hang from steel hooks. Paper plates, plastic cups, bowls, and storage containers nest. Christmas ornaments sparkle in a large wood bin. Toys fill another: dolls with painted-on lashes, cars with etched-on doors. A freezer case advertises ice cream. The single checkout lane is empty, red shopping baskets rising in a perfect column next to it. La La doesn't see any customers.

From the back emerges the man she assumes is the fence. His eyes bulge, a hazard, perhaps, of examining other people's property over the years. An ink stain blots the seam of his shirt pocket, and a shock of black hair rises from his egg-shaped head.

"I'm Zev's daughter," La La says. Her father called ahead.

The man, who goes by the name Raven, takes in her loose coat and swollen duffel, performs some inner calculation, and says, "This way."

La La follows him into a storeroom. Amid stock matching the merchandise in the front, computers and tablets rise in an oven-size box. A second box has swallowed designer clothing and purses. Sitting at a large metal table, Raven pushes aside overseas shipping labels. La La empties her duffel and pockets.

He takes the Longines in his reddened hands and studies it, then presses it to his ear. A real Longines is so finely calibrated it barely ticks. In his hooked palm, he weighs the watch. Too light means fake. Putting on a pair of black-rimmed glasses, he examines the manufacturer's stamp. La La performed the same tests in the car, wanting to know the value of what she stole. "How's Zev?" he asks, examining the TAG Heuer.

Zev told Raven about his arrest because the fence would have figured it out on his own or learned about it from other contacts. La La was surprised Raven was willing to put himself in the middle of a situation that had become hot. "He's okay," she says.

Raven sets the watch down. "I can give you three fifty for both."

So that's why the fence agreed. Knowing she's desperate, he plans to squeeze her. Even used the watches are worth over a thousand. "Make it four hundred."

"Someone else might give you more. If you could find someone else. Of course, that could take some time."

She's at his mercy, and he knows it. "Fine."

He offers three hundred for the jewelry after looking at the pieces through a loupe. It's less than a quarter of what they're worth.

"I'll sell them on Craigslist," she says, hoping he'll come back with a higher offer.

"Suit yourself." He hands them back. Craigslist is risky. Zev never used it, but she needs more cash.

They agree on fifty for the coat, one thirty for the clothing.

It's been forty-five minutes since she left the house. She imagines the mother in the photo returning home and noticing the open window. She'll rush to her dresser, then call the police. Someone might have seen La La's car. The police could be running the plates now.

Raven disappears into another room.

When a skinny orange cat hops onto the table, La La's belly growls. *If they're not overfeeding their animals, they're starving them.* The cat stretches his back leg until it's level with his body, an ice skater's pose. He rubs his wet nose against La La's knuckles. Petting him, La La feels ribs protruding and briefly forgets her own danger. "Hold on," she says. Retrieving a can of cat food from her veterinary bag, she pulls off the top and sets the can on the carpet. The cat jumps down after it.

The fence returns and hands La La cash. He sniffs. "What's that smell?"

"I had a can of cat food," La La says. "Thought he would like it."

"Don't fucking feed him again."

La La tucks the cash into her purse. "Have a good day," she says, nearly adding, "Kitty."

In a mall parking lot, she photographs the jewelry, switches on her phone's mobile hotspot, and opens her computer. Uploading the images to Craigslist, she asks for half of what she could get if she were willing to wait but still twice what the fence offered.

Within five minutes, a woman named Rochelle e-mails, offering five hundred dollars for the diamond studs and the ring. They agree to meet at a coffee shop in fifteen minutes. It's twelve o'clock.

La La waits at a table until twelve thirty. She considers giving up on Rochelle, who might have changed her mind. But she hates to lose the sale, and perhaps the woman has only been delayed. Or maybe she's the owner, and the police are on their way. Returning to her car, La La stakes out the coffee shop. Her knee bounces, knocking against the steering column because the seat strains so far forward to allow her feet to reach the pedals. She runs through treatment protocols for animal viruses: parvovirus, herpes virus, picornavirus, paramyxovirus, rhabdovirus, retrovirus, influenza virus, vesicular stomatitis.

At one, a woman wearing a puffy lavender coat arrives and glances inside the coffee shop. Hoping it's Rochelle and that she is who she says she is, La La meets her at the door. The woman's mouth is large and lipsticked, a waxy, unsettling peach. She apologizes for the delay, explaining she had trouble getting a cash advance on her credit card.

La La chooses a table next to a window. When she lays out the pieces, the diamonds sparkle in the sunlight. Rochelle examines them through a loupe. La La wonders if she works for a jeweler. "The quality is good," Rochelle says. As she fingers the studs, her mouth cracks open with desire.

Though grateful for it now, La La doesn't get the obsession with diamonds. Chemical compounds with refractive properties, admittedly pretty, but hardly worth the fortunes spent on them. The tiny engagement ring Clem gave her is perfect. If he had bought her something showy, she'd have been insulted.

"Earth to lady selling diamonds. Whose did you say these were?"

"Mine."

"That's strange."

A wave of heat rolls over La La. "Why?"

"Your ears aren't pierced."

Fuck. A rookie mistake, and La La's hardly a rookie. But she is nervous.

Rochelle removes her rectangular topaz earrings and inserts the studs.

Beneath the table, La La wipes her palms on her coat and reminds herself the buyer wants to believe her lies, preferring them to the truth, which she could guess without much difficulty. "I planned to pierce them," La La says. "But I changed my mind. I'm afraid of needles."

"I see." Rochelle counts out four hundred-dollar bills. "I know we agreed on five, but since you can't use them, maybe you'll take four." Lipstick clumps in the corners of her mouth.

La La is tempted to pack up the jewelry and leave, but O'Bannon expects her, and she wants to give him as much cash as she can. "Make it four fifty."

Smiling, the woman adds two twenties and a ten to the stack.

As La La marks the bills with a counterfeit detection pen, Rochelle says, "You should do it."

La La doesn't look up. "Do what?"

"Pierce your ears. It only hurts for a second."

The lines remain amber, and La La slips the money into her wallet.

La La perches on a fabric chair, thinking how much friendlier O'Bannon's waiting room would be if the seat swiveled. Dark Berber carpet, chrome light fixtures, and a gray couch complete the pessimistic décor, and it's a relief when the lawyer appears and accompanies her to his office.

After she lays two thousand dollars on his desk—the housekeeper's money, what she made that day, and all of her savings—he counts it and sweeps it into a drawer. She wonders if he'll tell his partners about it, or if he's like most people, dishonest when the opportunity arises. It's far less than he asked for.

As he taps his lips, the corners of his mouth sink. "I'm not running a charity."

"I'll get the rest."

He plucks a stress ball from the top of a stack of papers and kneads it.

La La unbuttons her coat. "Can you keep him out of prison?"

"I'm only talking to you because your father thinks you should know what's going on since you're paying."

"Can you?"

"Doubtful."

"If Claude Thomas is in a coma, how do the police even know anything was taken?"

"The house belongs to his son, Sean Thomas. He was away at the time of the burglary. When he returned, he told the police his silver and cash were missing."

"What about the fact that Zev saved Claude Thomas's life? Doesn't that count for anything?"

The lawyer rolls the ball between his palms. "He didn't save anyone's life, because he wasn't in the house. Zev's phone was stolen a few hours earlier, and the thief left it on the counter."

"My father said that?"

"Your father doesn't want to go to prison. A friend of Zev's will testify he was with your father, watching TV, the morning of the burglary."

A friend in the same line of work, La La guesses, and maybe not the most credible witness.

"At the preliminary hearing I'll get to cross-examine the cops about how careful they were in handling the phone to preserve fingerprint evidence," O'Bannon says.

La La hates for Zev's heroism to be erased. But she's not paying O'Bannon to second-guess him. On a shelf behind the lawyer, the Colorado penal code stands next to a volume on criminal procedure.

For as long as Elissa lived with La La and Zev, their house overflowed with books. Paperback mysteries topped hardcover biographies in bookcases that climbed to the ceiling. Dog-eared true-crime books obscured her mother's nightstand.

One night, proud to have put on her pajamas by herself, La La asked Elissa to read *Madeline* to her.

Her mother lay in a recliner, absorbed in a book of her own. "If you didn't keep me running all day, I might have the energy," she said, turning a page. "'Mom, I'm thirsty,' 'Mom, I'm hungry,' 'Mom, my dress tore.' Jesus, La La, you're exhausting."

La La shakes off the memory. "How can they threaten to charge Zev with murder if Claude Thomas dies? My father didn't try to kill anyone. The guy had a stroke. My father tried to save him."

"Even if your father was there, which he wasn't, and tried to save the guy, legally it could still be murder. The prosecutor is relying on something called the felony murder rule. If you accidentally kill someone while committing a violent felony, like burglary, you can be charged with murder. But let's not get ahead of ourselves. No one's being charged with murder while Thomas is alive. If it comes to that, we'll fight it."

"Maybe Thomas had the stroke before the burglar even got there. Maybe a good Samaritan just found him in distress and called for help."

"Good Samaritan. I'll have to remember that one," O'Bannon says. "Unfortunately, Thomas yelled something that triggered his Amazon Echo to turn on. The device recorded him screaming at a burglar."

"Fuck."

"That about sums it up." O'Bannon stands, indicating the visit is over.

At a hobby shop, La La buys the electric train set Zev asked for. He's never been interested in that kind of thing, but he must need something to keep him busy now that he's trapped in the house. She picks up groceries, too, the Pop-Tarts, microwaved burritos, and frozen pizzas that are all Zev eats since La La went to college. So different from her fiancé, who only wants food that's fresh, organic, and fair trade. But maybe a difference is what she's after.

Zev and Mo greet La La in the living room, the cat butting her leg. As always, Zev's hair is combed neatly, but he's cut it himself, and the bangs slope downward, like a graph of falling temperatures. She hands him half of the bags and carries the rest into the kitchen.

"I want to hear everything," Zev says, as he unpacks the food. If she's determined to return to that life, the least he can do is give her advice, maybe keep her from making a deadly mistake. He asks her about the neighborhood where she worked, the exterior and interior of the property.

La La lifts Mo into her arms. She starts to tell Zev about the hamster, but he interrupts. "For God's sake, don't waste time with that. You'll get caught." It's one thing to quiet a watchdog, another thing to set up an animal hospital inside a house. Even if she's willing to take such stupid risks for herself, she ought to think about him. "I don't understand you."

"He needed my help."

"*I* need your help. Forget the goddamn animals."

La La looks at Mo. "She can hear you, you know."

"How much did you make?" When she tells him, he says, "You would have done twice as good if you concentrated on stealing." He asks what she took. "Good that you left that computer behind," he says. Things have changed since she was younger. People are meaner, more likely to empty a magazine into your chest. There's no punishment for killing a burglar. Those who do become heroes, their faces broadcast on the evening news. When he realizes he's been holding open the door to the freezer, he closes it and rubs his hands together. He hopes she gets luckier than he did. Because in the end, no matter how careful you are, your fate is determined by luck. Look at him. Worked for years without getting caught only to get tripped up doing the right thing. If that isn't bad luck, he doesn't know what is. He's learned his lesson. If he gets off, he'll never try to help anyone again.

The stress of the day catching up to her, La La stifles a yawn.

"Am I boring you?" Zev says.

She massages Mo's spine. She could use a cup of coffee, but he doesn't have a pot going.

When she gets home, she changes into jeans that fit her and a button-down shirt, stashing her burglar's clothes in the trunk of the Mercedes. She stretches out on the couch, the deception making her feel thick and sluggish, as if she has the flu. She worked hard to succeed in veterinary school, and now she's separated herself from it, and from friends like Nat and professors she admires. In a year, she'll return, she promises herself. But she knows things don't always go according to plan. She groans, and Black, lying next to the couch, cocks his head. "It'll work out," she says, but the dog doesn't look convinced.

She shuts her eyes, and the next thing she knows, Clem is coming through the door.

"Home early again?" he says.

Sitting up, La La caresses Black's head. "Why don't people take better care of their animals?"

Clem hangs his coat on a hook. "They take good care of them. They bring them to you, right?"

"Not always."

"It's like people who wait years to see me for back pain."

"It's not like that." At her change in tone, Black's ears dart up. "Your clients choose to wait. Animals are at the mercy of their owners."

"Did something happen at the clinic?"

"No."

Sitting next to her, Clem takes her hand and rubs her finger above the engagement ring. "How about we set a date? What do you think?"

La La tries to swallow, but coughs instead.

Two and a half years earlier, in La Casa du Spaghetti, Clem ordered a carafe of the house cab-merlot and poured two glasses. La La had just finished her first year of veterinary school, and they were celebrating. He covered her small hands with his large ones on the red cotton tablecloth. "I can't imagine my life without you," he said. From his pocket, he withdrew a silk drawstring bag. He loosened the opening and plucked out a slim silver band with a tiny pear-shaped diamond in its center. "It was my grandmother's."

There was so much Clem didn't know about her and her family. Yet his impatience to claim her buoyed La La. She leaned forward and examined the ring he held out. "It's perfect," she said. She offered her finger, but Clem continued to talk.

"You don't think it's too small?" His ears turned pink. "My grandfather was a junior loan officer in a bank. He'd been saving for a year to buy a bigger diamond, but my grandmother got tired of waiting for him to propose and tried to break up with him. He had his eye on a certain stone, he explained. My grandmother said she wasn't marrying a ring. The next day, they bought this and went straight from the jeweler's to the courthouse." Clem slipped the ring on La La's finger. "I know school keeps you busy," he said. "So we don't have to get married until you graduate."

La La withdrew her hand. Perhaps she was making a mistake.

Clem tightened the drawstring. "You don't look happy."

"My father says marriage is for suckers. My mother wasn't a big believer in it either, obviously. I don't know what I think." She wondered if Zev had given Elissa an engagement ring, and if he had, where it came from.

"I would never leave you. Is that what you're worried about?"

La La wanted to believe him, but she knew people grew tired of one another.

Clem pushed his chair away from the table. "Would it help if I got on all fours? Maybe then you'd know how I feel about you."

La La reached for his hand and squeezed it. "I guess I know already."

When they returned home from the restaurant, La La motioned for Clem to join her on the couch. "I need to tell you something." Dusk's soft light trailed into the house, illuminating yellow floral curtains the last tenants had left behind.

Clem sat next to her and intertwined his fingers with hers. "What is it?"

Her confession emerged as a rasp. "My father's a burglar."

Clem's face tilted the way Blue's did when the dog was confused. La La imagined the apartment empty; Clem, the dogs, even the curtains gone. Only her and the waning light remaining.

"You said he was a locksmith," Clem said.

"He is. And a burglar. I robbed homes with him when I was

growing up." She pulled off the ring and held it out to him, admiring it before it was gone.

"Why did you wait until now to tell me?"

"I didn't want to lose you." A muscle in her cheek twitched.

"Do you still help him?"

"No! I'm going to be a veterinarian."

"You never go along as a lookout? Or to drive the getaway car?"

"This isn't the movies. He's not a bank robber. And I don't do it anymore." The dogs lay on the carpet, ears raised, as if waiting to hear La La's fate.

Clem's unfocused gaze swept the room. He smoothed his beard. When he looked at La La again, his eyes were the ones she knew, soft and full of compassion. "I guess it doesn't have anything to do with us, then. Does it?" He took the ring from her and for the second time that night, slipped it on her finger.

"I can't think about setting a date," La La says when she stops coughing. She pushes her hands under her thighs. "Too much going on at school."

Clem's shoulders sag. He adjusts his neck, releasing a sharp pop. "I thought you'd be excited. But we can wait, okay?" Glancing toward the front of the house, he says, "Whose Mercedes is parked out front?"

"I traded in my Honda. Since I'm going to be a veterinarian, I thought I should have a nicer car."

"I didn't think you went in for that kind of thing."

"What kind of *thing*? A car that shows I'm more than a veterinarian's assistant?" The dogs pace, tails high.

"Status symbols. But it's fine if you want one. You deserve it, right?"

"Nice of you to give me permission," she mutters, turning away.

"Jesus, what's with you tonight?"

Black climbs between them, panting, his muzzle in La La's face, his butt in Clem's. She hates to worry the dogs. Breathless, she says to Black, "We'll stop." He licks a wide swath across her nose and collapses across both of their laps.

4

After Clem leaves for work the next morning, La La retrieves from her car the loose jeans, the hardware store cap, and the men's winter coat and boots. She changes into them, taking off her clean scrubs and hanging them in the closet.

In a neighborhood southwest of Denver, she approaches a large property that borders the foothills. Though hot air blasts from the car's vents, as La La passes the house she shivers with cold, her fingers turning blue and aching. Towering ornamental grasses in winter gold knife through the snow; a life-size bronze elk rears, the expensive statue boding well for what she'll find inside. The shades are drawn and snowy footprints tramp from the mailbox to a neighbor's house and back. La La parks a block away and returns to the house.

Icicles descend from gutters, slowly dripping. With a soft *whump,* a tree releases a mound of snow. The street's only other occupant, a Steller's jay, chirrups, bemoaning the frosty covering that hides seeds, nuts, and berries. At the house, there's no sign of a security system. The temperature seems to plummet.

When she rings the doorbell, no one answers. She knocks for good measure, but still nothing. As she hunts for a spare key, she hears footsteps along the sidewalk, crunching a layer of snow. La La knocks like someone with legitimate business until the pedestrian recedes down the block.

Around back, La La jiggles a wrench next to a first-floor window and considers how long ago the pedestrian passed. Evergreens block the views of neighbors on either side of the house. You can get away with one noise, Zev taught her. Neighbors, even if they hear it, will just wonder where it's coming from. Only with the second disturbance will they narrow in on its location. But someone walking by may have an easier time placing the sound.

Wind brushes the trees. Wrapping her hand in a dish towel, La La hammers the wrench through the glass. Shards rain around her arm. She pokes her hand through the jagged hole and turns the latch. Climbing inside, she lands on a gray wool carpet and the remains of the windowpane. Six leather recliners form a semi-circle around a fireplace; the air smells of ash.

"Daddy's home! Daddy's home!" she hears. A parrot flaps and cries again, "Daddy's home!" The bird is freezing. La La hurries to unlock the front and back doors. She walks from room to room looking for the creature, passing through an immaculate kitchen with appliances as big as cars and a Mexican tile floor, a living room with a giant burl table. In the den, she spots the cage. The bird is an eclectus parrot, her feathers a palette of primary colors, as if painted by a child: red on her face, blue on her chest, and yellow in her tail. She's fluffed up her feathers to keep warm, and her water bottle is nearly empty. The house is too cold for the bird. La La raises the temperature from fifty-five to seventy-three degrees, refills the water bottle. She strokes the parrot's head, and the bird burrows into her hand. *What kind of people abandon a bird to cold and thirst? The parrot belongs with a mate in a lush tropical forest, not caged in suburbia, alone.*

La La checks the time. Five minutes have passed since she broke the windowpane.

In a walk-in closet in the master bedroom, she collects Louis Vuitton and Yves Saint Laurent handbags. A black lacquer jewelry box on a shelf plays "Somewhere Over the Rainbow" when she opens it. "Bluebirds fly!" the parrot squawks from the den. La La scoops up a thick gold chain, a diamond solitaire necklace, and diamond cuff earrings. A silver-plated yin-yang pendant lies tarnishing at the bottom of the box, a date engraved on the back. Hardly worth stealing, but La La remembers her mother wearing a similar piece. It swung from Elissa's neck when she bent to clip a rose, to tie her espadrilles, or to pick up a towel La La dropped on her bedroom floor despite Elissa's threat—which she made good on—to show La La the "sting of a damp towel against a tender behind." La La picks up the pendant. She'll wear it under her clothes, and no one will know.

When she climbs a stepladder to reach an upper shelf, an unlocked safe greets her, a Glock inside. Leaving the safe open gives the homeowners quick access if they need it, and makes La La's job easier, too. After unloading the gun, La La drops it into her bag.

From a fireplace mantel, she seizes a picture of the family in ski suits, goggles pushed on top of their helmets and giant gloves swinging from their wrists. The sun lights up a crowded and colorful slope behind them. In the center of the shot, two boys with windburned cheeks pose with snowboards. On either side, their parents gaze at them, pride lifting their middle-aged chins. Skiing is a rich person's sport, and La La's never tried it, her experiences limited by Zev's meager earnings. She returns the photo to the mantel, feeling that she is owed the stolen items in the duffel.

Passing the den, La La peeks in on the bird. Her feathers lie flat, and she's whistling. In the distance, a police siren wails. The time is nine minutes. Did the pedestrian call the police? "When you panic, you get into trouble," her father used to say, and it proved true for him. As La La races to the back door, the siren draws closer. The parrot sings *woooooo, woooooo*. La La pictures herself in handcuffs in the back of a squad car, like the time she and Zev were arrested. The tang of her sweat mingles with the floral fragrance emitted by a plug-in air freshener.

When she opens the door, the siren is almost at the house. She doesn't know whether to run or to retreat, and lingers in the doorway, letting in the cold she earlier tried to banish. Lacking another champion, she calls on God for help, though she isn't religious. Clouds hurry by on northerly winds, and she offers God a deal: she'll tend the animals of the poor if the police car passes her by. Why should the rich be the only ones to benefit from her knowledge? The siren weakens before fading altogether.

At the dollar store, Raven buys everything except the gun, and the yin-yang pendant, which she doesn't offer. He gives her the number of a guy named Cecil who might be interested in the Glock and she calls, then camps out at a McDonald's with a cup of coffee, waiting.

In the PlayPlace, a young mother in designer jeans catches a toddler at the bottom of a yellow tubular slide. Tenderness flows from the woman's hands. Two stubby-legged children chase each other over black rubber tiles. Captivated, La La doesn't notice a man approach.

"Are you La La?" Short and heavy, he sweats in a long down coat that hides who knows what. He keeps his eyes down, his aggrieved face studying the floor.

La La would rather do business out in the open. It's safer. But she can't sell a gun in a McDonald's or anywhere public. "Let's go to my car."

Cecil follows her to the Mercedes at the far end of the parking lot. Sitting behind the wheel, the canvas bag on her lap, La La unlocks the passenger door, and he gets in. When she hands him the Glock, he looks it over. His thumb angles unnaturally as if it's been broken. "How much?" he says.

"Like I told you on the phone, two hundred."

"I've got one twenty."

Would he try to take advantage of Zev this way? Pointing to the gold cross dangling in the hollow of his neck, she says, "I'll take that, too."

He fingers the cross, his mouth drawn. "It's the symbol of Our Lord, for chrissakes."

"The chain, then. I don't suppose that's a symbol of anything." She's pushing it, but she needs the money, and she resents the guy lowballing her.

He reaches behind his neck. After he gives her the chain, his hand disappears under his jacket.

La La tenses. Maybe she's gone too far. She wishes she carried her own gun, but it would increase the severity of the charges if she were caught, and she doesn't know how to shoot. If he pulls a weapon, she'll open the door and roll out, the car giving her temporary cover. Where she'll go from there, she doesn't know.

Cecil shoves a thin stack of twenties at her, and she pockets it.

It isn't until he gets into his car and drives away that she counts it. One twenty, like he said.

She recites veterinary antibiotics—aminoglycosides, beta lactam antibiotics, chloramphenicol, trimethoprim, glycopeptides, fluoroquinolones, polymyxins, lincosamides—cataloguing their uses until her breathing returns to normal.

O'Bannon counts the eleven hundred dollars La La hands him and deposits it in his desk drawer. "I said ten thousand. You've given me three. If we go to trial, the fees are going to run into the tens of thousands." The lawyer squeezes the stress ball in his fist.

"I have to pay Zev's mortgage." La La digs her nails into the leather seat cushion.

"We all have mortgages. Maybe I should withdraw now and transfer the case to a public defender."

"No! I'll get the money," she says, though she isn't sure how.

"What about Mom?" La La says to Zev.

"What about her?" He yanks a needle through a button he's resewing on a shirt.

"Maybe she could help."

"After all this time, I'm sure she's dying to pay my legal fees." He pushes the needle through again.

"Maybe she regrets leaving us."

"Ow!" He sets the shirt down and sucks on his index finger.

"Why don't we look for her?" In the past, La La considered hiring a private detective to find Elissa, but she never had the money. She was afraid, too, of how angry it might make her mother, who clearly didn't want to be found. When she was in college, La La searched the Internet for Elizabeth Gold and Elissa Gold—her mother had never taken Zev's last name, Fine—but there were so many results. Dozens of hits were for a city councilwoman on the West Coast; more than fifty were for a real estate agent in Florida. Neither picture resembled her mother. There was someone looking to rehome a dog, and La La got excited, until she saw it was a young person like herself. She discovered many old articles about the accident on the lake, but nothing about her mother after that time. Zev had cut ties with Elissa's parents, Ruth and Harry, but La La located a phone number for them in an online white pages. She tried calling it, but it was disconnected. Searching further, she found their obituaries.

"Bleeding over here." Zev holds up his finger, blood blossoming at the tip.

"Maybe she's changed." Though La La has fantasized a reunion in which her mother apologizes, she knows that's unlikely. Yet her mother might be the only one who can help her save Zev.

"Still bleeding," Zev says, sucking again. "Forget about her. I'd rather go to jail than accept her help."

La La doesn't believe him. Besides, if she finds Elissa on her own, Zev won't have to know.

After Elissa disappeared, Zev rarely mentioned her. Once, the week before Mother's Day, having seen a display for the holiday in a mall, nine-year-old La La made her mother a card. She folded a sheet of white paper into quarters and drew flowers in purple and black, Elissa's favorite colors, on the cover. Inside she wrote, *Happy Mother's Day*. Proud of her efforts, she rushed to show Zev, ignoring the small voice in her head that said it wasn't a good idea.

Zev was putting away laundry. "For her?" he yelled, gesturing with a fistful of white briefs when he saw the card. "I'm the one who stuck around!"

La La was embarrassed to see Zev's underwear, even if he wasn't wearing them. Her eyes filled. "Sorry," she said, backing out of the room. Later, while Zev read *Parenting,* La La stuffed the card into an envelope only to realize she didn't have Elissa's address.

"In all this time you never looked for her?" La La says.

"Why the hell are we still talking about her?" Though the needle still hangs from the shirt, Zev slams the sewing box shut.

Sitting alone in his living room later that day, Zev slips a photo from his wallet. It's the only picture of Elissa he kept, the image captured in the hospital after La La was born. When Elissa handed him the red-faced baby, he was terrified his grip would be too loose and he'd drop her, or too tight and he'd squeeze out the air that sustained her. But La La settled into his embrace with a sigh. He'd never felt as content, as sure of his purpose, as he did in that moment. He swayed and hummed "Jolene." La La's eyes closed. Elissa lay back in her cotton gown, her hair soaked. To Zev it seemed her anxieties about the unplanned child were forgotten. (He'd convinced her to keep it.) He crouched next to Elissa, and a nurse snapped their picture.

What happened on the lake was his fault. He all but insisted Elissa take La La skating. "Do something fun with her for a change," he said. "Give her a happy memory. It won't kill you." Zev had planned to take La La himself but then someone called for a locksmith.

"Okay," Elissa said.

Zev's memory of that time is a jumble of what he saw, what Elissa told him, and what he read. Where there are holes, his imagination fills them in.

Before he had left for the locksmith job, he dressed La La in a yellow snowsuit, a woolen hat, two pair of socks, and boots. Elissa wore a pair of Zev's snow pants over her jeans. Tossing their skates into the trunk of her car, she drove to the lake.

When they got there, Elissa pulled on La La's skates, the girl complaining they were too small. She always found something to whine about. Elissa considered taking her home right then. Later she would tell Zev she wished she had. Before she let La La skate, Elissa walked a ways out. The ice was thick and blue, safe. They'd had a warm spell earlier in the month, but the past week, temperatures had dropped again. She put her own skates on.

At first they stayed together, flying over the ice. La La's cheeks turned pink. The cold air sharpened Elissa's senses. Zev was right. She ought to spend more time with La La. She could take her on other outings, to the zoo or a farm. While Elissa imagined feeding straw to a baby goat, the animal's lips tickling her palm, La La skated away. By the time Elissa petted the pigs and cows, La La was at the far end of the lake. Elissa saw her briefly and then not at all. Fear threatened to immobilize her, but she forced herself to skate as fast as she could. La La had dropped into a hole in the ice, its edges jagged and thin, translucent. Ten feet away, Elissa stopped. If she went any closer, the water would swallow them both. Elissa didn't want to die on the lake. She'd barely lived, her life consumed by a family she didn't want. She turned and skated toward the car. She didn't carry a cell phone; they were less common then. She would find a nearby home. Call emergency services from there.

After Elissa left, a couple arrived at the lake to skate. They discovered a dog guarding an unconscious child half-submerged in the water. They called 911. While they waited for an emergency crew, a newspaper reporter who'd been listening to the police scanner appeared. He asked the couple what they knew.

Moments later, a fire rescue crew arrived, and an officer in a cold-water suit pulled La La out. It wasn't until they were loading her into a heated ambulance that Elissa returned.

"Didn't you see the sign?" the reporter asked her. He pointed to a small placard, that read DANGER—THIN ICE, half hidden behind bushes at the opposite end of the parking lot. Elissa hadn't seen it. The reporter tried to interview her, but she ignored him, climbing into the back of the ambulance where La La was naked and wrapped in blankets.

Though La La's vitals were normal, she was taken to the hospital for observation. Hours later, when they returned home, Zev put La La to bed. She seemed to have come through the ordeal unscathed.

The next day, the headline on the local paper shouted: MOTHER ABANDONS DROWNING CHILD. Featuring, as it did, a dog watching over an abandoned child, the story was picked up by newspapers across the country.

Zev was interviewed on a local TV news station, though Elissa refused to appear. He agreed only because the producer promised to get the word out about the dangers of skating on frozen lakes.

"Why did your wife take her skating on thin ice?" the anchor asked once the show began. The man's hair was slicked back. Hot lights blinded Zev. Before Zev could answer, the anchor asked another question: "Didn't she know the girl could die from hypothermia?" And then: "People are saying she should be charged with child endangerment," which wasn't a question at all.

"She thought the ice was thick," Zev said, doing his best to defend Elissa. "She didn't see the sign. It was hidden in a corner of the parking lot."

"I see," said the anchor.

"I'd skated there before and never had a problem," Zev said.

"Why didn't she go in after her?" the anchor asked.

Zev had asked himself the same question. "You aren't supposed to."

"That dog never left her side." The anchor looked into the camera. "If anyone has information about the pooch, please call the station."

Other stories came out. A neighbor had seen Elissa berate La La. "She's just a little girl," he said to a reporter. It was unfair, Zev thought, because what parent didn't make mistakes?

The city moved the sign to the center of the parking lot. "How could she have missed it?" people said when they drove by.

Zev tried to comfort Elissa, telling her the scandal would pass, but she didn't seem to hear. She moved as through a swirling snowstorm, her eyes downcast, her shoulders hunched.

"Certain people don't deserve to have kids," a bank teller said, raising her eyebrows at Elissa, while a loan officer nodded. Elissa ran out without making her deposit.

"Couples are dying to have children, and you abandon yours," a man in line behind her at the post office said, his voice carrying throughout the cavernous room. Mornings, Elissa left La La a block from school, avoiding other parents. She told Zev the whole town was against her, especially women.

Her life had overwhelmed her even before the incident at the lake. Though she thought his stealing was funny when she first met Zev, she assumed he would outgrow it. Early in their marriage, she decided to leave him but then discovered she was pregnant. "You'll regret it for the rest of your life," Zev said, when she brought up abortion. "You'll wonder who the child would have been." But it was Zev who would have wondered. Zev who would have felt regret. "It's my child, too," he said.

Even an easy child such as La La proved too much for Elissa, whose hair lost its luster, thinned, and clogged drains. She developed acne and clenched her jaw. "This isn't the life I wanted," she said to Zev, a week after the accident.

"There's nothing we can do about that now," Zev said. But there was something Elissa could do, and she did it three weeks later.

He knows where she is. Months after she disappeared, he got her number from her mother, Ruth, by claiming La La wanted to talk to Elissa. Ruth said Elissa was living in Queens and had changed her last name to Roberts, so no one would connect her to the mother in the news story.

"Don't contact me again," Elissa said, when he called her. "I'm finished failing at motherhood. I'm done living with a thief. Find someone else." Occasionally, he Googled the humane society where she had found work and looked at her picture in the staff directory. He watched the animal-training videos she'd made, trying to understand how she could be so patient with pets but impatient with her own daughter. Of course, La La prefers animals, too, but Zev always assumed that was because Elissa left.

Animals didn't disappoint La La the way humans did. Or maybe it's genetic, something La La inherited from her mother. He's never told La La where Elissa is, not wanting her to suffer any more at her mother's hands.

Looking up Elissa's workplace on his smartphone, he finds she's no longer listed in the staff directory. He calls the humane society and is told she took a job as executive director of the Mesa Animal Shelter in Arizona.

He returns the picture taken in the hospital to his wallet. On the dining room table, he arranges the train track. A motion detector in the ankle monitor activates if the device is still for too long, indicating it's been set aside or that the person wearing it has died. The movement of the train should satisfy the motion detector. When the track is complete, he pushes the duplicate monitor into an open freight car. It's a squeeze, but it fits. The ankle monitor needs to be charged daily, so Zev arranges it with the jack facing up and plugs in the power cord. By the train's second lap, the power cord stretches across the track and the train tumbles over it, derailing. Something to work on, the kind of puzzle he likes, though the stakes couldn't be higher.

The last time he talked to O'Bannon, the lawyer told him Claude Thomas was showing small signs of improvement. The swelling in his brain had gone down. He had opened his eyes and responded when the doctors tested for pain. If he continues to improve, the doctors might try short periods off the ventilator. Zev's glad something he did turned out well. Should Thomas recover, Zev won't be charged with murder. He just has to hope the guy doesn't remember him.

Zev misses being outside, watching homeowners until he knows their patterns, when they leave for work and when they return. Looking for houses with obvious signs of wealth, an expensive car in the driveway or elaborate landscaping tended by gardeners. Searching for secluded homes and ones with access from side doors. Because he kept the houses he robbed tidy, his burglaries often went undetected for days, time passing before they showed up on the police blotter, someone having finally noticed the damage to a back door or an out-of-the-way window. Stuck inside, Zev paces in rooms that seem to shrink by the hour.

As La La undresses for bed, Clem looks up from his phone and notices the yin-yang pendant. "I didn't know you were into Chinese philosophy. Is it new?"

La La's hands and face tingle. She meant to take it off as soon as she got home, but started to play with the dogs instead and forgot. "A store near the hospital had it in the window. My mom wore one like it." She strokes it between her finger and thumb.

"You sure you want a reminder?"

La La pulls on a nightshirt, the necklace disappearing beneath the cotton. "I can't help thinking about what my life would've been like if she stayed."

"Your life isn't so bad. Is it?" He lifts the necklace above her shirt. Bends down to kiss the spot where her jaw meets her ear.

La La's skin warms. She longs to tell Clem everything but is afraid if she does, he'll leave her. The woman Clem courted wasn't a burglar. In college, La La organized a volunteer program, pairing students with shelter dogs for daily walks. After a rape in an apartment near campus, she tacked up flyers with tips on how to keep intruders out. Her life wasn't without moral ambiguity. Her father sent money, and La La knew where it came from, but at

the time, Clem didn't, and at least La La wasn't the one breaking the law.

He starts to lift her nightshirt, but La La turns away. "Anything new on the blog?" she asks.

Backing off, Clem looks at her curiously, then checks the
blog on his phone. "Looks like someone's thruway toll was paid
by a prior driver. The Nobel Committee should be calling any
minute, right?"

La La snorts.

Thursday morning, unable to find a home with a sick pet, La La
settles for giving an elderly dog a potty break before making off
with the family's valuables. It's not until she's back home several
hours later that she remembers something about a promise to
tend to animals of the poor. Does the promise count if she was
under duress? She's tempted to forget all about it. To lie down for
a nap, embracing oblivion for an hour or two, the recent unhappy
changes in her life disappearing. If she were more help to an animal that morning, perhaps she would.

Instead, she decides to visit a dog park across town, where,
as a veterinary student, she'd informed owners of a free spay
and neuter day at the hospital. She'll clip overgrown nails, clean
waxy ears, and perform free exams to discharge her obligation.
Black bag in hand, she rides the bus, hoping it will handle roads
sloppy with new snow better than her car. In a neighborhood
of small ranch houses, La La pulls the cord for her stop. The
bus slides past a corner and lets La La off in the middle of an
intersection.

Walking toward the park, hood pulled over her head, La

La passes a property surrounded by a chain-link fence, and her shoulder tenses. She'd like to investigate, but a car idles in the driveway, and besides, she doesn't want to break into a home if she doesn't have to. Two blocks later, in front of a house with broken shutters, stiffness clamps La La's hips. The driveway is empty, and the interior is dark. A snowman next door waves a paper-towel arm and regards La La with silver-button eyes. Perched on a fence, a magpie shrieks about death—whose, La La doesn't know.

She walks on, ignoring her hips, which feel like shattered glass. But as she reaches the corner, she turns around. She'll be quick, she tells herself. She can keep her promise this way, too. When she presses the doorbell, it doesn't ring. She raps hard on the thin door, then raps again, but no one answers. Shuffling around back, she picks the lock on a sliding glass door. Inside, a heavyset German shepherd limps toward her across a stained olive carpet. Onesies, bibs, and a pink baby blanket drape across the back of a corduroy love seat. In a playpen squeezed between the love seat and the wall, letters dance on a plastic book cover. An electric menorah and a tiny artificial Christmas tree share a small tabletop.

"The temple priests had enough oil to light the menorah for only one night, but miraculously it burned for eight nights," Elissa once told her, touching a match to the candles on their brass menorah.

"Maybe they pinched oil from another temple," Zev said.

Elissa glanced at La La, then back at Zev. "She's six."

La La eases down next to the dog and reads her tag: PETUNIA. She runs her hands along the shepherd's tan-and-black fur, performing a gentle exam. The dog's joints are swollen; they grind as La La manipulates Petunia's legs. It's likely osteoarthritis.

An old refrigerator buzzes. Water sloshes in a dishwasher. Arranging Petunia on her side, La La massages her back leg, loosening the muscles with her palm. The dog relaxes and groans. Outside, a car hushes through the snow, slowly approaching the house. Grabbing her veterinary bag, La La starts toward the sliding door. How unfair to be caught when she isn't even stealing. But who would believe she broke in to help? Petunia's eyes remain shut, and she hasn't moved. La La hates to leave her, having attended to only one side. Fear stiffens La La's neck. Her head feels like it's attached with a pike.

As she clutches the door handle, the car passes. Returning to the dog, La La finishes the massage. She rummages in her bag for a bottle of glucosamine and chondroitin supplements. Another car approaches the house. Thinking it will pass like the earlier one, La La pulls out the bottle and opens it. Petunia stands and looks toward the street, her large ears erect. The dog's heart quickens. La La leaves the bottle on the coffee table. When the car pulls into the driveway, Petunia hobbles toward the front of the house. The car engine shuts off just as La La reaches the sliding glass door, but when she tries to open it, it jams. She pushes and pulls, pulls and pushes some more, but it won't budge. One car door opens, then another. The dog squeals happily. La La lifts the door, which has slipped from its track, back into position and opens it. "We're home," La La hears, as she races away.

At the bus stop, La La sweats despite the cold. The perspiration on her face turns clammy. Someone has sprayed red paint over the schedule on the sign, and La La can't make it out, but it hardly matters because the times are never accurate. A bus from a line different than the one La La is waiting for lets off an old man in a black wool cap and beat-up leather gloves. He looks at La La's veterinary bag. La La attached stickers to it—Grumpy Cat and Dog Is My Co-Pilot—so she could recognize it among those of other students. "You a veterinarian?" the man asks. Areas of gray stubble dot loose skin on his cheeks and neck.

La La shifts the bag to her other hand but too late to hide it.

"You make house calls?" he asks.

"Sometimes," La La says.

The man pulls off a glove and rubs a hand over his face. "My cat hates going to the vet."

La La peers down the street, willing her bus to arrive. It isn't safe to stay in the neighborhood where someone might have seen her enter the house.

"He needs to be put down, but when he sees his carrier he runs, and I can't catch him anymore. I hate to upset him on his last day." He puts his glove back on, stamps his feet, his thin rubber boots inadequate for the weather.

"What makes you think it's time?" she says.

"He doesn't eat. Cries a lot. Forgets where the litter is. I try to keep him clean, but I've got my own problems."

"How old is he?"

"Twenty-one or thereabouts. Maybe you could come over now. It's only a few blocks." He motions in the direction La La came from, then sticks out his hand. "Name's Sebastian. Cat's name is Neapolitan, Neo for short."

"I really can't. I have to meet someone." Clutching her bag to her chest, she looks down the street.

"I'll pay you. I'm not rich, but I've always taken care of Neo."

La La's bus turns the corner onto the street. "That's me."

"There'll be another." He grabs her arm. "Please."

La La shakes him off. Leaving her house, she made sure to

tuck the exact change needed for the round trip—two dollars each way—into her pocket. But now when she reaches for the fare, it's missing. Except for a useless credit card, her wallet is empty. When she grabbed the lockpicks from her pocket outside the sliding door, the money must have fallen out.

The air fills with the hiss of brakes, and the bus door opens. While La La ascends the steps, she tells the driver she forgot her fare.

The driver continues to look through the front window. "You and everyone else. No one rides without it."

She climbs back down.

"Thank you," Sebastian says, as La La follows him. She hates to think of the cat in pain, and this can be part of fulfilling her promise, too.

When she passes Petunia's yard, the shepherd presses her nose to the gate, but La La ignores her.

Sebastian's house smells of cooked beans and coffee. A piano fills half of a small living room. The cat lies motionless on a blanket in the bedroom, dozing. He's a calico, patches of red and brown bleeding into white. La La pets him, feeling his knobby spine and hips that jut out. Her kidneys burn. Though she performs a cursory exam, she already knows what's required. "I'm going to give him two shots," she says. "First one is to relax him."

Sebastian murmurs his assent. La La looks up dosages on a veterinary app on her phone. She fumbles in her bag for the medications she stole from the hospital and has carried since she came across a deer slowly dying after being hit by a car and had no way to help. Filling a needle with the sedative Telazol, she injects the muscle. Surprised, Neo lifts his head. His tail puffs. Sebastian holds him in place, rubbing the cat's chin.

As she waits for the drug to take effect, La La looks through the window. A sparrow hops on a patio table shrouded in white, the bird so light it leaves no trace in the snow. Blown off in the wind, a patio umbrella floats on a drift beneath an ash tree. La La's limbs grow heavy. Neo's pupils dilate; his head wobbles and drops to the blanket. "Ready?" she asks, the word catching in her throat.

Covering his mouth with his hand, Sebastian nods.

La La injects Nembutal to stop Neo's heart. The cat is still.

Sebastian caresses the cat's head with his hands. He kisses him, whispering, "Good-bye, Neo."

La La looks out of the window again. Gone is the sparrow. Silently, she asks the cat's forgiveness, despite thinking she's done the right thing. "I can't take him back to the clinic."

"I'll figure something out."

"Okay."

When Sebastian tries to pay La La, all she accepts is bus fare.

In the living room later that night, La La sits on the couch, cradling her laptop. She opens a people-finder website that Nat recommended. "Much more efficient than a Google search," her friend said. The thought of actually tracking down her mother is so unnerving, she types "Elidda Gold," then "Eliffa," eventually using one finger to get the job done. The name yields only one woman in her late sixties, but Elissa would be in her early fifties. La La searches for the only full name she has for her mother, "Elizabeth Gold." Sixty-two women. That's better.

From the overstuffed chair, Clem watches television, channel surfing until he lands on the local evening news. Black lies on La

La's feet, warming them, and Blue rests his chin on Clem's lap. A segment begins about an odd burglary, odd not because of the way the burglar entered the property or because he knew where to find the valuables—which were routine enough—but because he took care of the homeowners' parrot.

La La's skin prickles. She plunks her laptop on the coffee table and jumps up, disturbing Black as she scrambles toward Clem. She reaches for the remote control, but he refuses to relinquish it. "I'm watching this, aren't I?" he says. "Anyway, it's about animals."

Standing in front of the house, the bronze elk visible behind him and a large News 4 emblem on his microphone, a reporter says, "We know it wasn't a cat burglar. He would have eaten the parrot." He chuckles, a fake newsroom laugh, then frowns. "As of this afternoon, the police don't have any suspects."

Afraid to make a scene, La La returns to the couch. Since they don't know who the burglar is, the story can't do any harm.

Next to the reporter, the homeowner licks her teeth, presumably making sure the thick, red lipstick she applied for the interview hasn't migrated. She leans toward the microphone. "It's horrible knowing someone has been in the house. I keep thinking I hear someone in the next room."

La La bites a fingernail impatiently, wanting to know if the police have any leads at all, someone who saw her coming or going, or noticed the color of her car.

"He filled the bird's water bottle," the homeowner says. "Our neighbor was taking care of it while we were away. She's the one who discovered the break-in. The burglar turned up the thermostat, too. Why, I can't imagine."

It irks La La that the homeowner thinks the compassionate burglar is a man.

"One of your professors?" Clem says, and laughs. La La tries to join him, but what comes out is more like a grunt.

"The bird was happy when we got home," says the woman, who wears a yellow ski jacket and fiddles with a silver hoop earring. "He was singing that *Wizard of Oz* song." She runs her fingers through her hair. "The thief took a diamond necklace I inherited from my mother."

You'll buy another before the insurance check even clears.

The woman turns away, but the camera and mic follow her. "My mother wore it every Christmas Eve. Just seeing it in the jewelry box would remind me of her." She wipes her nose with a tissue she pulls from her pocket.

How was La La supposed to know *that*? If she did know, she wouldn't have taken it, or she might not have. She bends to caress Black, who licks her hand reassuringly. She glances at Clem, but he doesn't seem to have a clue. "Definitely one of my professors. Probably picking up some Christmas gifts. You know how crowded department stores are this time of year." Clem laughs.

"Of all things," the homeowner says, "he took a silver-plated yin-yang pendant. It was my college roommate's. When she died of cancer, her mother gave it to me."

La La's heart beats erratically. Clem looks confused. "That sounds like the necklace you were wearing last night, doesn't it?"

"They're pretty common," La La says, her face warming. "The store had a million of them."

He touches his beard. "Where did you say you got it?"

La La tries to come up with the name of a jewelry store, and when she can't, she invents one. "The Jewelry Basket," she says. "It's not far from school. There's a gas station across the street."

Clem looks absently at the TV. He shakes his head, and La La imagines the argument he's having with himself. His face turns pale and the corners of his mouth crimp.

"You okay?" she asks.

"I'm great. My fiancée is a burglar. That was you breaking into the house, right?" He squeezes the remote control, his knuckles turning white. "Wait—before you answer that. Are you in veterinary school? Have you ever been in veterinary school?" He rakes his beard with his fingers, scratching so hard La La's afraid he'll draw blood.

"I told you I don't do that anymore."

Clem rises. "Let's go to the jewelry store. Right now."

"They're probably closed." Sweat runs down La La's belly.

"Maybe they're open late for the holidays. You told me you saw it in the window, didn't you? Maybe they put another one in the display."

La La tries to think of an excuse. She can't tell Clem the truth without putting their relationship at risk. The mere thought of him leaving causes La La's vision to narrow, dimming the room. Yet she's reluctant to tell another lie that he's unlikely to believe. She looks toward the dogs, but they can't help her. "When I saw it, I thought if I had it, I'd feel closer to my mother." She touches her chest, imagining the pendant. "So I took it."

"Just like that? You took it?"

La La rubs her shirt against her stomach to absorb the sweat. "I was already in the house. For Zev."

"Why?" he cries, startling the dogs, who scurry to a corner of the room and huddle together, tails tucked.

"He got arrested. His lawyer costs a fortune. I can't earn that kind of money as a vet tech."

Clem sinks back into the chair.

La La tells him about her father's break-in. "He saved the guy."

"He nearly killed him."

"Actually, the guy's recovering. Slowly. Zev's lawyer said he's even breathing a little on his own." She leans toward Clem. "But this is why I didn't tell you. I knew you wouldn't understand. It was very courageous of my father to call nine-one-one. If he hadn't, we wouldn't be having this conversation, because he would have gotten away. He's very good at what he does."

"Good at being a burglar?"

"Yes." La La glares at him. The news has moved on to a story about child abduction.

Clem comes over and sits next to her on the couch. He pushes a strand of hair behind her ear. "I'm sorry about your father. I really am. But you don't want to throw away your life because of his mistakes, do you?"

"Sometimes you have to take a risk to help someone you love."

"What about the people you hurt?"

"They'll install better locks. Be more security conscious. Who knows, I might prevent something worse from happening to them."

Clem looks toward the darkened window. "You don't believe that. And you promised me you were finished with stealing."

La La studies Clem's profile. "I didn't know he'd get arrested."

"You could have asked me for help. I don't like Zev, but I would have done it for you."

"You can't afford his lawyer. Besides, I'm not just stealing. I'm taking care of animals."

"You've done this more than once?"

"A few times."

Standing up, Clem towers over her. "You're insane. You think you're some kind of Robin Hood, stealing from the rich to help animals. La La of Goldstone Forest. Where's your bow and arrow?"

"You're mocking me."

"I want you to hear how ridiculous you sound." He walks to the window. "We're engaged. You should have confided in me. Did you ever think about how this would affect me? What if you get caught?"

He's shouting, which causes La La to lower her voice. "I won't."

"Your father thought that, too."

La La runs her hand over the depression in the cushion Clem vacated. "I took a leave of absence."

"What?"

"You asked if I was still in veterinary school. I was, but I took a leave."

"What did you tell the school?"

"That my father is sick."

"You lie to everyone."

Joining Clem at the window, La La touches the glass and feels the cold, a fragile barrier away.

"Why can't Zev rob a few extra houses and pay for his own lawyer?" Clem asks.

"He's under house arrest. And it wouldn't be a good idea while he's awaiting trial." She grasps his wrist, catching dark hairs beneath her fingertips, already missing the small intimacies of their relationship. "It's only until his case is resolved. Then I'll go back to school, and everything will be like it was."

Clem pulls his hand away. "You really think you can get a temporary job as a criminal?"

"I love you."

"You have to stop, or I'm moving out. I have a kindness blog, for God's sake! I want people to be more loving. I thought you wanted that, too. That you showed it by helping animals. I don't know what to think now."

"My father took care of me."

Clem closes his eyes. "What about us?"

Having made her choice, La La has no answer.

5

After La La quiets the barking dog during her first job with her father, Zev thrusts his chin toward a security decal in the window. "You see that?" he whispers. "Fake. Real ones have the alarm company name." A blue backpack hangs from her father's shoulder.

When no one answers the doorbell, they go around back. Zev pulls a crowbar from under his coat and shows La La how to insert it above the lock. He pries open the door, splintering the frame. Worry buzzes through La La's arms and legs, sits like a helmet on her head. She longs to run but is afraid to leave Zev. Breaking into a house seems wrong, but how can it be if her father is doing it?

In the master bedroom, Zev goes through drawers carefully, dropping items into his backpack. An Irish setter observes them from his bed in a corner of the room, chin on his paws. La La scratches his ears, then stations herself next to a window that faces the front yard as if by watching for trouble she can keep it away.

A mail carrier walks up the street, shoving envelopes through slots. Will the woman notice something amiss? Hear them inside through the narrow opening? La La tugs her father's sleeve and points. Putting a finger to his lips, Zev continues searching the room. The mail carrier stitches a path from house to house, her cart scrabbling along the sidewalk. La La peeks from behind a curtain, fingers clenching the red muslin. When the woman turns up the walk, La La wraps herself in the fabric. *Chunk chunk* comes the mail. Frightened, La La wets herself, the first time since she was a baby.

In the car, soggy and cold, La La hides her condition from her father.

At a truck stop, Zev breathes on a diamond, fogging it. "See how it doesn't stay misty? That's how you know it's real." When La La barely nods, Zev shoves the diamond in his pocket. She can at least pretend to be interested, he thinks, after insisting he take her with him.

"La La's too busy to come to the phone," Zev says later that afternoon when his daughter's friend Charlotte calls, though La La's just watching *The Price Is Right*. When the two girls get together, they don't shut up, telling each other the smallest details of their eight-year-old lives. After Zev hangs up, he fills a bucket and mops the kitchen floor. Then he finds La La in front of the TV. "You can never tell anyone what we do."

"You told me that already. Who was on the phone?"

"No one," Zev says. "Let's play War. I'll get the deck."

Although La La usually loves to play cards, this time she's slow to flip them over. "It had to have been someone."

The next afternoon, La La's friend Ananda appears at the door. "Can La La come out?"

"She has the measles," Zev says, and he closes the door before Ananda can reply.

La La charges down the hall. "I'm fine!"

"Your life is different from Ananda's now," Zev says, still grasping the doorknob.

"She's my friend."

"I'll be your friend." He knows it isn't the same. The girls play Cat's Cradle, knitting strings over their fingers in elaborate patterns. They jump rope, chanting, "Cinderella, dressed in yella, made a mistake, kissed a snake." Yet he can't take the chance La La will slip and reveal their activities. He's prepared to be vigilant to keep other kids away, but as soon as they hear La La's sick, they stop coming.

When the school secretary phones a few days later to check on La La, Zev says he wants to homeschool his daughter. Soon after, a large manila envelope arrives in the mail from the school district. Zev completes the paperwork, surprised there's so little to it. It seems just about anyone can teach their child at home if they want to. He studies with La La when they're not on a locksmith call or robbing a home, hoping he'll be more successful as a teacher than he was as a student.

At La La's age, he was called into the principal's office regularly for making off with devices he was curious about but couldn't afford to buy: a teacher's handheld calculator, an audio cassette player, bicycle and combination locks, and transistor radios belonging to his classmates. He intended to return each device after dismantling it and putting it back together but sometimes was caught before the reconstruction was complete. Then his father, a toll collector on the New Jersey side of the George Washington Bridge, was made to pay for the item, and the pieces were thrown away. Sputtering curses, his face as red as the tomatoes he grew every summer, Sam would beat him, but Zev's curiosity was un-deterred.

Over time, Zev's skills as a thief improved, and he learned to evade detection. When six months passed without a call from the principal, his father, who had developed an affinity for the belt, found other excuses to thrash Zev: dust under his bed, dirty fingernails, a description of their family as poor to a cousin. His mother, who suffered from constant migraines, tried but couldn't protect him. When she died in a car accident, Zev barely noticed her absence. He doubled his efforts to keep his room and his body immaculate, but even that didn't stop his father.

At fifteen, tired of welts that burned along his ass and back and kept him on his feet all day, Zev ran away to Manhattan, where he slept in abandoned buildings, wrapped in newspaper. He picked pockets and broke into bus station lockers to survive.

A year later, after he had picked a coin-operated locker, someone slammed a hand on the locker door. "Nice work," said a man in mustard coveralls, EMERGENCY LOCKSMITH sewn across the chest. He licked the bottom of his yellow mustache, then smoothed it with his fingers. "Who taught you?"

"I figured it out."

"I'm Elijah." The man's voice, like his neck, was thick. "You have a name?"

"Stan," Zev said.

"Well, Stan, mind the cop out front. Or if you'd like to put your skills to better use, apprentice for me. I've got more work than I can handle, and you seem like a quick study. Be at this address tomorrow at eight." He handed Zev a card.

"Sure," Zev said, never intending to see Elijah again. But

when he woke the next morning stiff with cold, he realized it would be nice to have a regular job. One that would allow him to rent a room with heat.

Elijah taught him to pick common locks—cams and dead bolts and ratchet bars—and to install them. When locks defied picks, Elijah demonstrated how to open them with a bump key or by drilling through. He had Zev copy keys. The man took him out for hamburgers and milkshakes, letting Zev order as many as he liked. He bought him sturdy shoes and a warm winter coat. In Elijah's eyes, Zev saw a measure of kindness intended for someone else, a measure of pain Zev didn't cause but that his presence evoked.

On the days Zev wasn't working, he stole. Employing his new skills, he broke into homes. He didn't need the money, but he enjoyed the challenge, and it was more exciting than being a locksmith.

The cry of a kitten, like the sound of a hinge before Zev oils it, wakes La La. She shivers, and her nose drips as it used to on frigid winter mornings when she and her mother walked the three blocks to school, Elissa tugging on her hand, while La La struggled to keep up. She can still picture her mother, who has been gone a month: coffee-brown hair that fell into her eyes, pale cheeks, long fingers that were expert at removing splinters. But the room in La La's mind that holds the image is growing darker over time, details disappearing.

The kitten squeaks again, a sound meant for a mother cat but that finds La La, instead. Hurrying to the entryway of her house, La La pulls open the front door and steps barefoot into the brittle cold. A foot of snow has frozen to a hard crunch on the lawn. In a basket on the landing, swaddled in a baby's fleece blanket, the kitten trembles, her face—brindle fur and yellow eyes—and her pink tongue exposed. La La wonders who could have left her. She brings the basket inside to her room. As she lifts the animal out, she discovers a book, *Caring for Your Cat,* beneath the blanket. When La La dives back into bed, the kitten grazes her chin with a tiny, sharp claw. La La opens the book.

She's read three chapters when the smell of pancakes floats into her room. La La wraps the kitten in the fleece blanket and carries her into the kitchen. She holds the cat up for Zev to see. "Someone left her for us. In a basket."

He rests a plastic spatula in the hot skillet. "Like Moses in the bulrushes."

La La doesn't know what he's talking about. "She was cold. She doesn't have a collar."

"We'll bring her to the shelter," he says, as he retrieves syrup from the refrigerator.

La La clasps her arms around the kitten. "I warmed her up."

"You did a good thing."

"Maybe she's from Mom."

Zev unscrews the cap from the syrup. He has no doubt that's who the kitten is from, a twisted good-bye gift from Elissa, who knows he doesn't like animals. The fleece blanket is one he purchased for La La when she was an infant that Elissa took to keeping in her car for rescues such as this one. The thought of Elissa hiding somewhere in town a month after she left, setting the basket down on their landing but not bothering to come in to see him or La La, infuriates Zev.

"Mom loved animals," La La says.

"Yeah, that's all she—"

"I'm going to call her Mo."

"For Moses?" Zev says, as he sets the table.

"For Mother."

"The shelter will name her."

"The pancakes!" La La says. But it's too late. Smoke drifts toward the ceiling, setting off the alarm.

Zev turns off the burner and removes the skillet. "Cats cost money," he shouts. He climbs on a chair and pulls the batteries from the alarm. "They shed."

La La turns the kitten toward her. "She can be my friend."

With the melted spatula, Zev scrapes burnt pancakes into the trash.

"I don't have any friends," La La says.

Zev stares at the ruined pan. It's true. No one appears at the door for La La anymore. No one calls, inviting her to sleep over. He can't remember the last time she asked him to buy a gift for a birthday party, but of course he wouldn't let her go. It's what he intended, but seeing her face pressed toward the kitten's, her shoulders curled into her chest, he has second thoughts. Yet he can see no other way to ensure their work remains secret. He feels as he did when he used to find her standing alone in front of the cavernous, nearly empty school building because Elissa forgot to pick her up, except now he's the one neglecting her.

La La raises her head. "The book says she needs shots."

"What book?"

"The one that was in the basket."

Zev retrieves a fat telephone book from the hall closet and opens it on the kitchen table. "My daughter found the thing half frozen," he says into the receiver. "It's an emergency."

La La clutches Mo while they ride to the clinic. As she steps inside the brick building, a sharp pain runs down her belly, like the time she tripped and fell on the corner of a box of dominoes she was holding. Her left arm freezes, immobilized in an invisible cast. Her joints stiffen with age. Illnesses, half a dozen or more, ravage her small body, and her eyes itch and tear. She begins to shake and nearly drops Mo.

A young veterinarian with a cartoon character's round head and acne scars has just returned a cat to his owner. The vet wears the top of his blue scrubs inside out, the label visible and a thread trailing off a seam. After introducing himself to La La, Dr. Bergman scoops Mo into his arms. He has La La sit down and asks her what she's feeling. "It could be that you're allergic to something in the clinic," he says, and he makes the unorthodox suggestion that he examine Mo in Zev's car.

As soon as La La exits the clinic, she feels better. She climbs into the back seat of her father's car, while Zev gets into the front. He starts the engine and turns up the heat. When the veterinarian joins them, he carries a black bag. He listens to Mo's heart and lungs, looks at her ears and toes, and pushes on her abdomen. "Well, Mona, you're healthy," he says.

"It's just Mo," La La says. "I named her after my mother."

"A fine name." Dr. Bergman puts away his otoscope. "We'll give Mo her initial vaccinations today." He writes what the cat needs on a prescription pad. "When you get home, call to schedule her spay surgery," he says to Zev.

"How much is *that* going to cost?" Zev asks.

"We offer monthly payment plans."

"Monthly payment plans," Zev repeats, drawing out the words as if they're in a foreign language.

A man steps out of the clinic, a husky limping at his side, and La La flinches, grabbing her knee.

"Did you injure yourself?" the doctor asks.

"No."

"Think carefully. You're sure you didn't hurt yourself?"

"I don't think so."

The vet regards La La with renewed interest. "We just did surgery on that husky's anterior cruciate ligament."

"English," Zev says.

"His knee." Dr. Bergman follows the husky's progress through the parking lot before turning back to La La. "Do you always feel what animals around you feel?"

Just that week, she shared the thirst of a poodle chained outside a coffee shop, his fear of a passerby's wide-brimmed hat, and the trembling excitement of a cat on a hunt. "I guess so."

"I've heard about animal empaths, but I've never met one," the veterinarian says.

Zev glances over his shoulder. "Animal what?"

"You're a remarkable young girl." The doctor nods, agreeing with himself.

Remarkable, La La mouths, the *m* like a kiss.

"I'm glad you're keeping Mo," Dr. Bergman says. "I'll visit you sometimes if it's okay with your father. Bring a patient. To help with treatment, but also to allow you to develop your skills." Clicking his pen open and closed, the doctor asks Zev, "No school today?"

"I homeschool her."

"That explains it." The doctor takes Mo inside for shots, forgetting his black bag on the seat. Ten minutes later, a vet tech brings the kitten back. She grabs the bag. "He's been looking all over for this."

"What a nut," Zev says, as they drive home.

La La is sorry the appointment is over. She likes Dr. Bergman.

About once a month, Dr. Bergman stops by the house. When he calls to say he's coming, La La tenses, her muscles contracting in anticipation of the pain his visit might bring. She's felt the aching belly of a dog who ate a sock and the broken leg of a cat who tumbled from a window, and a rabbit with a respiratory infection made her wheeze. Nevertheless, she looks forward to seeing Dr. Bergman, to the treats he brings for Mo and the books for her, *Black Beauty, Charlotte's Web, Lassie.*

On one such visit, the doctor arrives with a dog who won't stop scratching. "He has allergies," the veterinarian says. The Weimaraner was the runt of the litter, and the breeder couldn't get rid of him. His tail is docked, and his ears hang like flags on a windless day. The side of La La's head and her ribs throb where the breeder kicked the dog. "He has to eat a special diet, duck and potato, no corn or wheat," says Dr. Bergman.

"They gave dogs leftovers when I was growing up," Zev calls from the hall. He always stays close by when the doctor visits.

"Add two fish oil tablets to his dinner," Dr. Bergman tells La La before stepping out of the room. "Weimaraners make excellent watchdogs," he says to Zev.

Returning to La La's bedroom, the vet scratches Mo under the chin. "Looking good, Mona," he says. La La has given up correcting him.

"Hell of a nerve dumping a dog on us," her father says after Dr. Bergman drives away, though Zev agreed to take the Weimaraner and is already cutting a length of rope for a leash. La La names the dog Tiny.

Mo and Tiny sleep with La La. On nights when La La thrashes with a recurring nightmare, her mother flying away in a silver spaceship that recedes until it isn't even a dot in the sky, Tiny wakes her, nudging her ankles with his cold, wet snout. La La clasps Mo to her heart, the cat's softness soothing her.

At the dining room table, from a book like the one she used in school, Zev tries to teach La La math. Explaining fractions for the third time, he breaks his pencil point. "Ask Dr. Bergman," he says, shoving the book away.

For her reading lessons, La La goes through the newspaper's crime section, checking to see if their burglaries were reported. She reads wedding announcements and scans obituaries for funeral times, then looks up the addresses of family members in phone books. While families celebrate and mourn, Zev and La La rob their homes.

Zev's idea of physical education is to have La La climb through their dining room window and scale their fence. With Tiny beside her, she does sprints in the backyard, training for a time when she and her father might have to run.

During his next visit, Dr. Bergman shows La La the crusty scales on a parakeet's feet and describes how to treat them. La La squats to scratch her toes and notices the doctor wears one brown sock and one blue.

Returning the parakeet to its cage, the doctor says, "After you treat the bird, clean out the cage to get rid of the mites."

"Blech," says La La, but even as she says it, she can feel them crawling beneath the scales, feeding on the bird's skin, their hunger no different from the parakeet's or hers at dinnertime.

"I'm pretty sure the bird doesn't like them, either," Dr. Bergman says.

"They're nasty to the bird, but nice to themselves." La La wonders if all creatures are like that, taking care of themselves at the expense of others.

"Well put."

With her finger, La La spells out the words "well put" across the top of her desk, adding a five-pointed star at the end. Then she touches her math textbook. "My father said you could help me."

The doctor scratches his ear. "I'm not really a teacher. At least not that kind." But when he explains fractions, La La understands. "What does your father teach you in science?" he asks.

La La thinks for a minute. She wants the doctor to like Zev. She remembers her father explaining how a crowbar works. Drawing a diagram, she presents it to the doctor. "We're studying force and leverage," she says, proud to have remembered the fancy words. In the hall, Zev coughs so hard La La wonders if she should get him some water.

The doctor studies the diagram. Lines appear between his eyes as he reaches for his pen. *Click, click, click, click.*

After the veterinarian leaves, Zev tears up the image of the crowbar wedged between door and frame. "He asks too many questions," Zev says. "Maybe he shouldn't come over."

"I *like* him," La La says. "And no one else visits me."

Zev drops the shredded paper in the trash basket. "He's so flaky, he probably doesn't remember anything, anyway."

La La doesn't think the doctor is flaky, not in the ways that count.

"She's here. I smell her," La La says, standing in a stranger's master bedroom.

Zev smells it too, the rose fragrance he bought Elissa every year on her birthday. "It's just her perfume." Still, he can't help imagining his wife lying on the enormous bed, reading the mystery on the elegant white nightstand.

"It's her." La La remains in the middle of the room, though normally she stands watch at a window. She lifts her nose.

Examining the contents of a dresser drawer, Zev says, "It's not her."

La La pokes her head into a cavernous walk-in closet.

"You're in the way." Zev pushes past her. Cherry-picks the most valuable pieces from a jewelry box. Elissa wore tie-dyed shirts and roughed-up cowboy boots, but the woman of the house owns high heels and designer silks. Yet who's to say Elissa didn't buy a new wardrobe to go with her new life?

"We should leave her a note."

"No," Zev says.

"To let her know we're not mad," La La calls after him, as he exits the room. "We just want her to come home."

He catches La La moments later in the den, writing on a mono-grammed pad. *Dear Mom,* she began, followed by three hearts.

Zev snatches the pad. He tears off the top sheet, balls up the paper, and stuffs it into his pocket. "You'll get us caught. Your mother doesn't live here. Even if she did, why do you think she would want to come home? She knows where to find us."

"Maybe she has amnesia."

His daughter's been watching too many soap operas. La La runs back toward the master bedroom.

"We have to go!" Zev examines a photo on the desk. The woman in the picture—stiff, blond hair falling over a crisp pastel blouse—looks nothing like Elissa. He feels like smashing it. "Now!"

In La La's room later that day, her blanket, clothes, even the damp towel on the bed smell of roses. Zev bought the perfume to please Elissa, and occasionally she wore it to excite him. Her casual touches transferred it to his skin. Closing his eyes, he inhales deeply. When he opens his eyes, loss coats him like a tarnish no amount of polish can remove.

His daughter knows better than to take items from homes. That's his job. And they never keep anything that can link them to the burglaries. He'll punish her, take away TV for a week and refuse to buy the expensive treats Tiny loves. Searching the room, he finds the bottle under her pillow. He's about to put it in his pocket when he changes his mind. Removing the cap, he pumps a cloud above his head and lets the fragrance rain down.

That night, La La has the dream, her mother soaring away, but this time the rocket fuel smells like roses.

In La La's bedroom, Dr. Bergman assembles a set of anatomical models he says are being replaced in his office, though they look new. After they examine the leg on the canine model, Dr. Bergman has La La feel the bones in Tiny's leg. He shows her how to exert just enough pressure on the skin, moving her fingers to the femur, fibula, tibia, and patella. The doctor's hand is large; his fingers, rough and caring. The world grows smaller when he removes them.

"Domesticated animals have survived by understanding humans. What's more unusual is to find a human who understands animals," the doctor says.

He means her, and for once she feels like more than an outcast.

"You have a gift," he says, "and with a gift comes responsibility. For now, that means taking good care of Mona and Tiny, but there will come a time when you'll have a chance to help more animals. Try not to let anything get in the way." Pinching the bridge of his nose, the doctor looks toward the hall.

La La wants nothing more than to take care of animals the way Dr. Bergman does. She can't see anything stopping her.

6

After a sleepless night, La La tries again to make Clem understand why she has to help her father. "Zev will die in prison," she says.

"Don't you think that's a bit of an exaggeration?" He shoves khakis, cotton pullovers, walking shoes he can stand in all day, and a toiletry bag into a suitcase.

When La La can't bear to watch anymore, she practices her examination skills, running her hands over Black's fur, checking his skin, feeling his abdomen, looking at his eyes and lids, stretching his lips to see his molars. Blue's turn arrives, but he hops away.

Clem jots the name of a motel on the back of a used envelope and holds it out to La La. She refuses to accept it, so he sets it on her dresser.

"Don't go," she says, while he zips up the suitcase. "I'm sorry," she tries, as he tucks his orthopedic pillow under his arm. He grabs his keys from the hook in the entryway. "We're engaged," she says, but he doesn't seem to hear. And maybe they're not engaged anymore. Her breath comes shallow and fast as he shuts the door behind him.

In the bedroom, Blue sniffs the spot where Clem's pillow used to be and whines. Black gnaws a shoe Clem left behind. La La curls up on the floor next to Black, her head on his flank. Why does she always end up with animals as her only companions? Clem's actions seem cruel. She's surprised by the depth of his anger. What has she done, after all, other than try to help her father?

When she gets up, she surveys the closet, reluctant to spread out the clothes that remain. To fill the gap would be to accept that Clem isn't coming back. She prefers to keep the hole and hope.

Around lunchtime, she texts Nat, loads the dogs into the Mercedes, and drives to a park, where she sits on a bench cleared of snow. She unclips the dogs' leashes. Blue takes off, and Black hops up beside her.

As she waits for Nat, her cell phone plays "Honky Cat," and again she lets Dr. Bergman's call go to voice mail. Wrapping an arm around Black, she listens to the message. "You're hard to reach. I shouldn't be surprised. I remember how crazy vet school was. Maybe you and Clem want to join us for brunch on Sunday. Nothing fancy. Charlotte makes a mean meatless chili, and I've been known to bake fresh bread on the weekends. A break might be good for you. I'd love to hear how you're doing, and of course the dogs and even Zev. I think about him more than you might imagine. Interesting fellow. Well, I've gone on too long. I hope you get this. Oh, it's me, Ronald Bergman, you know, Dr. Bergman. Anyway, it would just be you and Clem and me and Charlotte. I better sign off; my vet tech is waving at me. I must be late for an appointment." He forgets to disconnect and the message continues as he greets his next patient.

There's nothing La La would like more than to give Dr. Bergman good news about her progress. As it is, she'd rather he think she's busy in the hospital.

Nat shows up twenty minutes later with her leashed ferret, Casey. He sits on her lap, while Nat brushes his shadow-colored fur. "Sorry it took a while. I stopped at home. Casey could use the air."

"We broke up," La La says, suppressing a smile, her emotions haywire from the shock of Clem leaving. If she starts to laugh, she doesn't think she'll be able to stop. Cars pass, their tires churning through wet streets. A girl in a green jacket tosses a tennis ball for a flat-coated retriever, and the ball disappears in piles of white. Though next to her on the bench, Nat and Casey seem miles away. La La scratches Black's neck, the dog's pleasure erasing the memory of Clem's bulging suitcase, but not for long.

The wind whips the pom-pom on Nat's hat. "What happened?"

La La examines the dirty, boot-flattened snow at her feet. "He found out." Ever since they became a couple, La La worried Clem might leave her. Yet she feels as unprepared as if she never imagined it.

"Not easy to keep something like that a secret," Nat says.

"It's not like I want to be a burglar. I'd rather be in the hospital with you."

"I wonder."

"I have to help Zev. I know what it's like to have someone give up on you. I know it even better now."

Nat sets down Casey's brush. She fishes antibiotic ointment

and arthritis medication from her purse and hands them to La La. "That's all there was. You didn't get them from me."

"Thanks," La La says, relieved the hospital still throws the expired medications into a donation basket meant for shelters. She doesn't know in what condition she'll find animals and wants to be prepared.

Cold spreads upward from the bench. When La La scratches Casey's belly, the ferret climbs onto her shoulder. "Would Tank leave you over something like this?"

"Tank might offer to help. Sometimes I think he misses the adrenaline." Nat pulls her hat over her ears, the wind having picked up again.

Darting over, Blue drops a tennis ball at La La's feet. The flat-coated retriever and his owner aren't far behind. La La lifts the ball, damp with snow and drool, and wipes it on her jeans. She hands it to the girl.

"Your dog gets around pretty good on three legs," the kid says.

"You don't need everything you're born with."

The girl scratches Blue under the chin and runs off, the retriever following.

When she's out of earshot, Nat says, "You want me to tell you the truth, right?"

"You're going to anyway."

"I haven't lived within a thousand miles of my parents since I was seventeen." Nat worries a blemish on her cheek. "My father's a perfect gentleman in public who's in love with Wild Turkey in private, and I have imperfectly healed bones to show for it. Every time my mother sees me, she reminds me I'm responsible for ending the family line. Ask me, I'm doing the world a favor. Personally, I've found it's better to stay away. I definitely wouldn't risk my marriage and career for them."

"My father never hit me," La La says.

"No, he taught you to break into homes."

"I insisted."

"You were eight!"

Tired, Blue collapses at La La's feet. La La regrets getting together with Nat, who can't seem to see beyond her own troubled upbringing.

At the kitchen table, Zev dismantles the duplicate monitor. Removing the one strapped to his ankle would interrupt the fiber-optic beam that travels its circumference, triggering an alarm at the monitoring company. But Zev read online about someone beating the device. Monitoring companies often ignore disruptions of less than a minute because they can be caused by accidents, such as banging the contraption against a tub or chair leg. A man who removed and reassembled the device within that time was able to escape without alerting authorities.

Later he'll time himself, but now Zev just wants to get to know the monitor. He's removed two screws when Mo hops up and bats them away. Zev crawls on the floor, searching for them. He'll have to remember to put Mo in a carrier if he ever takes apart the real thing. He's not in a hurry to flee, doesn't know where he'd go or what he'd do. Committing burglaries in a strange city would be hard. He wouldn't be able to contact La La, not until law enforcement stopped looking for him, and who knows how long that would be. On the other hand, if he ran, La La could stop robbing houses. She's the best part of his life.

The worst is having dragged her into his problems. Finding the screws, he returns to the table.

Mo paws at the window above the sink, a finch on a bush safely beyond her reach.

"I'd let you out," Zev says, "but La La thinks you'd make an owl or a fox a nice dinner. Me, I don't think you'd let them catch you."

La La would have taken Mo when she returned from college, but the quack is allergic to cats. Zev knows he isn't the best owner. Never teases Mo with any of the feathery toys La La's bought over the years. Killed the pot of catnip La La grew, forgetting to water it. At least he keeps the litter clean.

As if she can read his thoughts, Mo returns to his lap. Zev feels sentimental, thinking of leaving, and rubs the bottom of her chin. Nothing is certain yet. He removes the rest of the screws. The device is in pieces when he hears a car drive up. Scooping the parts into a brown paper bag, he stows them in his bedroom closet.

La La parks in front of her father's house. He's the one person she can count on not to defend Clem. She lets the dogs out, and they follow her to the back door. Inside, they spy the cat on top of the couch and press their snouts to her bottom. La La registers Mo's annoyance and the soreness of her joints as she jumps to the top of a bookshelf.

"What's wrong?" Zev says. "I wasn't expecting you."

On the dining table, rattling a steady beat, a locomotive pulls a single open freight car around an oval track. Zev hasn't bothered with the lights, trees, or station house that came in the box.

The setup is downright barren, and La La wishes for a tiny engineer or some plastic riders waiting to board.

She sinks onto the couch, which smells of piney fabric freshener. Rubbing her neck, she tells Zev about Clem discovering one of her burglaries and moving out.

Her father plucks lint from a chair's sailcloth cushion. "Good riddance."

La La wants to be angry at Clem but remembers the way he enfolded her in his arms after she'd helped put an animal down in the clinic. How he massaged her feet when she was tired, though he had every reason to be exhausted himself. "I love him."

Zev carries the lint into the kitchen. "You're just attracted to his chemical scent," he calls out.

La La hears the garbage can open and shut. "Where'd you read that?"

"What does it matter if it's true?"

Her father never dated anyone after Elissa. Once, on a job, he looked at a dusty wedding photo and said, "They're deluding themselves." La La expected that would be the end of it, but he lifted the picture and cleaned the glass with the tail of his shirt before replacing it and continuing to rob the couple. As a child, La La would watch romantic comedies with Zev, and he would scoff at the happy endings, but he never fell asleep as he did during other movies.

La La looks at her diamond ring, imagining Clem will ask for it back before too long. Mo has returned to the couch. When Black barks at the feline interloper, La La shoos him away.

"You're too good for him," Zev says, returning to the room. "You're going to be a real doctor, even if your patients have four legs." He cuts the power to the train, and the room falls silent.

La La buries her nose in the cat's fur, the smell as subtle as tree bark.

Retrieving a feather duster from a closet, Zev swipes the coffee table. "Can you trust him?"

La La sits up. "What are you talking about?"

"Maybe he'll go to the police."

"Why would he do that?"

"How do I know?" He lifts a lamp from an end table and dusts under it.

"He wouldn't."

Abandoning the duster, Zev gets out the vacuum cleaner and turns it on. The dogs hide under the dining table.

"Do you have to do that now?" La La shouts. She lifts her feet, so he doesn't run them over.

"I thought we agreed you wouldn't tell people what we do," Zev yells.

"He figured it out," she says, but she doubts he can hear her over the noise of the machine.

The vacuum rams a table leg, and the dogs scramble onto the couch. "Who else have you told?"

Mentioning Nat would upset Zev even more, and she can't think of anyone more trustworthy than her friend. "No one."

"Thank God."

La La remembers how they hid in the house for days, shades drawn and doors double-locked, the few times Zev thought someone had seen them on a job. He laundered the same clothes over and over, the colors fading, and watched TV news morning and night, until at last he decided it was safe to work again.

Putting away the vacuum cleaner, Zev takes out furniture polish and a rag. An artificial lemon scent infuses the room as he squeezes out the cleaner. Shifting Mo back to the couch, La La gathers Black and Blue and begins her exit. Zev is so absorbed in his cleaning, he doesn't seem to notice.

As she walks to her car, La La gets a call from Dr. Porter, dean of the veterinary school. "I've got a tricky case, and I thought of you," he says.

Even in veterinary school, La La tried to hide that she could sense what animals feel. But certain professors noticed her ability to diagnose illnesses sometimes before lab tests came back and began to rely on her. "I'm glad to help," she says, the words tumbling out of her mouth, she's so grateful not to have been forgotten.

"I'm treating a cow that's been losing a lot of weight. She's got diarrhea and her milk production's down," Dr. Porter says. "The thing is, she's been eating and her temperature is normal. I've run some tests, and I've got my suspicions, but I'd like to know what you think."

When La La closes her eyes, she can almost see the animal, skin stretched tightly over her bones.

At the hospital later that afternoon, students and professors in scrubs hurry to afternoon classes and to see patients. A few stop to greet La La and to ask after her father. La La didn't think to put on scrubs but wishes she had, to remind herself she isn't merely a burglar and to reclaim her place among her classmates if only for an hour.

Dr. Porter, an older man with a stiff gait and ears grown large from listening, is studying a chart in his office. Together they walk to an isolation stall in the area behind the main hospital where large animals are received.

The cow is a Guernsey, the color of rich earth, and ordinarily twelve hundred pounds, though nowhere near that now. La La feels a cavernous hole in her belly, as if she hasn't eaten in a week, though she just had a bowl of rice and beans. She also feels the cow's abdominal pain. She strokes the animal's side. "If it's not showing up in tests yet, maybe Johne's disease?"

"That's what I'm thinking, too."

"She's scared and starving," La La says, revealing too much about herself in service of the animal.

On Saturday night, La La bowls with Nat and Tank at The Alley Cat. They used to be a foursome. She and Clem would laugh at the sour smell of the rental shoes and the giant mural of pins floating among shooting stars and planets.

Sitting on an orange bench, La La wishes the night were over and she were in her house where she could be miserable in private. Black and Blue are with Clem. He texted that afternoon to see if he could have them for the night, and La La agreed though she hated to part with them. She thought when he picked them up, she'd have another chance to convince him she was doing the right thing. But once he arrived, she couldn't think of a thing to say that she hadn't already said, and he loaded the dogs into the car and was gone.

Tank is the embodiment of a New Year's resolution, with glowing skin and muscles so defined they could be used to teach anatomy. Nat once confided that he makes her feel safe. His head is shaved, and he wears sleeveless shirts with aphorisms like "sweat is fat crying" and "pain is weakness leaving your body." Three months before, he was fired from his job as a personal trainer at a health club for booking appointments with members at their homes without going through the club. Although he's been looking for another full-time job, he's managed to find only a handful of private clients.

Every time Tank wraps his arm around Nat, she squirms away. She's probably trying to protect La La's feelings, but it just serves to remind La La that she's alone. Once, interrupting her approach, La La turns around to ask her friends if they think the place is hotter than usual. Catching them in the middle of a kiss, little more than a peck, her ball grows heavier. She resists the urge to drop it in the gutter.

After Nat bowls her sixth frame, she gathers their empty cups and heads to the concession stand.

Though it's his turn, Tank doesn't pick up a ball. Instead, he sits next to La La. The crash of pins creates a wall of sound around them. He leans over and whispers, "I admire what you're doing for your father. It takes guts."

"Thanks?" La La presses her knee to keep it from bouncing. Nat didn't say anything about telling Tank.

"You're welcome. They call prison hard time, but what's really hard is living the rest of your life with a record. It isn't easy making less money than your wife. It's humiliating. But I've got an idea for how we can both make some money."

La La's feet sweat in the suffocating shoes. "Yeah?"

"Prescription drugs. Oxycodone, Percocet, Valium, Ritalin, you name it. Medicine cabinets are stuffed with them. Bring them to me. I'll get a good price for them. We'll split it fifty-fifty. Grab everything. I'll sort it out later."

"Have you told Nat?"

He runs his hand over his scalp. "Nah. You should have heard what she said about you breaking into homes."

"What did she say?"

"'I'm surprised at La La, blah, blah. What she's doing is crazy, yada, yada.' Doesn't understand you have to help your father. Not her fault. Her father scarred her. Still, you'd think she'd be a better friend. So, what about the drugs?"

"I don't know. People need their medications." La La glances at the concession stand. Nat has reached the front of the line.

"Don't worry. When they file a police report, the doctor will order an early refill. No one gets hurt."

"I feel weird about stealing medicine. I'm almost a doctor."

"The people I sell the medications to need them. In a bad way. If they were professionals with insurance, they could go to a fancy pain specialist. But because they're junkies or college students, they can't get what they need. Think of it like helping an animal that's suffering."

"My father never stole drugs. It's narcotics trafficking on top of everything else." La La stands and studies their scores, hoping to end the conversation.

"Just think about it. If you change your mind, bring them to me."

"What should she bring you?" Nat sets their beers on a table and sits next to Tank.

"These articles on animal fitness she read. I thought maybe I'd branch out. Help animals stay fit, too."

"That's actually not a bad idea," Nat says. "You could go on runs with them. Take them swimming. Animal obesity is a huge problem. Shortens their life spans. Leads to diabetes, arthritis, heart disease, even cancer. I'm proud of you." Tank runs his fingers through Nat's hair. When Nat catches his wrist, he sighs.

La La considers telling them she's not feeling well and calling a cab. It's not a lie; her head is throbbing. She hasn't felt so isolated since before she met Clem. In college, her freshman roommate paired up immediately, the couple having sex constantly in the single bed that was an arm's length from La La's. They thought nothing of walking around the tiny room naked, the guy coming so close to La La, she was afraid he would accidentally brush her with his junk. She began staying at the library until two in the morning when it closed and would gladly have stayed later.

At campus parties everyone seemed to know everyone but her. She couldn't find the courage to insert herself into the conversations of drunk girls, or to attempt to dance to the slow grunge that blasted from iPhone speakers, so she stopped going. Embarrassed to be eating by herself, she hurried through meals in the cafeteria. Except in the veterinary clinic where she worked, someone talking to her was apt to startle her.

When she began dating Clem, everything changed. Her thoughts about classes and current events—withheld for two years—poured out faster than Clem could keep up. He grasped his large chin as he listened and didn't let go until she slowed down enough for him to comment. They ended most nights in the double bed in his apartment. Of the two, La La was the more inexperienced and the more energetic. He awoke in her feelings of lust and belonging, a combination so powerful she was reluctant to leave his apartment each morning and wouldn't have if he hadn't promised to see her that night.

Nat's hands are on La La's shoulders. "You look a little pale. Maybe this wasn't such a good idea." Nat gathers their things.

"But I'm bowling a personal best!" Tank says.

La La and Nat put on their coats. "I'll drop La La off," Nat says, "and come back for you."

"That's okay. Knowing me, I would just screw it up, anyway."

They drive La La home, but if she thinks she'll feel better when she gets there, she's mistaken. The place is unnaturally quiet. The smell of laundered cotton that lingered around Clem has disappeared.

Taking a walk outside, she tries not to slip on patches of black ice. Ribbon-like clouds weave between the stars. Venus burns a pink hole in the sky.

Is it a mistake to try to save Zev from prison? He once did the same for her. Of course, he was the one who got her involved in crime in the first place. Setting their history aside, don't all children owe their parents something? Though he isn't religious, Zev taught La La passages from the Old Testament for the bat mitzvah they celebrated when she was twelve, just the two of them in the kitchen, drinking Manischewitz from tumblers and eating sponge cake. He recited a few of the Ten Commandments: "Honor thy father" (Zev's version), "Thou shall not murder," and "Thou shall not take God's name in vain," conveniently skipping, "Thou shall not steal." La La came across that one in the Cecil B. DeMille movie. But even if she hadn't, it was something everyone knew.

When the cold grabs the tips of her fingers through her gloves and they begin to sting, she turns around, walking slowly to delay her return. Back in the house, she doesn't need Clem to check that the doors are bolted or the heat is turned down. Zev taught her how to take care of those things. But alone, her skin hurts, her lungs thicken with grief. She wanders from one room to another as if she might have simply misplaced her happiness, left it on a dresser, or absentmindedly stuck it in a kitchen cabinet. She has no one but herself to blame for her isolation. She drove Clem away, just as she did Elissa years before. Though Zev never blamed La La, she knew she was responsible.

A month before Elissa vanished, she brought La La to a frozen lake. While La La sat on the bumper of their Ford Escort, her mother yanked the laces on La La's skates so tight her toes began to tingle. "If you're going to cry, we're going home," Elissa said.

La La wiped the corners of her eyes with a fat black glove.

"Stay away from thin ice, or anywhere you see a slick of water." Elissa pulled up La La's hood. "We'll skate together. Don't let go of my hand."

La La wasn't a baby. She understood about ice. When Zev took her skating, they raced from one end of the lake to the other. Being tethered to her mother was awkward, and when Elissa relaxed, La La plucked her hand free. In the distance, a brown duck waddled. The duck's confidence reassured La La, who never bothered to consider the animal's weight or that it could float in freezing water. Against a flat blue sky, geese flew in formation overhead, honking hello. La La followed them, joining their orderly family and putting distance between herself and Elissa.

It seemed everywhere people heard the story. How a girl— what a wonder it was her they were all talking about—fell through the ice. How a mysterious black dog watched over her until help came. Newspapers ran articles about it. Though her parents tried to hide them, La La saw. The TV news covered it, too. It was easy to condemn a mother for abandoning her child. It was natural to feel outrage. Elissa stopped leaving the house except to go to work at the shelter, until one night she disappeared for good.

La La wished she had listened that day on the lake, holding fast to her mother's hand. In La La's memories, time moved backward and forward, but in reality, it moved in only one direction, giving birth to regret.

7

It's Sunday, a good day to rob churchgoing families. Driving through a well-to-do suburb northwest of Denver, La La passes a house and feels a tickle on her arm. Little more than an itch. Still, she wonders.

A large side yard bordered by thick bushes provides access to the back. La La parks at the end of the block and waits to see if the family will emerge. Her patience is rewarded when an Audi pulls out of the garage, parents in front and children in back, father and son in overcoats, mother and daughter in shearling jackets. La La pauses to make sure no one has forgotten anything.

Clouds gather, layered and gray, their edges dissolving into mist. They touch down in the mountains, where it's raining. A pair of squirrels dart around the trunk of an ash tree, chirping friendly taunts. Stopping, they groom each other. La La looks away.

She moves the car to a spot around the corner. Making sure no one has stayed home, she rings the bell, then walks to the back of the house, where she assesses her options. The windows rise high off the ground, and there isn't a patio table or ladder to climb on. Pulling a crowbar from her bag, she jams it a few inches above the back door lock and pushes. When the frame shatters, the door opens to a recreation room. A stair-stepper and tread-mill face a TV. A signed Avalanche jersey hangs above a water dispenser. Hockey sticks, pads, and other gear tumble over one another in a corner of the room. At the sight of skates, La La flashes back to icy water pulling her down and covering her. She bends over, struggling to breathe.

A Great Dane lopes toward her, pushes his head under her hand. The smoothness of his coat—that and his concern—relax her. She sucks in air as he rubs his fawn-colored flank against her.

When she's recovered, the dog lies on the floor and licks his front leg, and the tickle in La La's arm returns. She'll examine him quickly, she tells herself, then hesitates. The police are al-ready aware of an animal-loving burglar. She should rob the place and get out. But fate seems to have put her there to help.

From his tag she learns his name is Riley. Running her hand over his front leg, she feels it before she sees it: a small, irregu-lar bump. The red-and-gray mass resembles the ones in her text-books. She hates to leave a note, which could give her away. And there's hardly time. If someone heard her jimmy the door, the po-lice could be on their way. She imagines them taking positions in front and back, aiming pistols at the doors. The law is on their side. Her love for her father, a common criminal, no match for it.

Yet if his owners get him to a vet soon, Riley might have a chance. She pulls a drug company pad from her veterinary bag but realizes it won't do. Upstairs, she enters a library. Surrounded by leather-bound and hard- and soft-cover books, she doesn't see anything to write on. In a child's bedroom, the pop star P!nk stares from a poster. La La picks up a spiral notebook and a purple pen from a desk. She flips to the first blank sheet and tears it out. *Riley has a lump on his right front leg,* she writes. It's likely a mast cell tumor, but she doesn't include that. *Get him to a vet right away.* In the living room, she sets the note on the coffee table.

Eight minutes have passed since she entered the house. Crystals dangle from a chandelier above a long mahogany table in the dining room. La La grabs a candelabra displayed in a walnut cabinet and silver flatware from a drawer. As she drops them into her canvas bag, the doorbell rings, then rings again. She pictures Jehovah's Witnesses, a Boy Scout troop raising money, or a housekeeper who uses her key only when the family isn't home. Returning downstairs, she waits by the back door and listens. A motorcycle roars past. Next to her, the Great Dane reaches well above her waist. She caresses his ears, her hand trembling, until quiet falls over the house.

In the master bedroom, a nightstand that smells of orange oil gives up a diamond tennis bracelet and gold earrings. In a medicine cabinet, drugs line up like infantry in her fight to save her father. She touches Ativan, Ritalin, and a generic statin drug, sweat popping out on her neck. But she can't bring herself to take them. Back in the library, she sees a book protruding farther than the rest and free of dust. She snatches it, confirms her instinct that it's a safe, and picks it in under a minute, recovering a roll of hundreds. A photograph in an ebony cabinet has captured a girl in a hockey uniform lying on the couch next to Riley, the dog filling most of the furniture. In another picture, the family hikes with Riley on a mountain trail. She hopes they won't be the last photos the family takes with the dog.

•   •   •

At the kitchen table that night, La La examines the Elizabeth Golds listed on the people-finder website. She excludes women too old or too young to have given birth to her, leaving fifteen possibilities. Zev would know Elissa's exact age, but La La's afraid to ask, since he made it clear he didn't want Elissa's help.

She calls the women whose phone numbers are listed, leaving voice mails from a script she prepared. "Hi, my name is La La. I'm looking for my mother, Elissa Gold. She left a long time ago, and I have no idea where to find her. Maybe you're my mother. Or maybe you're related to her. It's urgent." None of the voices on the recordings are familiar, but so much time has passed La La doesn't know if she would recognize her mother's voice.

The first time someone answers the phone, La La is so surprised she forgets to speak.

"HEL-lo," the woman says.

La La panics, but whether she's afraid of finding her mother or of being disappointed, she doesn't know.

"Hel-LO?" the woman barks. In the background, Rachel Maddow gives her spin on the news. "Is this a prank?" the woman says.

Remembering her script, La La reads it, stumbling over the word "mother" each time it appears.

"Sorry, hun, no relation. Zippo, zed, nada. My kids don't speak to me. I'm sure you wouldn't cut your mother off just because of a little political disagreement or some things I posted on Facebook. I won't be around forever. Maybe you could call my kids and tell them they should be grateful just to have a mother. You'd be doing us all a favor. Can you do that? Can you call them?" After a pause, the woman begins to read names and numbers. "Are you getting this?"

La La hangs up, crossing the woman's name off the list.

Monday morning, La La has an e-mail from an Elizabeth Gold. She's so excited, she squeals. Black's ears shoot up. But then La La reads the message. *You seem like a lovely young woman, but I'm not your mother. I hope you find her.*

It's disappointing, but there are still thirteen more names on her list. Surely one will turn out to be her mother.

La La robs a home and gives O'Bannon part of what she makes, a total of $5,500 now. The more she earns, the more it seems she owes the lawyer, who's working steadily, running up billable hours. Zev's personal needs aren't small, either, and since Clem left she's responsible for all of her own expenses, too.

More e-mails come in from Elizabeth Golds. All from strangers. La La blackens their names on the list, using far more ink than necessary and with enough force to press valleys in the paper.

On Tuesday, Clem texts. La La hesitates before reading the message. *I rented a place. I'd like to get the rest of my stuff, okay?*

Not okay, she thinks. She doesn't reply, thwarting his efforts to be finished with her.

He tries again the next morning.

When do you want to come over? she responds.

Tonight? I worked out a schedule for the dogs, he texts.

Great. I'm going to lose them, too, La La texts back.

You're not the only one who cares about them, Clem responds.

La La doesn't argue. Clem's devotion to the dogs is one of the things she loves about him.

That night, while La La waits for Clem, Zev phones. "Claude Thomas had a second brain bleed. A bigger one. O'Bannon sounded worried."

She shuts her eyes. "He could recover."

"Or he could die, and they'll charge me with murder."

"You tried to save him."

"Big mistake."

Through the phone, she hears the train circling the track and then a crash.

"*Fuck,*" Zev says.

"What are you doing?"

"Nothing."

"I'll be over tomorrow," La La says. "I'd come over now, but I'm waiting for someone."

"Someone more important than your father."

She could call Clem and cancel, but she's looking forward to seeing him, despite the reason for his visit. Maybe if she tells him about the developments in her father's case, he'll feel sorry for her, though she doubts it. "I'll see you in the morning."

Clem arrives carrying a pile of supermarket boxes, another dozen in his SUV. The boxes save them from an awkward embrace or the equally uncomfortable absence of one. His beard looks scraggly, as if he's forgotten to trim it. Black and Blue attack him with their tongues, their frenzied joy irritating La La, until thankfully they move on to sniffing the cardboard.

Setting the packing materials on the kitchen floor, Clem goes through cupboards and drawers, pulling out dishes, flatware, glasses, and mugs that were his before they moved in together. He might as well erase all the meals they lingered over, the glasses of wine that eased their way into the bedroom. He fills a box and sets it to one side. La La could help, but she doesn't, sitting at the table, staring at the words RIGATONI, HONEY NUT CHEERIOS, and RICE-A-RONI emblazoned across cardboard.

Clem packs an eggbeater and tools for grilling. On the counter, he lines up things they bought together. "Why don't you keep the blender?" he says. "You'll use it more." La La nods, and he returns it to the cabinet. "And the food processor, too," he says.

She fantasizes running him through the blades.

"How about you keep them all?" he says.

She doesn't need additional reminders of their life together. "Whatever. What should we do about the furniture?"

"I've ordered new stuff."

He doesn't seem to care about all the time they spent combing through neighborhoods to scavenge pieces. Or maybe he knows she can't afford replacements.

There's the matter of the engagement ring, which she's wearing. Clem's too polite to ask for it back, or he forgets to, and she doesn't offer.

From his shirt pocket he takes a paper, unfolds it, and hands it to La La. It's the custody schedule for the dogs. Twenty-six weeks with La La, twenty-six with Clem. La La grabs the paper and it tears across the holidays, splitting La La's turn with them on Christmas, and Clem's next Easter.

His new address is written above the schedule. It's in a town similar to Longview, about a fifteen-minute drive away. "Does your place have a yard?" she asks.

"A small one." He lifts an empty box and examines the inside, removing the outer peel of an onion and dropping it into the sink.

"Stairs?" she says. "You know they can be hard on Blue."

"Only a few." He presses on the bottom of the box and then presses again, making sure it's solid. He seems like he'd rather be anywhere other than with her. "There's a park nearby," he says, as he scratches his beard.

Going from room to room, he fills boxes with country CDs, chiropractic textbooks, cotton T-shirts whose softness La La can still feel against her skin, jackets and boots she helped him pick out for Colorado winters. There's more, but she stops watching, ignoring Clem's questions about who owned this album or that book, until eventually he quits asking.

"They'll lock me up forever if he dies," Zev says. A coffee stain the size of a hand blots his sweatpants, but he doesn't have the energy to change.

La La gives him a puzzle book she must have picked up at the supermarket. "No one said he's going to die."

He tosses the book on the table without opening it, then pours La La a mocha latte. Looking at the ceiling, he says, "If you're listening, God, don't punish me for saving a guy's life."

La La wraps her hands around the mug. "Maybe you should pray for Claude Thomas."

"Don't you think I already have?" Just last night, he unearthed the prayer book he bought for La La's bat mitzvah and recited the section for healing.

"Think about something else. Try one of these puzzles." She opens the book.

"I can't concentrate." He wishes she didn't spend the money. They need every penny for O'Bannon. He's hoping the lawyer, concerned about his ability to pay, doesn't drop him, especially since it's looking like the whole case will soon get more complicated.

"Watch *Sopranos* reruns."

"I don't like the way it ends." Why they had to ruin a perfectly good crime series, he'll never understand. They seemed to foreclose any comeback for Tony or a sequel for the network. Mo rubs against his leg.

"She knows you're upset," La La says.

"For once let's not talk about Mo, okay?" If he goes to jail, he'll never see Mo again. By the time he gets out, she'll be dead.

"Sure." When La La stretches out a hand, Mo rubs against her finger. "Her back legs are pretty stiff."

"What did I say?"

"Okay."

The cat purrs, and Zev tries to imagine life without that sound, one of the few constants in his life over the last decade. There will be other, harsher sounds in prison.

La La sips her coffee. "I can't stay long."

"You never stay long." He holds up a hand to silence her objection. "I'm not complaining. With all you're doing for me, how could I complain? I just miss you." There's a chill in the house, or maybe it's inside him, what the beginning of the end feels like. What Tony must have felt in that last fucking scene.

Three weeks pass, and with them the holidays. Zev didn't feel like celebrating, so La La spent Christmas Eve with Nat and Tank, feeling like an orphan. Tank pulled her aside at one point to ask if she'd thought more about his idea. He looked thinner than he had at the bowling alley, and she supposed he must not be working out as much. "I can't do it," she said, but she wondered how much the drugs might bring.

Claude Thomas is still alive, but the doctors are pessimistic about his chances for improvement. Thomas is unresponsive to stimulation, voices, or pain. Only a ventilator keeps him breathing.

Looking at O'Bannon's latest bill, La La doesn't see how he has time for any other clients. But since Thomas's condition has worsened, the stakes have grown higher. She can't risk O'Bannon resigning. She starts looking for someone to sublet the house and for a cheaper place to rent.

She's just about given up on hearing from her mother when she gets an e-mail from ElissaOnMyOwn one night. *You found me. What's so urgent?*

La La reads it, so excited she nearly drops the phone. It's just like Elissa to be so short with her. The people-finder record shows an address of Dallas, Texas, for the woman with that e-mail. How did her mother wind up there? She'll know more after they talk. But the record doesn't include a phone number.

I can't believe it's you, La La replies. *I'm including my phone number. Please call.* She waits up, glancing at the phone every three minutes. Watches the news, then the National Geographic Channel. To pass the time, she looks up the *One of a Kind* blog and is pleased to see very few new posts and all for the sorts of small acts of kindness that drive Clem crazy: a child sharing her lunch with a classmate, a man holding open a door for a woman. (*What had that taken—ten seconds?* she can hear Clem complaining.)

At three in the morning, realizing her mother must have gone to bed, she pulls on an old T-shirt and washes up. Getting beneath the covers, she closes her eyes, but Elissa's e-mail lights up like an elaborate Christmas display behind her eyelids. She thinks of all the things she'll tell her mother—how she's almost a veterinarian and back in Colorado with two rescued dogs. She imagines flying to Texas. Elissa probably won't meet her at the airport or invite her to stay at her house, but they could have dinner somewhere. Then Elissa could give her the money for attorney fees. La La would promise to pay her back once she's a vet.

The next morning, Friday, there's nothing more from Elissa. La La e-mails her mother again. Perhaps the first e-mail went into Elissa's spam folder.

She gets a text from Tank. For the past three days, he's been texting over and over. Vague messages only she would understand that she ignores. He has too much time on his hands. But maybe he's right that his customers require the medications as much as the people whose names are on the bottles. The cash they'd bring could only help.

Driving to a job, La La hums "Mama Rock Me," the ringtone she'll use for Elissa's phone number. She doesn't even mind that when she's in the house and cuts a cat's nails, grown so long they curl into his flesh, the animal spooks, and she has to chase him down to finish.

She opens a medicine cabinet in the master bathroom and fingers orange plastic bottles of Wellbutrin, Oxycodone, Percocet, Valium. Childproof containers that raise your blood pressure when you try to open them.

When Sunday arrives, and La La still hasn't heard from Elissa, she leaves herself a voice mail to make sure her phone is working: "Hi, La La. You found your mother. Isn't that wonderful?" She receives the message right away.

What are another few days after she's waited so many years?

But now that they're about to be reunited, every hour that goes by without Elissa pricks La La as painfully as a thorn from the untended rosebushes.

On Monday, La La e-mails a selfie she takes with Black to Elissa.

Pretty dog, Elissa replies. La La can't remember anyone complimenting Black's looks before. Her mother always loved animals. She sprinkled seeds for squirrels, tossed bread for birds, and didn't care when raccoons knocked over the trash, telling La La, "They have to eat, too," and, "Why should food go to a landfill when animals are hungry?" It was her mother, La La is pretty sure, who left Mo. La La prints the e-mail and ponders the address ElissaOnMyOwn. It has to be her mother.

The next day, she gets another e-mail from Elissa with a picture of a cat and the word "Buster."

Your cat is beautiful, La La writes. *How old is he?*

La La waits but nothing arrives from Elissa.

Please call me, please, La La writes. *You owe me at least that.*

I don't owe anyone anything, Elissa replies. *Anyway, my phone is broken.*

Can't you get it fixed? Or get a prepaid phone? La La writes.

"I thought you needed the money." Tank stands in La La's doorway, sweating though it's thirty degrees out.

His visit is a surprise, and La La hesitates to invite him in and prolong a conversation she wishes he never started. But she doesn't want to talk where they could be overheard, either. She motions for him to enter and closes the door behind him. "I tried

to steal the medications. But I couldn't. I kept imagining someone having a crisis."

"Jesus. You're already robbing them."

"It's different." Her phone buzzes against her palm.

I went to buy a phone, writes Elissa. *The one I want costs two
hundred dollars. I don't have that, and they won't give me a payment plan, because I still owe fifty dollars on the old phone.*

"What is it?" Tank says.

"Nothing."

"If it's nothing, why do you look so upset?"

La La scans the e-mail again, ignoring Tank's question.

"Is it from Zev?"

"You better go," La La says.

Tank leans against the door, his pallor gray. "Some of the
drugs are for me."

La La puts the phone in her pocket. She wonders if Nat
knows. "How would Nat feel if I helped you?"

"You'd be taking care of me."

"She wouldn't see it that way."

A bead of sweat drips down the side of his face. "Fuck Nat."

Surprised by the bitterness in his voice, La La backs up.

"I'm not asking anymore." When he steps toward her, the
dogs growl and bare their teeth, and he stops. "If you don't get
them, the police will get a tip about a veterinary student burglar."

After Tank leaves, La La curls up on the bed. The dogs press
themselves to her, but despite their presence, which would normally reassure her, she can't seem to banish the thought of Tank's
threat. She glances at her phone. She knows it isn't smart to send

money to Elissa even before they've talked. But the woman isn't a Nigerian scammer. La La contacted *her*.

For the first time in years, La La dreams Elissa is rocketing away, but this time, La La follows in a smaller ship. When she wakes, she still hasn't caught her mother.

In the morning, La La shows the house to a couple interested in subletting. The man's hand lingers on the woman's back, teasing her hair as they walk through the rooms, discussing whether their furniture will fit. When the woman remarks on the size of the yard and how it will seem like the grounds of a castle to their Pomeranian, the man laughs. They tell her they'll take it, starting February first, two weeks away.

When the couple is gone, La La e-mails Elissa, *Where should I send the money?*

To the Dallas Western Union. The one on Kiest Blvd.

La La wires funds she set aside for O'Bannon. From the sound of things, her mother won't be able to help with Zev's legal bills. But now that she's found Elissa, La La doesn't care if her mother helps or not.

Sunday morning, La La and Nat make their way around the reservoir, clomping on packed snow. It still feels odd to walk without the dogs. Like she's forgotten something. La La considers telling Nat about her mother but decides to wait until she and Elissa have talked. "How's school?" La La asks.

"School's fine. It's Tank I'm worried about." Nat hugs herself, feeling the cold or perhaps anxious about the direction her marriage is taking.

"Why?" La La won't be the one to tell Nat about Tank. Her friend might blame her, as though La La's crimes have given Tank license to commit some of his own. Tank might find out she told Nat and make good on his threat to inform on her. It's Nat's fault Tank is blackmailing her. Nat never should have shared with Tank that La La was stealing.

"I don't know. Maybe I'm seeing things that aren't there," Nat says.

La La looks away from her friend toward the surface of the reservoir, where a fresh coating of snow conceals the bumps and ridges beneath. "Once he finds work, I bet things will get back to normal."

"Maybe you're right. Thanks."

For nothing, La La thinks.

Later that day, La La scours online listings until she finds a rental house she can afford that allows pets. She arranges to tour the place and when she gets there, the owner lets her in and then returns to her car. La La wanders through the house alone, no need to hide her disappointment. The carpets are so stained, little remains of their original pink color. Black mold streaks the tiles in the shower, and hard water deposits coat the fixtures. There's a hole in the kitchen wall the size of a man's fist. La La has just about decided it won't work when the backyard, silver maple towering over a snowy lawn, comes into view through a window. She pictures the dogs napping under the tree in the summer or chasing squirrels who dash along the top of the chain-link fence. A dog door opens to the yard from the bedroom. La La goes out to the owner's car. When the woman opens the window, La La tells her she'll take it.

"You will?" the owner says. She unlocks the passenger door, and La La gets in. Rather than having La La fill out an application, she pulls a lease and a pen from a messenger bag, as if she doesn't want to give La La even the briefest chance to change her mind. La La wasn't expecting to sign right away. She tells the owner she'll have to come back the next day with cash for the first and last month's rent. (The woman doesn't have the nerve to ask for a security deposit.) Using the money from the next day's job will put her further behind with O'Bannon, but what choice does she have? She signs on one of the two lines marked "tenant," the other remaining depressingly empty.

8

When she's fifteen, La La accompanies her father to a mall one Sunday afternoon. A group of girls her age roams the long corridors without their parents, clutching frozen drinks. While her father buys shoes, La La waits on a bench and watches the girls wander in and out of a too-bright Hallmark store, then try on earrings in a jewelry shop, gazing at themselves in countertop mirrors, holding their long hair back in their fists. La La rubs her earlobe, as smooth as if Zev himself polished it.

When Zev returns, La La drags him to the jewelry shop and begs to get her ears pierced. Elissa's were pierced, and she wore dangly beads and dream catchers. "Why don't you wear what I got you instead of that cheap crap?" Zev once complained.

"What you *got* me came from fences in exchange for—never mind," Elissa said. At the time, La La didn't understand what her mother meant, but now she does, and she understands, too, that her mother would disapprove of her life.

Zev peers into the shop. "The place isn't clean. You could get an infection."

"Those girls," La La says, pointing, "don't have infections." She presses her fists to the window. A girl waves, and La La opens her hand, surprised to have been noticed. She often feels invisible.

"You don't know what they have. I'll buy you clip-ons."

"Why does everything we do have to be so weird?"

"What's weird?" Zev says.

"Oh my god, you're serious. We make a living robbing houses."

"LA LA!"

"Sorry." The girls pay for their jewelry. As Zev hurries La La away, she waves to them again though their backs are turned. In a department store, her father selects clothes for her, baggy carpenter pants and button-down shirts in browns and tans, colors that fade into the landscapes of the homes they rob. It's barely spring, but girls are wearing short skirts in pink and purple with matching high-heeled sandals.

Returning from a job the next day, her father stops at a light. At the corner, a long-necked boy presses a freckled girl against a brick building and kisses her, his hand disappearing beneath the girl's sweater. La La's chest flushes. Back in her bedroom, she reaches under her shirt, pushing her fingers beneath her bra. She longs to experience what the girl felt, but her own flesh is too familiar, and like a book she's already read, empty of surprises.

Tiny watches with curiosity, scratching his ears, and Mo dozes on the bed. They're getting on her nerves. With Tiny's allergies acting up, La La's skin itches. Nocturnal like all cats, Mo is sleepy during the day, and La La can't stop yawning. Over the years, she's learned to control the effects of Dr. Bergman's patients on her, to amplify their symptoms when diagnosing a problem and otherwise to quiet them. Visiting his clinic, she's been able to stay longer and to help with more patients before tiring. But La La is too attached to her pets to tune them out. It does little good to eject them from her bedroom because she can sense them throughout the house. Nevertheless, she herds them through the bedroom door and slams it shut, nearly catching Mo's paw. They whine to be let in, and though La La feels the pain of their exile, she refuses to comfort them, ignoring them well past dinnertime, when their confusion turns to hunger.

When La La started high school, Zev hired a college student, Deja, to teach La La subjects Zev himself never managed to learn, but now the studious college junior begins to aggravate her, too. La La doesn't see the point in calculating the area of shapes, how it will help her treat animals, or how the woman can describe math solutions as elegant with an airy grin on her face. The novels she gives La La are even more useless, the hunting of whales in *Moby-Dick* cruel and unnecessary. La La's excited to read *Animal Farm*, but then angry to find pigs and sheep maligned to illustrate political systems invented by people. If that's satire, she can do without it. Only biology interests her. They study the cellular structures of humans, who are after all just a type of animal. Not an animal La La admires particularly, nor one whose inner life she can read. Why that is, she doesn't know.

She no longer looks forward to Dr. Bergman's visits. She's sick of being invaded by the trauma of each animal he brings. She has her own problems. The doctor talks endlessly about her responsibility to animals. *Who's responsible for me?* she'd like to ask. The next time the doctor calls Zev to say he's coming, La La sneaks out before he arrives.

In the early spring warmth, children whiz by on bikes and skateboards, their jackets unzipped and flapping behind them.

Robins peck at gray lawns. Months of snow potholed the streets and fissured the sidewalks. La La levers her foot into a crack and sprays out rubble, widening the hole.

A year later, the last of the snow melting and fuzzy gray buds appearing on aspens, La La refuses to go out with Zev anymore. She needs to study if she hopes to get into college and veterinary school, she says. She tells him to fire Deja. She can learn what she needs to know from textbooks, and he should save his money. But when he leaves the house, La La seeks company a mile away, in the alley behind a 7-Eleven, where she often finds the same crew.

Tamara first spotted La La in the store, shoplifting two packs of gum. Outside, she motioned for La La to accompany her around back, where she held out her hand for one of the packs. "You're lucky the owner didn't see," she said. "He always calls the police."

If Tamara hadn't dropped out of high school, she would be a senior. She wears black jeans to match her boots and a giant black sweatshirt that swallows her fragile hands. Her hair is black in the shade and purple in the sun, shaved on one side. Leonard is older—La La doesn't know how old—with round plugs in his earlobes and a spiked chain around his neck. He sits on the asphalt, Tamara on his lap, leaning her head back when they kiss.

Max is La La's age. He's always texting his friends in school, even when he talks to La La, and she wonders why he bothers being a truant. His fingernails and wrists need cleaning.

They're all broke, so La La suggests robbing a house. Leading them through the neighborhood, past warped shake roofs, and bikes and plastic toys on yellow lawns, she comes to a garage that's open and empty of cars. At the end of the block, a garbage truck raises a plastic bin in its metal claw. La La herds the group into the garage, uncertain if the operator of the truck has seen them. Standing before the door leading into the house, she pulls a tension wrench and a pick from her pocket. She pokes the wrench into the keyhole and turns, the play in the lock allowing the cylinder to move slightly. She inserts the pick and rakes the descending lock pins, bumping them up and trapping them above the cylinder. When she traps all the pins, the lock releases.

Leonard whistles. "Nice."

La La lifts a finger to her lips and points toward the street. The garbage truck nears the house.

"Whatever," Leonard says, without bothering to lower his voice. He takes Tamara's hand and pulls her inside.

For once Max has put his phone in his pocket. "This way," La La whispers, leading him through an overheated hall to a master bedroom that smells like dirty laundry. Sheets pretzel on an unmade bed. It's mid-morning and the sun shines through the window. Water rings dot a dresser. Shoving aside stockings and thongs in the top drawer, La La doesn't find any valuables. Then she notices a tube sock bulging at the toe and holds it up. "People are idiots," she says. Max laughs. She passes him the sock.

Drawing out a velvet box, he opens it to find a sapphire engagement ring. "Cool." They gather a laptop, too, and an Xbox.

The phone rings, startling La La. When a machine answers, a man's voice tells the caller to leave a message. After the beep, the same voice says, "I thought you'd be home by now. I'll try your cell."

"Let's go," La La says.

In the dining room, Leonard holds a portable CD player and

discs in one hand and a bottle of Dewar's in the other. He swigs the Scotch and hands it to Tamara, who takes a sip.

"We should get out of here," La La says.

"Tamara wants to see if there's any lingerie she likes," Leonard says.

"She likes or you like?" Max says.

"Same difference."

"This isn't a department store. The owner's on her way home." La La's neck stiffens. Committing a crime with people she hardly knows is starting to seem like a bad idea. "Leave that," she says to Tamara, indicating the bottle, "and let's go."

Leonard takes the bottle and tilts it back again. He wipes his mouth with the back of his hand. "What about the flat-screen TV? I could use a new TV."

"You think we might look suspicious carrying that around?" La La says. You don't have to grow up robbing houses to understand certain things. A car alarm shrieks, jangling La La's nerves. "I don't know about you guys, but I'm leaving."

"What the fuck. Let's go," Leonard says, planting the bottle on the table.

They exit through the back door. The garbage truck is gone, but the car alarm continues to wail. When did the neighborhood get so busy? A silver-haired woman wearing a visor pushes a baby carriage. A man in an ill-fitting suit drags a wheeled sales case. A skinny teenager hops out of a laundry van and glances at them before turning up a walk with a box of shirts.

La La wishes she had worn sunglasses and a baseball cap. She sweats through her shirt, the cotton sticking to her back, a clammy second skin. Robbing homes with her father, they always had the car as cover.

After they duck behind the 7-Eleven, she suggests selling everything at a nearby cleaner's that she's heard runs a fencing operation out of the back. It's a place Zev uses as a last resort, preferring not to work so close to home, but she doesn't tell the others that. She insists on going alone.

"We'll kill you if you rip us off," Leonard says.

"Easy," Max says. "She doesn't want the guy to get nervous, dealing with a crowd."

"Thanks," La La says to Max. He's looking up, his eyes yellow and green. Cat's eyes.

When La La enters the store, Erik is behind the counter. A skin condition paints his cheeks with a permanent blush, as if he's ashamed, though La La's never seen any other evidence of that. He looks past her, expecting Zev.

"My father sent me," she says. The place smells of chemicals. Clothing entombed in plastic hangs from a motorized rack. On a chalkboard, someone has scrawled in green, *Happy Spring— Comforters Dry Cleaned $19.99.* He leads her to the back, where giant washers and dryers spin. A woman who's ironing doesn't look up. The room always appears exactly as the back of a cleaner's should. La La wonders where the fence keeps the merchandise he buys.

"I'll give you one sixty for the lot," Erik says, after examining the stolen items. It's ridiculously low.

Back at the convenience store, La La says the fence paid one twenty and hands the others thirty each.

"Doesn't seem like much," Leonard says, fanning out the bills. "You sure that's all he gave you?"

La La shrugs. "What do you think you get for a used CD player?"

From the 7-Eleven, Leonard purchases two six-packs. La La, Max, and Tamara buy plastic-wrapped pastries. They sit in the alley, pulling apart cheese Danish, chocolate horns, and jelly donuts, filling their mouths and washing down the sticky dough with beer.

La La's on her second beer when Max presses a donut, painted with white icing, into her mouth. After she swallows, he leans over and licks her lips, setting them abuzz. She feels aroused, but greater than that is the pleasure of being wanted.

When the food and beer are gone, she and Max walk to her house. Alone with him, La La doesn't know what to say. She shoves her hands into her pockets to keep them from trembling.

Max looks at his phone, a string of texts rolling across the screen. "It's all bullshit," he says, but he doesn't look up.

La La is counting on Zev not being home yet and is relieved to see the driveway empty. She can't imagine introducing Max, with his torn white T-shirt and spiked hair, to her father.

Fresh cat droppings glisten in the litter box in a corner of her room. Books about wild and domesticated animals fill shelves. She once pored over them, preparing to become a veterinarian. Mo hides under the dresser, only the tip of her tail showing.

"Do you like animals?" La La asks.

"I like other things more." Max pulls off his T-shirt, revealing an ivory chest and nipples pierced by silver rings. He sits on the bed. "You can lick them if you want." The metal is cold and strange against La La's tongue, but it doesn't matter. She gladly takes them in her mouth to feel she belongs to someone other than Zev. Max unbuttons La La's shirt and unclips her bra. He cups her small breasts, his fingers dry. When his lips replace his hands, she forgets to breathe, and freezes for fear of interrupting the warm rain of sensations now on, now underneath her skin.

"You should get them pierced," he says.

"Does it hurt?"

"Only a little." He sets her hand on top of his pants and shows her how to move it. Lying back, he closes his eyes and grunts. Then his pants are wet, and he's quiet.

"Are you okay?" she asks.

"Better than okay."

La La stretches out alongside him, vaguely dissatisfied. Awake in parts of her body she isn't used to noticing or naming, and certainly not discussing with a boy who's still for the most part a stranger. "The fence gave me one sixty." She reaches into her pocket and takes out cash, handing him another twenty.

"You didn't have to tell me." He puts the money away.

"I wanted to."

They kiss, Max pressing hard and biting her lip. She doesn't know if she likes it, if it's punishment or reward.

"How'd you know how to pick that lock?" he asks.

"My dad and me, we're burglars." It's the first time she's thought of herself that way. It's something her father does. Something she got stuck doing with him. But now she's done it without him, for pastries and beer, and to impress Max.

"I guess I am, too." Max's phone pings in his pocket. "My father says I'm nothing. At least now I'm something. Maybe you'll teach me to pick locks."

"Sure. But you better go. My dad will be home soon."

When he leaves, she misses the taste of salt on his chest and sugar on his lips. She closes her eyes and, imagining Max is still with her, touches herself.

• • •

They rob homes whenever they run out of money, meeting in front of the 7-Eleven, Leonard driving his brother's car. La La directs them to cities and towns thirty and forty miles away. Sometimes she secretly chooses properties she's been inside with Zev, the owners having replaced whatever was stolen. Her father always says a good home to hit is one you've already robbed, because you know the layout and have been successful. One family installed new security. When La La sees the alarm company sign, she steers the group to a neighbor. Several owners alter where they hide their valuables, choosing new, equally obvious spots. Lightning doesn't strike twice, people figure, but it does.

She always lies to Leonard and Tamara about how much the fence gives her, making up the difference to Max in her room. Mo never gets used to Max, hiding under the dresser whenever he arrives, the cat's anxiety heightening La La's fear that her father will catch them. Max has begun to unzip his pants and to present himself, scarlet and veiny, head like a little wool cap. At his urging, she tastes him, the soapy flavor surprising. Tiny hops on the bed, eager to join a game that involves hands and tongues, but La La orders him off and he sulks, ears back, La La feeling his affront at being treated harshly.

Once, Max shoves her head down until, feeling him at the back of her throat, she chokes and pulls away. He comes on her face and hair, and she lifts her shirt from the floor and wipes the slippery stuff away. As always, he leaves her with a hot need that she satisfies after he's gone.

The next time the four of them meet, Leonard arrives at the 7-Eleven on foot. "My brother changed where he hides the key,"

La La's new driver's license nestles in her wallet, and Zev is home, his aging Lexus in the driveway. "I'll be back," she says.

In the living room, Zev is reassembling an antique padlock.

"Can I borrow the car?" La La says. "The bookstore has some new stuff on animals."

He reaches for a rag. "I'll drive you."

"I can drive myself. I'll be there a while, and I don't want you to have to wait." Mo rubs against La La's legs, but La La can't be bothered to pet her.

Zev wipes his hands. "Be careful, please. And get home in time for dinner." He pulls the key fob from his pocket and holds it out.

Grabbing it, La La starts toward the door.

"Here," Zev says, slipping a twenty from his wallet. "If you want to buy something."

La La shoves the money in her pocket.

"How about a 'thank you,'" Zev says.

"Thanks," she mumbles over her shoulder, letting the screen door slam behind her. Minutes later, she pulls up to the convenience store.

Leonard and Tamara climb into the back seat. Max joins La La in front. "Nice car," Leonard says. "What are you, rich?"

"Why bother robbing houses?" Tamara says. "Just ask your daddy for money."

"We're not rich," La La says, pulling away from the curb. "My father's a locksmith."

Tamara lights a cigarette.

"You can't smoke in the car," La La says. "My father will kill me."

Tamara takes a deep drag and blows out a cloud.

La La pulls over. "Get out if you're going to smoke."

"What a bitch," Tamara says, but she tosses the cigarette out of the window.

La La drives to a neighborhood where she and her father worked a few months before.

"What about that green house?" Leonard says, indicating a ranch with a three-car garage, lawn nicely kept, and little cover.

"Say cheese," Max says, pointing out security cameras.

"Smartass," Leonard says.

A block later, Max points to a dark house, blinds down and circulars piling up on the driveway.

"That's a good one. When me and my dad were there, we found three thousand dollars in the back of a file drawer." As soon as the words are out of her mouth, La La regrets them. But it's too late to take them back.

"Locksmith, huh?" Tamara says.

La La looks in the rearview mirror. Tamara holds an unlit cigarette between her lips. Leonard plays with a plastic lighter, flicking it to life, letting it go out, and flicking it to life again. "So that's how you learned," Leonard says.

La La can't focus, and by the time they pick out a place, it's late. They grab what they can, and La La takes it to the fence. When she pays Leonard and Tamara, she forgets to hold back any money.

"The guy was feeling generous all of a sudden?" Leonard asks, staring at the eighty dollars La La gave him.

Another mistake. Rattled, La La says, "He must have had a good day." She decides to take a break from robbing houses.

•   •   •

Two weeks later, La La and Zev are eating dinner in the kitchen when there's a knock at the front door. "Police!"

Zev opens it to two uniformed officers. La La stands back in the entry to the living room.

"I'm Officer Gregson, and this is my partner, Officer Maines," the older of the two cops says. He lifts his hat to scratch his head, revealing a white buzz cut. "Mind if we come in?"

"Yes," says Zev.

"We have a warrant." Gregson pulls it from his jacket pocket and hands it to Zev, who examines it. "Are you Zev Fine? Is that your daughter, Louise Fine, also known as La La?" The officer looks toward La La.

Zev ignores the questions.

Glancing around the living room, Officer Gregson asks Zev, "Is that your Lexus in the driveway?" There's irritation in the question, as if the officer himself would like such a car, but honest work doesn't allow for it.

"If you're going to search, get it over with," Zev says.

"Any reason the two of you would have been in Cherry Creek on a Wednesday afternoon two and a half months ago?"

"Don't say anything," Zev says to La La.

"Two witnesses say your daughter told them you both robbed a house there. She knew the exact amount of cash that was taken." The officer looks at La La. "Isn't that right?"

Pain gives Zev's eyes a sunken look. "Don't answer."

La La's neck warms. Blood rushes to her cheeks. Three pairs of eyes take in her reaction, but she can no more control it than she can control the past.

"Maybe you better sit down," Officer Gregson says to her.

"You, too," he says to Zev. La La takes the opposite end of the couch from her father.

Officer Maines looks at a curio cabinet. "Quite a collection of locks you have." His thumbs loop in his belt. His thick fingers seem capable of violence.

"I'm a locksmith," Zev says.

"Convenient," the officer says.

"Stay put while we have a look around," says Officer Gregson.

La La closes her eyes. Remembering the conversation with Tamara and Leonard, she wishes she were born a cat or dog without the ability to speak. She counts the beats of her rapid pulse. Tiny and Mo have disappeared.

After a while, the officers return with a crowbar and lockpicks. They show them to Zev.

"I told you, I'm a locksmith," Zev says.

"You did say that," Officer Gregson says.

They put Zev and La La in handcuffs.

"Don't say anything," Zev repeats.

He doesn't have to worry. La La is too frightened to talk.

La La spends the night in a juvenile facility, separated from her father, who's locked up in the county jail. The next day, O'Bannon secures their release. Zev found the lawyer's name in the yellow pages.

"Your friends Leonard and Tamara got into some trouble," O'Bannon says, looking across his desk at La La. Zev sits to her left. An interior window with a view of a secretary is to her right. It isn't safe to look anywhere, so she looks at her lap. "Brilliant characters, those two," the lawyer says. "They tried to burglarize a house at night. When the cop who lives there came downstairs with her Glock drawn, your man Leonard started to cry." He isn't her man, but there's no point saying so. "In exchange for lighter sentences, they told the police about a house in Cherry Creek they say you robbed. It appears La La told them what was taken. When the cops originally canvassed the neighborhood, they learned a Lexus was parked around the corner at about the time of the burglary and people who match your descriptions knocked on a neighbor's door and tried to sell them magazine subscriptions.

"Leonard and Tamara are lousy witnesses. They'll say anything to avoid jail time. And they have prior convictions. Leonard forged a few thousand dollars' worth of checks, and the girl was caught shoplifting candy and makeup numerous times. But it doesn't look good that the car and people matching your descriptions were seen in the neighborhood. Or that La La knew what was stolen. Luckily, they didn't find much when they searched your house. The crowbar and lockpicks are of little help because entry was through an open window."

Acrid sweat dampens La La's armpits. As the one who gave the information to Leonard and Tamara, she should take responsibility. She can say she robbed the house alone, using Zev's car. O'Bannon described the possible consequences for her and Zev if they're convicted. A minor without a prior criminal record, La La might be tried as a juvenile and face a lighter sentence. Eventually, her record might be expunged. Zev probably won't let her take the blame, but she'll never know because she doesn't offer.

To speak up is to risk her dream of college and veterinary school. Though she's been neglecting her future, now that it's in jeopardy, she discovers she hasn't given up on it. Zev stole her childhood. What can she possibly owe him?

"My daughter wasn't there," Zev says, though he knows it will change his life in ways he can't control, and not for the better. Why did he ever make La La his partner? He thought she could help him avoid exposure by quieting dogs, and he longed to share that part of his life with someone he loved. When she refused to go out with him anymore, he was secretly happy, thinking they got away with all the jobs they did together. He imagined she'd go to college as if none of it ever happened. He thanked God he didn't ruin her as he ruined so much else, his own life and marriage, and Elissa's life, too, if she was to be believed.

Out of the corner of his eye, he sees La La shaking her head, but he continues to look at the lawyer.

O'Bannon taps his lips. "Bad idea. Noble. But a bad idea."

"She had nothing to do with it," Zev says. "I did it alone. I'll tell the district attorney that if they drop the charges against her."

"Go home and think about it," the lawyer says. "Call me in a couple days."

"I don't need to think about it. That's how it happened."

Three weeks later, Zev agrees to plead guilty to burglary of a non-dwelling building, a Class 4 felony. The charges against La La are dropped. Since it's his first offense, Zev is sentenced to four years' probation and forbidden to work in people's homes during that time. He takes a night job washing dishes at a restaurant, attacking the relentless grease while mulling the fact that he's on the cops' radar now and will have to be even more careful. He trades the Lexus for a used Mercedes and continues to rob homes during the day.

La La applies herself to schoolwork, spending hours in her bedroom with Mo and Tiny, catching up on subjects kids her age have already mastered. Max drifts away, having little interest in studying. La La never returns to the 7-Eleven or sees Leonard and Tamara again.

Stuck on a chemistry equation one afternoon, La La walks a mile and a half to Dr. Bergman's office. The receptionist lets her wait in the doctor's office, where diagrams of animal anatomies and an enlarged photograph of Dr. Bergman with two Boston terriers hang on the walls. It's been a while since La La has been to the clinic, and she's happy to discover she isn't overwhelmed by sensations. Instead, they linger at the edge of her awareness, waiting for her to draw them into focus. Babies—she isn't sure what kind—shiver. A paw burns, perhaps from a cut.

As soon as he has a break between patients, Dr. Bergman joins her. La La looks for a sign that he's angry about all the times he stopped by the house only to find she wasn't there, but his face is untroubled. He missed a spot shaving, and the shadow on his chin makes La La happier than she's been in a long time, though she can't say why.

She describes the difficulty she's having with her schoolwork. "You're probably too busy to help." Grasping the strap of her backpack, she waits to be turned away.

"After all the help you've given me, I wouldn't be much of a friend if I didn't reciprocate. Let's see if I remember any of this." He pushes aside patient charts and prescription pads to make room for her textbook. Sitting next to her on the client side of the desk, his knees pressing against the pine, he demonstrates where she went wrong solving the equation. He reviews more of her work, correcting mistakes she didn't know she made.

When she stretches, he laughs. "Not as interesting as animals." He retrieves two bottles of apple juice from a small refrigerator in the corner of the room, one for each of them. "Stop by once a week, and we'll go over your work. While I've got you, I'll tell you about my patients." Siamese kittens are in for their first appointment—the shivering she felt—as well as a dog who tangled with metal landscape edging.

Grateful for the doctor's help, La La nearly confesses everything. But worried he'll think she isn't fit to be a vet, she thanks him, instead.

9

Wearing an oversize T-shirt that reads WELL ADJUSTED—
something she bought for Clem that he left behind—La La
checks to see if she missed any calls from her mother. Since she
sent Elissa money, her mother e-mailed another picture of her
cat, Buster. She also requested a photo of Blue, and then compli-
mented La La on adopting a special needs dog. As happy as that
made La La, she wishes her mother would call.

The television is tuned to *Cat Whisperer,* a reality show about
an animal behaviorist who helps cats get along with their people.
The starchy smell of the noodles she had for dinner hangs in the
air, accompanied by the musty odor of cardboard boxes from the
move that she still hasn't unpacked and the mildewing carpet.
Under the dining room table, Blue chases dust balls.

When the behaviorist mistakes a physical ailment for a psy-
chological condition, La La wants to shake him. Instead, she
e-mails the network to complain.

Three weeks have passed since Tank threatened her. The
memory of him coming toward her, sweaty and agitated, is never

far from her mind, but she's betting he won't reveal her activities to the police and call attention to himself. He'll buy what he needs on the street, stealing the money from Nat's purse or taking it from their joint accounts, making an excuse if Nat notices.

When the phone buzzes with an e-mail, La La hopes for good news. *My wireless service was cut off while the phone was broken because I stopped paying the bill,* Elissa writes. *I owe three hundred dollars more.*

Slipping to the floor, La La weaves her fingers through Black's fur. With her other hand, she types a reply. *Mom, If you don't mind my asking, what's my real name?* When Elissa says *Louise,* La La will have proof. Then she'll give her mother all the money she needs. Steeling herself, La La touches Send.

She watches another episode of *Cat Whisperer.* As the behaviorist explains to a couple that they've failed to bond with their calico, an e-mail from Elissa arrives: *I'm looking forward to talking to you.* La La tries to scroll down, but that's all there is.

Rough sounds escape from her throat as one by one she deletes the e-mails from ElissaOnMyOwn. Blue hops over and noses her elbow. When petting the dogs fails to soothe her, she dials Clem's number. "I thought I found—," she says when he picks up, but her throat tightens too much to continue.

In the background, country music plays. "Found what?"

She tries again. "I found—"

"Oh, God, did one of the dogs run away?" A heavy door closes and the music disappears.

"They're right here." La La glances at them, reassuring herself.

"Then who did you find?" Full of concern, his voice calms her.

"My mother, only she isn't."

A car honks. "Start from the beginning."

While she tells him about Elissa, she scrolls through e-mails, looking for the ones she thought were from her mother, forgetting she deleted them. "She didn't know my real name," La La says, ashamed to have been duped.

"I'm sorry."

La La swipes through photos until she comes to one of her and Clem, taken by the manager of the restaurant the night they got engaged. In it, she holds out her hand, showing off the ring, which she wears now, too. "I sent her money."

"I guess I shouldn't ask where you got it, right?"

"That's all you care about." Moonlight illuminates bird droppings on her window.

"Not all."

Through the phone, La La hears a door open and a woman's voice. "Everything okay?"

"Be back in a minute," Clem says.

La La's finger hovers over the trash can icon. "You're with someone." It hasn't been even two months since they broke up. Had their engagement meant so little to him? She deletes the photo.

"I can talk."

"I shouldn't have called."

"I'm glad you did. We're friends, aren't we?"

The last thing she wants is to be Clem's friend.

Afraid she's forgetting much of what she once knew, La La reviews one of her third-year textbooks. She heard from O'Bannon that there was no change in Claude Thomas's condition, and that he didn't know how long the family would wait before making some decisions. That was how he put it, as if they were deciding what to have for lunch or where to go on vacation, rather than to end the old man's—and for all purposes Zev's—life.

"It's immoral!" Zev had said when they talked about it. "Give the guy a chance to get better. What's the big hurry? The son must want his inheritance, greedy bastard."

La La didn't argue. If Zev were in a coma, she'd never make that kind of *decision,* not as long as there was a chance he'd recover.

A knock startles her. Rising from the couch, she glances through a window and sees Dr. Bergman. Her car is in the driveway, and lights blaze in the house. There's no use trying to pretend she's not home.

"You had me worried," he says, after she opens the door. He looks around, his gaze lingering on the peeling paint and the stained carpet. His mouth hangs open for a moment before he speaks again. "I went to your old place when you didn't return my calls. They gave me this address." Taking off his scarf, he kneads it, his lips pursed, his face not the optimistic one she knows.

"Things have been crazy. My father got arrested."

He doesn't look surprised. "Sorry to hear that."

"I had to leave school to work and pay his attorney fees." She stands at the door, reluctant to take his hat and coat or to offer him something warm to drink, actions that would prolong his stay and encourage questions she'd rather not answer.

"So close to graduating. What a shame." He shows himself in and stuffs his scarf in the pocket of his coat, which he throws over the back of the armchair.

"I'll go back when things get settled." La La grabs a dirty plate and glass from the dining room table and carries them into the kitchen, setting them on the counter because the sink is full.

"Of course you will," he calls to her. "You should have contacted me," he says, when she returns to the room. He lowers himself into the chair. "I can always use another vet tech, especially one who's almost a veterinarian."

"I got a job."

"Good, good. Where are you working?"

She hesitates before answering. "It's kind of a mobile vet position."

"Oh yeah? I thought most of those were one-person outfits. Which one is it?"

La La thinks back three months to the last time she talked to Dr. Bergman. Ronald, he told her to call him. They discussed a new heartworm prevention medicine. The conversation they're having now would have been unimaginable then.

"Is it Dr. Larsen?" he says. "I remember when he was just getting started. Good man."

"No one you know."

He looks around, taking in the decrepitude of her new place again. "Where are Clem and the dogs?"

At the mention of Clem, her shoulders sink. She turns her engagement ring around, concealing the stone.

"Oh, no." Standing, he pulls her into his arms, and she buries her face in his misbuttoned shirt. "What happened?"

She extracts herself from his embrace. "We had a fight."

"About what?"

"He didn't want me to drop out of school. But I needed to earn money. A lot of money. My father's lawyer charges a fortune."

"Please tell me you're not—"

"I don't have a choice." She turns away from him, noticing a brown stain on the wall, food or perhaps more sinister stuff.

"I was afraid something was wrong when I couldn't get ahold of you."

"I'm helping animals. In every house."

"That isn't the way to help animals." He takes out a handkerchief and wipes his neck. "My daughter's apartment was burglarized last year. It was her first time living alone. She couldn't sleep afterward even though we put in a security system. She can't bear to touch the clothing that was ransacked. She broke the lease and moved back home but still thinks she hears someone prying open her window every night. I just don't think you're considering the pain you might be inflicting."

"I don't rob apartments."

"That's not the point."

"If Zev goes to prison, I'll have no one."

"That isn't true, but even if it were . . ." He hesitates. "Humans are animals, too."

When he starts to put on his coat, she tries to help, but he shrugs her off.

"I really am helping animals."

"I know you think so," he says, and then he's gone.

10

"The family disconnected Claude Thomas's life support yesterday morning," O'Bannon says. "He died two hours later. The DA is charging Zev with felony murder."

In her mind, La La ticks off pharmacological and behavioral treatments for canine separation anxiety, until her pulse slows. O'Bannon warned her and Zev this was a possibility, but she never really let herself believe it. "What happens next?"

"We talk to the DA. Argue the family's action in terminating life support is what caused the death, not the burglary. Our experts will maintain that it's unclear whether the fright during the burglary even triggered the stroke. It won't be cheap. It's a stretch to use the felony murder rule when someone dies months after the crime, but since the initial injury happened during the burglary, I can't guarantee anything." The lawyer taps the edge of a file, perhaps her father's, but he doesn't bother opening it.

La La slides a wad of cash across the desk. "Don't give up on him."

"I'm not, but I don't want to give you false hope, either." O'Bannon counts the money. "I hope you go back to school when this is over. I'd hate to see you as a client."

"Just keep Zev out of prison."

La La finds Zev in bed, lying on top of the covers, the shades in the bedroom drawn. As she approaches, he opens his eyes.

"I'm sorry," she says.

He closes his eyes again. "They're really coming after me now. Just a small-time thief. You'd think they'd have worse criminals to worry about."

"O'Bannon's a good lawyer." Mo hops on a dresser and La La scratches behind her ears.

"It won't matter. When they're out to get you, they get you. Especially if you're a nobody. They make an example out of you because who's to stop them?"

"O'Bannon has a strategy."

Zev rolls onto his side, facing the darkened window, his back to La La. "You'll be glad to get rid of me. I was a lousy father when you were growing up, and now I'm a burden. You'll be better off with me in prison."

"Don't say that." La La wonders if he'll try to run. The ankle monitor would be an obstacle, but perhaps not an impossible one. Not for him. Because she might lose him, La La's desire for her mother presses with renewed urgency. Elissa wasn't the best mother, but she's the only one La La has. She wishes Zev would get out of bed, dust or polish something. "Don't you ever wonder where Elissa is?"

Zev jerks his head back toward La La. "Why are we talking about her?" he shouts. "I'm the one who just got terrible news."

La La's done everything she can, but it's not enough.

When she leaves, La La calls Nat but gets voice mail. Though she knows she'll regret it, she texts Clem about the developments in Zev's case, her fingers heavy as she types.

You can come over if you want, he replies.

It's his week with the dogs, and as she steps into his house, Blue hops to greet her. Black spins a single, slow circle before thumping down at her feet. She sits next to them and rubs Black's chin and scratches Blue's belly. She isn't sure who she needed to see more, Clem or the dogs.

"I'm sorry about your dad," Clem says, standing over her. "Are you finished robbing houses now?"

"Zev needs his lawyer even more now. He may go to prison, but I have to support him until he does."

As Clem turns away, he scoops a bone from the floor. Sitting in an armchair, he drums it against his knee. "People manage without stealing."

La La doesn't want to get into an argument, especially not one they've already had. The engagement ring nestles in her pocket, and she rubs the band. It's the first time she's seeing his place. He never invites her inside when she delivers the dogs. A black leather armchair and matching couch are new, and so is a flat-screen TV that takes up half a wall. Images of Jonas Salk, Louis Pasteur, and Hippocrates stare grimly from hospital-blue walls. Dog beds checker two corners of the room. In a third corner, a rolled-up yoga mat leans against the wall. Alongside a pile of chiropractic texts on a shelf, a photograph shows Clem standing next to the dogs at a reservoir southwest of town. A larger reservoir than the one where she and Nat regularly walk. But who took the picture? Clenching her jaw, La La lowers her forehead to Black's flank. "Place looks nice," she says. Could the day get any worse?

"I was depressed after we broke up. Decorating cheered me up. And when I bring someone here, I want it to look nice, you know?" He avoids La La's eyes, looking around the room as if he, too, is seeing it for the first time.

"Someone."

"Naomi, okay?" He smacks the bone against his palm, and the dogs regard him with concern.

"I haven't dated anyone." Black taps La La's hand. Well trained, she pets him.

"You should. Find yourself a nice bank robber."

"I don't remember you having a sense of humor," La La says.

"Pain will do that to you."

Blue snatches a plush skunk and carries it from the room.

"What's she like?" As soon as she asks the question, she realizes she doesn't want to know the answer.

"She's a massage therapist. Volunteers at a women's shelter on Saturdays, working on the residents. Pretty amazing, right? And she's a real dog person. You'd like her."

La La pictures a woman with the head of a golden retriever, like in a YouTube video she once saw, the dog scarfing down food with a fork and knife. It's spring. La La thought she and Clem would be back together by now. But instead he's dating Naomi. "Great," she says, yanking fibers from the wool carpet.

"We like the same routines on the yoga channel."

"Since when do you do yoga?"

"She's teaching me. She says it's about letting go. How perfect is it that we both make a living doing body work?"

Perfect for Naomi. "Let's take the dogs for a walk," says La La, standing.

"Why don't you go? They'll like that, and it will make you feel better."

"I guess your girlfriend wouldn't like you hanging out with your ex-fiancée. Or maybe you haven't told her about us."

La La means it as a joke, but Clem shrugs. "I told her we lived together. I didn't get into the rest."

At the thought of their engagement being erased, she stiffens. "You can't deny what we had."

Clem tosses the bone into the basket. "You need to return my grandmother's ring."

"It's at the house," La La says, as she bends to leash Black.

11

Zev sits on a dining room chair and rests the ball of his foot on the edge of another. Knee bent, he can reach the ankle monitor easily. Earlier, he trapped Mo in her cage and lined up a #0 Phillips head screwdriver and his cell phone on the table. He's investigated the monitor so thoroughly, he's memorized it. The train waits on the track.

Setting the timer on the phone to a minute, he lifts the screwdriver and looks toward the ceiling: "Help me out here. I'm one of your chosen people. We can't all be heart surgeons, you know."

He pictures the order in which he'll attack the monitor. While practicing, Zev never managed to take it apart and put it back together in less than sixty-two seconds. He's counting on adrenaline and on knowing that if he fails he'll go to prison to help him shave the last two seconds. A hearing on the DA's request to raise his bail to $100,000 to reflect the murder charge is set for next week. When the bail bondsman won't agree to cover the higher amount, they'll lock Zev up. He can't wait any longer.

He starts the timer and turns the first screw. Working fast, but not so fast that he'll drop the tool or a part, he disassembles the device, laying the pieces out in the correct order for reassembly. He's got it off in thirty-three seconds. Putting it back together should be faster because he isn't sitting with his leg raised, and he has 360-degree access to the monitor. But knowing time is bleeding away causes his hands to shake. All the times he practiced, his motions were fluid. Now that a mistake could cost him his freedom, he lurches from one step to the next. With three seconds left, a single screw remains. When he presses it to the device with the screwdriver, it leans away. As it's about to fall, his hands tingle in a rush of nerves, and he gets a glimpse of his future: shivering in a prison yard, packed earth beneath his feet, a quorum of ill-intentioned men surrounding him. The vision passes. He adjusts the angle of the screw and is still tightening it when the timer goes off, but perhaps he's done enough to reconstitute the fiberoptic beam.

After depositing the ankle monitor into the open freight car, he plugs the power cord into the monitor's jack, the other end already in the wall. A scaffolding he built from wire hangers and secured to the table suspends the cord above the train, allowing the cars to circle unimpeded. He throws the switch for the train and watches the whole neat package travel round three, four times before he's satisfied it's working.

Clutching the cat carrier, the green duffel he packed that morning slung over his shoulder, his phone—battery removed—tucked away, Zev shuts the front door behind him. Mo yowls. Traveling with her will be hard, and La La will miss the cat, maybe more than she'll miss him. But if he leaves Mo behind, he can't be sure when she'll be found, because he hasn't told La La his plans. He's spent eighteen years with Mo. Since Tiny died, she's been his only companion. He raises the carrier to his face. "I'm not hot about going either."

The rosebushes scratch his cheek one last time. He's in too much of a hurry to consider how he feels about abandoning the place he and Elissa called home. That will come later. Earlier in the week, he sold his car and van on eBay Motors for four thousand dollars. Together with a few hundred dollars in savings, it's all the money he has. The day before, on a college rideshare site, he found the phone number of a student named Brian who was headed to Albuquerque, the first leg of Zev's trip. The kid was glad to take him, as long as they split the gas.

Brian picks Zev up in front of a local coffee shop in an old gray Camry, its right signal light flickering unsteadily. Zev knows a burglar who was caught with stolen property because of a broken taillight. But finding a new ride would take time he doesn't have.

Brian is handsome in the way some young people are, a glow to his skin and the confidence to overcome a flaw. The gulf between his eyes could accommodate a grapefruit, but he doesn't seem to know it. A red cap with a political slogan is clamped to his head, crushing short black curls. "You didn't mention an animal," he says when the cat moans.

"You didn't ask." Zev tosses his duffel in the back and attempts to stack the jumbled, coffee-stained papers on the passenger seat, before giving up and shoving them into the glove box. Climbing into the car, he settles the cat carrier on his lap.

The kid grips the steering wheel. "Is it going to cry the whole time?"

Zev buckles his seat belt.

"You ought to give it something to knock it out," Brian says. He raises the volume on the radio, presumably to drown out Mo's unhappiness.

"If I had something, I might."

Pulling away from the curb, Brian cuts off a driver, who leans on his horn. "That cat is annoying."

"You're a real animal lover."

"I like animals, all right. Ducks, deer, an elk if I can get one. Never shot a cat, although right now I wouldn't be opposed."

Zev wraps his arms around the carrier. The radio is tuned to conservative talk radio, and the host is interviewing a candidate. All politicians—liberal or conservative—are crooked, but this one is a bigger blowhard than most.

"You voting for this guy?" Brian says.

"None of your business." Zev has never voted. The way he sees it, the less he has to do with government, the better.

"Country would be in better shape if he was in charge."

When the kid merges onto I-25 South, Zev suggests they listen to country music.

"My dad likes that," Brian says, but he doesn't change the station. "This guy's got it right. There won't be anything left for my generation if we don't change Washington."

Zev resigns himself to hearing the candidate and the kid talk.

"I grew up on a ranch near here," Brian says, as if Zev were the least bit interested. "We weren't making much from the cattle, but we were sitting on oil and gas. Big company contacted my dad, wanting to drill, and for a while it looked like we'd be rich. Then the government passed restrictions. Made it expensive to get the minerals out of the ground. I had to take out student loans for college. Can't even afford to go to Cancun for spring break. That's bullshit."

"That's tough." Zev's never been to Mexico, but if the cops track him to Phoenix, his ultimate destination, he might make a run for the border.

"Whatever happened to free markets!" the kid says, turning to Zev, the car drifting over the lane line.

"Watch the road!"

Brian looks forward and straightens out the wheel. "My dad started raising alpaca. Funny-looking animals."

"Is that right?"

"I'm going to open a grow operation. I'm majoring in agriculture, but they don't offer classes on marijuana cultivation yet." He fishes a joint out of his shirt pocket, lights it, and holds it out to Zev.

Smoking pot is legal in Colorado but not while driving. The last thing Zev needs is for a cop to pull them over. "You could get arrested for that."

Brian takes a deep pull on the joint, holds it in his lungs, then releases it, filling the car with sweet smoke. Mo sneezes. "It relaxes me."

Spotting a state trooper's car at the side of the road, lights flashing, Zev feels cold creep up his arms and legs. But the cop is too busy giving someone else a ticket to notice the Camry. The kid puffs out another thick cloud, and Mo sneezes again. Farther along the highway, some other officer is just waiting to fill his quota. He'll see the joint in the kid's hand, and all of Zev's careful planning will be destroyed. At least Mo has settled down. When Zev peeks into the carrier, her eyes are closed.

Brian glances at Zev's lap. "Cat likes it, anyway."

Opening the window to clear the smoke, Zev says, "It's a shame."

"What's a shame?"

When the smell is gone, he closes the window to keep Mo from getting cold.

"What are you talking about?" Brian says.

"It's too bad you won't be able to vote for that guy you like."

"Why won't I?"

"A cop catches you smoking that, you'll get a DUI, which is a felony." Zev doesn't know if it's true and doesn't care. "Felons can't vote."

Brian looks at the joint and frowns. For a moment, Zev thinks the kid is going to ignore him, but then he licks his index finger and thumb, pinches the end of the joint, and returns it to his pocket. "Whatever."

The Rocky Mountains roll past to the west, peaks still wrapped in snow. Zev won't feel safe until he's out of Colorado. He's trading mountains for desert. As he gets older, he'll fit in among the Arizona retirees. The idea of finding an apartment with a swimming pool, taking a dip after work, appeals to him.

He met Elissa in Arizona. Both twenty-two, they worked at a National Park Service concession in the Grand Canyon, and he stole valuables visitors locked in their cars at night. Elissa had just graduated from college. She told Zev she was looking for a brainless summer job in a beautiful place. For Zev, it was another in a long line of dead-end jobs. Restless, he'd been chasing around the country since Elijah, who'd taught him how to be a locksmith, died of a heart attack when Zev was twenty. Elijah's children had sold his business to another locksmith who didn't have a need for Zev's services.

Before Elissa was assigned to his workstation, Zev had considered quitting because the pay was shit and the hours deep-frying chicken and fish dragged, oil spattering his sweaty face and arms. The first day she worked alongside him, time disappeared as fast as the food he served. He imagined freeing her hair from the net that was part of their uniform, her fingers from latex gloves. He showed her how to short a rude customer at the register, and she laughed, flashing brilliant, oversize teeth, as if she'd waited her whole life to be a thief. "We're the Bonnie and Clyde of saturated fats," she said, pocketing her take. As they cleaned the station after closing, Zev brushed his lips against the auburn fuzz on the back of her neck, her skin flushing a satisfying crimson.

Their first night together, they slept on top of his sleeping bag, their heat keeping the cool weather at bay. Another evening, as they walked the canyon rim, Zev presented her with a cashmere sweater. "The owner left the park, so it's okay to wear it," he said, and again was rewarded with a glow of teeth. By the end of the season, they'd made plans to move to Colorado. A year later, they married in Sedona, home of Elissa's spirit animal, the ringtail cat, and a bed-and-breakfast that had a discounted weekend. Zev tells himself his return to the desert state has nothing to do with Elissa's recent move there.

Brian unwraps a chocolate bar labeled *incredibles* and eats two squares. "These are healthier, anyway. Want some?"

"Maybe I should drive."

"Nah, I'm fine."

There's little Zev can do except hope they reach Albuquerque before a trooper pulls them over. From there, he'll catch a Greyhound to Phoenix and disappear. His forehead is damp. He considers getting out and hitchhiking, but he doesn't know if the police are looking for him, if his picture has gone out over the wire. "Cops could arrest you for that, too."

"Don't be so nervous, old man."

The kid is driving fifteen over the limit. Zev counts down the miles to New Mexico, gripping the cat carrier, scanning the road for cops. When they pull into a gas station in Pueblo, Brian pumps gas and heads for a fast-food counter.

In the bathroom, Zev leashes Mo and lets her stretch. He removes the towel liner, wet with piss, from the carrier and drops it into the trash. Wishing for a sponge and some bleach to scour the carrier, he settles for foam soap from a dispenser and a damp paper towel, instead. After scrubbing his hands and face, he fills a small dish with water and another with cat food. Mo takes a few sips but refuses to eat. She moves slowly, whether from arthritis, the stress of the day, or inhaling, Zev doesn't know. On his way out, he buys two candy bars and a can of Coke, and they get back on the road.

He hands Brian a twenty for the gas and resumes his watch. His eyes are itchy and dry, tired from the strain. When lights flash behind them, the candy bar sinks in his gut and he thinks he might pee. Did someone recognize him at the gas station and alert the authorities? The kid pales, but manages to pull over. Zev considers his options. Running will signal he's guilty of something, and he doubts he's faster than the trooper. Besides, he can't leave Mo. The officer takes his time, probably running the kid's plates. Zev hopes Brian doesn't have a warrant for some drug-related offense or a year's worth of parking tickets.

One hand clutching his weapon, the other, a ticket pad, the trooper approaches the car. Brian removes his license and registration from his wallet. At least the car isn't stolen. Zev sniffs, certain he can still smell the pot, though it's been hours since he aired out the car. To stop his hands from shaking, he sits on them, then realizes he should keep them in sight and hooks his fingers in the air holes on the cat carrier.

The kid opens his window. "What seems to be the problem, Officer?"

"You failed to signal when you changed lanes, and you were speeding."

Zev keeps his face down. While it might seem suspicious, it's better than the cop recognizing him. He watches the officer out of the corner of his eye. Sweat soaks Zev's underarms, and he waits for the officer to notice.

"My turn signal may be out," Brian says.

"That's a violation." The trooper flips open his pad.

"Sorry, sir." Offering his license and registration with his left hand, the kid adjusts his red cap with his right.

"You a fan of the candidate?" the trooper asks.

"Yes, sir. A law and order fan, generally. I admire what you guys do."

"How 'bout your dad? Is he a fan, too?" The officer indicates Zev with his chin. It pains Zev to keep quiet, but he knows better than to correct him.

"Big-time. We saw him at a rally in Denver. Most exciting night of my life. It seems like the country may be getting back on track, if you know what I mean."

"I think I do," the trooper says. "You're wise for your age. A lot of young people don't seem to get it. Maybe you can have some influence on your friends."

"I try."

The officer examines the documents and shuts his pad.

"Everything seems to be in order. Ever think about trying out for the force?"

"I'm studying criminal justice."

"Glad to hear it. We need more young people like you. Try to be more careful. And fix the light."

"Yes, sir. I will. You be safe out there."

"Thanks."

When Brian pulls away from the shoulder, Zev's head drops to his hands.

"You gotta relax," Brian says. "It was just a traffic stop. You aren't even driving."

Mountains that loomed gray and green and jagged all day, soften and round, glow red as they pass the Sangre de Cristo range at sunset. Small, bushy piñon pines crowd the side of the road. When they cross into New Mexico, Zev envisions a future in which he's free.

He stayed in Colorado all these years because it was where he had lived with Elissa, where she could find him if she had a change of heart. Every room in the house evoked memories of her. She picked out the dining room chairs, cushions covered in sailcloth fabric, and the matching drapes. In the kitchen, he could smell meals she had made: brisket, baked chicken stuffed with lemons, lasagna with vegetables instead of meat, which she called her "kind dinner." In a corner of the living room, in the small drawers of the olive wood secretary she inherited from her grandmother, she concealed notes written on the backs of napkins. *This is not who I am,* read one. *I don't get a moment's peace from that child,* read another. The secretary was always locked, the key hidden, but she had to know that wouldn't keep him out. He read them years before she left but brushed them off as insignificant, a way for her to let off steam.

He got used to her absence but never accepted it. If he couldn't have her love, he could have his anger, which he tended like a fire. When it died down or threatened to go out, he examined the cuts on his face and arms, and if they were healing, he walked among the thorns for new ones, remembering how she lavished care on the bushes—pruning, fertilizing, deadheading, and filling vases with blooms that perfumed the house all summer.

At ten at night, Brian drops him off at the Albuquerque bus terminal. Inside, gate announcements crackle over a loudspeaker. People doze on chairs, plastic bags, suitcases, and backpacks at their feet and on adjoining seats. If the police question ticket agents in Colorado, they won't have seen him.

In the bathroom, he tends to Mo again, trying to make her comfortable. His bus departs a little after midnight. Zev boards first and sits at the back, Mo next to him. Relieved to be out of the kid's car, he doesn't mind spending the night sitting up. Though he brought copies of *Car and Driver* and *This Old House,* he leaves them in his bag, unwilling to turn on the light and risk someone getting a better view of his face.

12

La La pulls up to Zev's with a bag of groceries, the same items she buys every week: frozen foods, Pop-Tarts, coffee, cream, and a variety of household supplies. Noticing his car and van are missing, she wonders if he sold them to help pay O'Bannon's bill, or if there's another reason the vehicles are gone. Their absence unsettles her.

She lets herself in the back and calls out, but her father doesn't reply. Mo doesn't appear, either.

On the dining room table, the train circles the track. Zev's ankle monitor rides in an open freight car, indicator light flashing as it transmits GPS data. Pain gathers at the base of her head. She isn't surprised he found a way to remove it. And she understands now why he wanted the train. If she weren't overcome with loss, she might feel a bit of pride. A second ankle monitor, one that isn't blinking, secures a note to the table. She lifts the note, though she doubts she'll like what it has to say.

Dear La La, I'm going away. You're the only one I'm sorry to leave. If not for me you'd be graduating from

veterinary school right now. I won't let them lock me up.
I can't live that way. I never have and I'm too old to start
now. Those places aren't clean. You're the best daughter
I could have asked for. You never looked down on me
even after you went to college. I mopped all the floors and
vacuumed. If I can avoid the bounty hunters, the bonding
company will foreclose on the house. Take anything you
want before they do. I'm sorry about all this. I love you.
Dad

Except for the soft scraping of the train's wheels against the track, the house is unbearably quiet. Gone are the sounds that always surrounded Zev: the swish of a mop; the crinkle of a magazine page; the *click, click* of a lock being worked. For the second time, a parent has left her without saying good-bye. She rereads the note, hoping to have overlooked something. It contains everything (he's gone) and nothing (where? How can she reach him?). She balls it up and sticks it into her purse. She hates the thought of her father in prison, but at least there she could visit him.

As far as she can tell, the authorities don't know he's gone. They'll figure it out when he doesn't appear at the bail hearing. La La hopes he gets away, except for a small part of her that wants him caught and returned to her.

She wonders if she'll ever see him again or hear him misquote a magazine. He was the only one who needed her. Except perhaps for Black and Blue, who miss her when Clem has them. And she's responsible for Mo, now, too. But is it possible Zev took the cat?

She turns toward the couch. When she doesn't see Mo, she rotates her arms and shoulders, alarmed to find they move freely and without pain. Perhaps the cat is dozing on the dresser next to

the window in Zev's room, as she does sometimes. La La rushes
down the hall, catching her wrist on the doorknob as she turns
into Zev's empty bedroom. She calls to Mo by name and when
that fails to produce her, with a hissing sound. In the kitchen, she
shakes a jar of treats and waits.

Why would he take Mo? The cat carrier isn't in the bedroom
closet or under the stairs. Though La La hasn't lived with Mo for
years, she's always known where to find her. Since Zev's arrest,
she's imagined losing him to prison, but she never thought Mo
would disappear, too.

From the top of the sofa, she collects three strands of brindle
fur that escaped the vacuum and pushes them into her pocket.
She presses her nose to the couch, hoping to inhale the cat's deli-
cate scent, getting a lungful of fabric freshener instead. If not for
Mo, she never would have met Dr. Bergman. She can still hear the
cat's muffled purr, her yowling cry on seeing a tom through the
window. She longs to feel those sounds in her body.

And then there's the house. Though she often felt trapped
inside, at other times—playing with Mo and Tiny, diagnosing
an animal with Dr. Bergman, even planning robberies—worlds
opened to her there. It was the only place she knew her mother.
They gardened together in the back, La La digging holes eight
inches deep and six inches apart, inserting tulip bulbs in the fall
before the ground froze. Bright flowers came up year after year,
long after her mother disappeared, the red ones suggesting blood
and foul play, the orange ones, fire, calamities La La imagined
kept Elissa from returning.

She'll search the house for clues about Elissa before the bond
company forecloses. Something with her mother's address on it.

She's always had the feeling Zev knew more about where Elissa was than he was saying.

In the bag on the floor, groceries thaw. Looking for Zev is out of the question because she might lead bounty hunters to him. She considers calling John O'Bannon but wants to give her father time to get away and doesn't know what the lawyer's responsibilities would be. She starts to dial Nat, then stops. Nat will tell Tank.

Though she'd like to go on sitting in the house, soaking up the smell of well-oiled locks, it's a bad idea to let the police find her there.

Soggy groceries beside her, she eases the car away, her eyes drawn to the rosebushes in the rearview mirror, their first buds appearing. There's no longer any reason to enter homes that aren't hers. She owes O'Bannon nearly eight thousand dollars, but she'll pay it off slowly now that she's not worried about him dropping Zev. She releases a breath she's been holding for months, only to discover relief isn't all she feels. She enjoyed raiding the homes of strangers, whose lives—rich and full of family—she coveted. She'll miss tending to other people's pets, neglected, as she was.

On the other hand, she can tell Clem she's stopped. La La imagines he'll greet the news with relief. He might insist on coming over to see her. They won't mean to, but they'll end up spending the night together, after apologizing to each other. The next day, he'll break up with Naomi. It's not her fault, he'll tell her. It's just that he's never stopped loving La La. It may not happen exactly that way. Perhaps it will take a bit more time. But time is something La La has, and she's willing to wait. Though she'd like to, she can't call him yet. Not until Zev is out of harm's way.

At home, Black licks her hand and Blue climbs her side. She drinks in the scents of dried mud on their paws and sap in their fur and briefly forgets she's an orphan.

She phones Dr. Bergman the next day, though she doesn't know if he'll talk to her. "I was wondering if that job offer is still open," she says, when his secretary puts her through.

He doesn't respond, and La La wonders if it's a mistake to have called, if he's written her off as a failed experiment, a person with whom he no longer wishes to associate. "I've stopped," she says.

"That's good. I never want to visit you in prison."

"I could work until school starts in the fall." Someone asks Dr. Bergman a question about a medication, and when he replies, La La is pleased to discover she knows the answer, too.

"I can't pay you what I imagine you were . . . uh . . . making."

She relaxes her grip on the phone. "No, of course not. I wouldn't expect . . . just a vet tech's salary."

"A very experienced vet tech with special skills."

La La doesn't know what to say. Doesn't know why he's forgiven her. Why he's willing to trust her with his patients and give her a job that will last for only a few months. Although she ignored his calls and followed a path he disapproved of, he still treats her as family. "Thank you," she says, doubting she deserves his kindness.

The following Monday, La La starts the job that will sustain her until she can take out student loans in the fall. It's strange to be back in a clinic, vaccinating a mastiff under bright lights and the resentful eye of a senior tech named Kali, who is also the office manager. The woman learned about animals growing up on a dairy farm. She has little formal training, but twenty-five years' experience, and Dr. Bergman trusts her.

"I wasn't aware we needed another tech," she says, while La La mixes the vaccine and inserts a needle into the vial.

The phone in La La's pocket begins to play "Lawyers, Guns and Money," the ringtone for O'Bannon. Zev's bail hearing isn't until Wednesday. Afraid the police have caught him, La La yanks the needle from the vial, nearly inoculating Kali against rabies. The tech crosses her arms, while La La steadies herself and prepares to feel the stick, then administers the shot. When Kali walks the dog out, La La darts into the bathroom to listen to the message.

"The police went to your father's house this morning after receiving an alert from the ankle monitoring company. Your father wasn't there," O'Bannon says. La La sits on the toilet. In her mind, she traces a rabbit's skeleton—cranium, maxilla, mandible, atlas, scapula, spine, fibula, tibia, femur, ilium, sacrum—until her heart rate slows. She washes her face, drying it with paper towels.

At five o'clock, she calls O'Bannon from her car. "What happens next?"

"We hope they don't find him."

The days have gotten longer, but the air still holds a chill. From high in the mountains, melting glaciers swell the creek alongside the parking lot with icy, turbulent water.

"He didn't want to be locked up," O'Bannon says. "For now, he isn't. You'll be all right. What do you want to do about the balance on your bill?"

"I'll pay it over time if you don't mind. I'm going back to school."

"I suppose it's better that way."

After she hangs up, La La runs her hand over the passenger seat. The car isn't her style. She considers getting rid of it and buying something simpler but decides to keep it a little longer. She doesn't plan to rob any more houses but likes to imagine she could.

While she gathers the courage to dial Clem's number, she watches the creek's tumultuous journey. "I'm working at Dr. Bergman's clinic until school starts. That's all I'm doing," she says when he picks up.

"I'm so glad to hear that. I never want anything bad to happen to you."

The kind words give her hope. "I thought, maybe, we could have dinner or something."

Clem is quiet for a moment. "I'm not sure I'm ready for that. I'm sorry."

The air in the car feels heavy. It presses down on La La like an avalanche. Nevertheless, she tries again. "It could be like it was."

"You know I'm seeing Naomi. We're talking about opening a bodywork clinic together. You'll meet someone wonderful. I'm sure you will."

Country music plays on a radio station and a motorcycle engine revs. Clem must be in his car, too. A bitter taste fills La La's mouth. She's already met someone wonderful, and it's him.

A week later, as La La is about to sit down to dinner, she sees through a window a tall woman with an AR-15 hanging from her shoulder and a pistol nosing into a holster at her side. AGENT glows white on the sleeve of her black jacket, a garment that fails to hide she's well-endowed. She shows something to a neighbor. La La assumes it's a picture of Zev and that the woman is a bounty hunter. The neighbor examines the photo and shakes her head.

When the woman knocks, La La steps outside and closes the door behind her. She's curious to find out what the agent knows. Since La La has no idea where Zev is, there's no risk she'll reveal anything.

"You'd be doing him a favor turning him in," the woman says. A silver shield hangs from a chain around her neck, and her hair is gathered in a brown ponytail.

"Can I see the picture?"

The woman holds up a copy of Zev's mug shot. "If he surrenders, he won't get shot."

"He doesn't carry a gun," La La says, her voice unnaturally high. "There's no need to shoot him."

The woman folds the photo and tucks it into her back pocket. "How do you know he doesn't carry one now? When was the last time you talked to him?"

Neighbors have begun to watch. "He's never carried one."

"It's no fun looking over your shoulder all the time. That's how it'll be as long as he's on the run."

"I'll let him worry about that."

"They all get caught eventually. Call me if you want to save his life." She holds out a business card.

THE FINDER is printed in bold letters on the card, then *Fugitive Recovery Agent* and a phone number. La La keeps her hands at her sides, refusing it.

The agent starts to go but turns back. "You wouldn't have him inside?"

"That would be a pretty stupid place for him to hide."

A hand on her pistol, the woman says, "Harboring a fugitive is a crime."

"I watch *Law and Order,* too."

"This isn't a TV show. Your father's in danger, whether you realize it or not. I understand he's the one who called nine-one-one. There could be extenuating circumstances."

"I'm not talking about his case."

"Suit yourself. But if you change your mind, call me." As she leaves, the agent deposits the card in the mailbox, then climbs back into her 4Runner.

"Why not tell Clem you're working as a vet tech?" Nat asks. She missed their Sunday walk around the reservoir and invited La La for dinner Wednesday night, instead.

La La didn't want to see Tank but couldn't think of an excuse fast enough, so here she is in their kitchen, surrounded by white cabinets, a double oven, and a coffee maker that could have been designed by NASA. "I did tell him. On the phone. He reminded me that he's seeing Naomi."

"He was engaged to you. Maybe they're not serious." As Nat chops mushrooms, her ferret, Casey, hops on the counter and steals one.

"The woman loves dogs. They're thinking about working together. Clem never even bothered to tell her we were engaged."

"Sorry."

Tank opens a bottle of red wine. She hasn't seen him since he threatened her. He looks gaunt, and his clothes smell sour. Nat told La La she refuses to do Tank's laundry, especially since he's hardly working.

"If you love someone, shouldn't you stick with them? We have one fight, and Clem takes off." La La checks her phone though it's been weeks since she heard from any of the Elizabeth Golds she contacted.

"It was a pretty big fight," Nat says.

"I'm with La La," Tank says, his first words since she arrived. "You don't leave. You stay and work it out." He looks at Nat.

"We're talking about La La and Clem," Nat says.

Perched on the back of a chair, the ferret nibbles on the mushroom, then throws it at Nat.

"Get her, Casey." His hands trembling, Tank pours three glasses of wine, then disappears.

Nat sprinkles shredded soy cheese on premade pizza dough. "You must be happy to be back in a clinic."

"I guess."

"What's the matter?"

"I assisted on an emergency surgery the other day," La La says. "A dog with bloat. We saved him, and later the whole office went out for beers. I felt good about it until I realized if it wasn't me helping, it would have been another vet tech. The animal didn't need me at all."

"It was you, and you were in the clinic legitimately, not in some stranger's home where you could get shot. Sometimes it's okay to do things in an ordinary way."

La La sets the table. When Tank returns, she walks a wide circle around him as she lays out napkins.

"Did you ever think about working out?" Nat says to La La. "It's a good way to burn off stress. It used to help Tank."

Tank shoots her a nasty look. He reaches under his shirt and scratches feverishly.

"Gyms are great places to meet people, too." Nat adds the chopped mushrooms to the pizza.

"I can't imagine anyone wanting to date me. Especially if they knew what you know."

"You're a veterinary student. People love animals." Nat finishes her wine and pours herself another. "Start thinking of yourself that way. Forget the rest." She refills La La's glass, ignoring Tank's though it's empty, and slips the pizza into the oven.

While the pizza bakes, Nat excuses herself to use the bathroom. When she's gone, Tank says, "Don't keep me waiting too much longer."

La La straightens a fork. "I'm not doing that anymore."

"You will. You'll return to your old life, just like I did."

La La wonders if he's right. Some days she feels as if gravity itself is pulling her into other people's homes.

13

The bus arrives in Phoenix at nine in the morning. Not having slept, Zev stumbles into the terminal. He asks a stranger for directions to the nearest diner, and on the way buys a prepaid smartphone that doesn't require him to give his name.

In the restaurant, the smells of bacon and coffee sharpen Zev's hunger. A server wipes the table, pushing crumbs onto the booth's ancient leather seat. Zev orders black coffee, a double stack of pancakes, and three scrambled eggs loose. Above the door hangs a large, dusty clock, its second hand moving steadily around the dial. Zev looks forward to a leisurely breakfast.

It isn't until his food arrives, and Zev thinks about slipping a bowl of kibble into Mo's carrier, that he realizes the cat isn't with him. Throwing three fives on the table, he runs back to the store where he bought the phone. The carrier isn't on the counter, and no one has seen it. He races to the bus station. It's hot, a kind of heat he isn't used to. Sweat rolls into his eyes, collects behind his knees, and drips down his calves. His side cramps, but he's afraid to slow down.

In the station, all the buses look alike. He has no idea which gate they pulled into. At the information counter, he tells the clerk he's looking for his cat, that she's in a carrier he left on the last seat of the bus from Albuquerque.

The clerk looks up from his computer, his hand cradling a mouse. "We don't allow animals on the bus." His fingers are long, the nails trimmed.

"I'm trying to take her *off* the bus."

"Unless it's a service dog. Then you can bring her on."

Zev sets his duffel down, his shoulder sore from carrying it. "She's a cat, and I don't want to travel with her, I want to find her."

"I suppose you could try the lost and found."

"Where's that?"

Reaching down, the man retrieves a beat-up cardboard box that holds a Desert Museum cap, plastic sunglasses, a makeup case, a single earring, a book of kids' jokes, and a key dangling from a mini flashlight.

Zev massages his shoulder. "She was in a carrier."

"It's not here."

"Could you look again?"

The clerk scans the area below the counter. "No cat," he says. "The bus might be in service. Check the rear of the station."

Five identical buses are parked in service bays. As he starts to board one, a woman in a driver's uniform approaches and tells him he's in a restricted area.

"My cat's on the bus."

"We don't allow animals on the buses."

"Except for service dogs. I know. I'm trying to get her off the bus."

The driver looks around. "Make it fast."

Zev scrambles up the stairs and down the aisle. When he gets to the last seat, it's empty. It's the wrong bus. The headrest on the seat in front of his was broken, but this one's fine.

He boards the second bus. What he wouldn't give to hear Mo crying. If he finds her, he'll buy her a case of the most expensive canned food the supermarket stocks and a giant planter of catnip. The back seat is empty. La La will never forgive him if he's lost Mo.

She isn't on the third bus, either. Clutching the handrail, he pulls himself into the fourth bus, his legs wobbly. A copy of *Motor Sport Magazine* has been abandoned on a seat, but he doesn't stop to pick it up. Nearing the back of the bus, he smells urine, just like on his bus, and quickens his step. He can't wait to hold her. To hear her complain about being abandoned. The headrest on the second-to-last seat is broken. But Mo's not there. He gets on his hands and knees, disregarding the layers of filth on the floor, and looks under the seats but sees only a crumpled tissue, a candy wrapper, and a pair of earbuds.

Though he knows it's hopeless, he tries the fifth bus.

He drags himself outside, his body heavy, except for his hands, which might float away without the carrier, their emptiness a reproach. Back pressed to the station's concrete wall, he sinks to the ground, one more vagrant populating the plaza, uncertain what to do next. Women in sleeveless dresses and men in business shirts gawk as they pass. Though he hates to stand out, he can't bring himself to find a bathroom, to shave and change from his wrinkled clothes. The morning has grown still hotter, and hunger pangs rattle his belly. Mo, too, must be hungry, not having eaten since yesterday morning. He hopes she's okay, wherever she is. Not everyone means animals well, La La used to warn him.

He's about to doze off, when he hears: "Sir! Sir!" The information clerk runs toward him, swinging the carrier.

Zev jumps to his feet. "Easy! She's not a bag of potatoes."

"I'm glad you're still here."

Zev clutches the carrier and looks through the holes. Mo trembles, her face pressed into a corner and hidden by her paws. He would take her out, reassure her, but he's afraid she might run. "Where was she?"

"Last seat of the bus, just like you said. Maya, one of the service personnel, found it. She gave it some water in the restroom and then brought it to lost and found. Lucky you didn't leave."

His first piece of luck in his new town.

When he stops back at the diner, a woman in a grease-stained apron holds up his breakfast in a Styrofoam container. "We kept it for you, just in case. But it's cold. Want me to microwave it? I'll get you some fresh coffee, too." She starts to lead him to a table, but then glances down and stops. "That's going to be a problem. I like animals as much as the next person, but the Health Department doesn't. You'll have to wait outside."

Back on the street, Zev puts a bowl of kibble in Mo's carrier, but she still won't eat. Trying to avoid the stream of pedestrians, he presses himself into a doorway. The waitress brings his food. Container in one hand, plastic fork in the other, he eats as neatly as he can, now and then reaching for his cup of coffee on the sidewalk.

When he finishes, he walks half a mile to a motel the waitress mentioned. Leaving Mo in the shade of the building, he registers, then retrieves her and unlocks the door to a room that smells of stale cigarette smoke. The polyester bedspread whistles as he sits on it. He returns to the front desk and asks to borrow cleaning supplies.

"Maid did that room an hour ago," the manager says. Her hair is the color of ash, short as a marine's, and she gives him a look that says she won't tolerate nonsense.

"I'm very particular." He slides a five-dollar bill across the desk.

She pulls a key from a drawer. "Down the hall, last door on the left. I better have this back in an hour."

When he steps into the maintenance closet, the odor of bleach hits him, as pleasing as the scent of fine cigars to other men, and he breathes deeply. Back in his room, he wipes the cracked toilet bowl, the mildewed shower walls. After vacuuming the stained carpet in the bedroom, he douses it with freshener. He removes a layer of dust from the TV screen and polishes the laminate night tables. Mo hides under the bed, coming out only to eat and to relieve herself in the litter box Zev improvised by scattering shredded toilet paper in a cardboard box he emptied of Borax.

Stepping gingerly into the barely clean shower, he washes himself, then changes into fresh clothes. He searches on his phone for a cheap apartment that's furnished and in a complex with a pool. A place on the ground floor, since he might need to exit through a window. When he finds one, he rides the bus to a property manager's office and fills out an application. He lists his name as Roger Cohen, whose social security number and driver's license he bought in Colorado from an associate specializing in identity theft. He crosses his fingers that Roger hasn't done anything lately to ruin his credit.

As he lies on the motel bed that night, he looks up the Mesa,

Arizona, shelter where Elissa works. He clicks on her picture in the staff directory. Despite the air-conditioning and fanning himself with a copy of *Car and Driver*, heat pricks his skin. He hasn't been this close to her in nearly twenty years.

Three days later, he signs the apartment lease, pays a deposit, and moves in. When he frees Mo from the carrier, she presses herself under the dresser and refuses to come out. Perhaps the streaked vinyl flooring and sagging mattress depress her as much as they do Zev. If he inspects, he's afraid he'll find bedbugs, but if he doesn't, he won't sleep, imagining them there. A scorpion waves its tail when he lifts a pillow. Zev bats it to the floor, crushes it under his heel, and wipes up the mess.

In the bathroom, cartoon roadrunners dash across the shower curtain. A man pees into a lunar crater in a framed poster. Preferring the pink wall with a nail hole, Zev takes the picture down. The rest of the art in the apartment is the kind found in office lobbies: a sunset over the Sonoran Desert, a flicker nesting in a saguaro. Once white, the kitchen appliances are gray. A small washer tops a dryer in a closet. The place comes with a twenty-four-inch flat-screen TV, cable included in the rent, and Wi-Fi.

He's sorry he forgot La La's castle drawing. He would have hung it above the apartment's only table, an unsteady butcher block. Pushed into a corner of the tiny kitchen, the table barely sits two. He leans a photo of La La holding a plastic stethoscope to Tiny's heart against the nightstand lamp where it will be the last thing he sees before he closes his eyes.

With supplies he took from the motel, Zev scrubs the apartment and washes his clothes. He walks a mile to a used car dealer, where he pays cash for an old BMW, registering it to Roger. The manager of the lot barely glances at the stolen license.

Zev has an instinct about the man. "I have some jewelry I might be looking to sell and some silver."

"I know someone who'd be interested," the manager says. He gives Zev the name of a gas station and directions to the place. "You want Arturo."

When he returns to the apartment, Zev reaches under the dresser and runs his fingers along Mo's cheek. "This is pretty weird for us both." She raises her chin, and he scratches her neck.

The next morning, he inspects the pool. Mesquite and paloverde trees border the property. Agaves, chollas, prickly pears, and a knife-edged plant he can't name dot the rocky landscape. The water is a light, artificial blue, lanes separated by ropes and buoys. The intense sun has burned off the chlorine, and he can barely smell it. He has it all to himself.

Stretching out on a lounge chair, he imagines what it would be like to retire. He doesn't have the money, and he'd get bored, watching birds and still water. There isn't a door he can't get through, a window he can't open. It would be a shame to waste his skills. He enjoys rescuing stranded homeowners, and he might even miss the burglaries, the surge of adrenaline giving way to satisfaction once he's safe.

He never intended to hurt anyone. And who can say it wasn't Claude Thomas's time? That he wouldn't have had a stroke on the landing even if Zev weren't there?

Zev's jeans and long-sleeved shirt, fine for spring in Colorado, trap the Phoenix heat and make him sluggish. He closes his eyes to the sun. Listening to the hum of the pool filter, he falls asleep.

When he wakes, he's startled to find the chair next to his occupied by a woman. Out of habit, he touches his back pocket, checking for his wallet. He raises his backrest, so she isn't looking down on him. "I didn't hear you sit down." She smells of the sunscreen that streaks her cheekbones. Reading glasses pinch the end of her nose.

"You were out." She pushes her glasses to the top of her head, flipping back blond hair cut in a bowl, gray roots beginning to show. Wet from a swim she must have taken while he was sleeping. A facelift hollows her eyes, but her expression is open, poised to take in more than what's on the surface. Under a blue one-piece bathing suit, her belly rises gently. Not wishing to be caught staring, Zev looks away. "Are you visiting someone?" she says, lowering a copy of *Psychology Today*.

The magazine is one of Zev's favorites, providing insight into human nature and helping him answer questions such as who will turn a blind eye to his activities and who among his contacts he can trust. He's already read the issue. "The cover story about fathers and daughters is interesting," he says. "In the magazine. Anyway, I moved in yesterday."

She looks at the cover, then pulls a water bottle from a cloth bag decorated with a Chihuahua, an image that makes him think of La La. As she sips, Zev realizes he must look out of place, sitting by the pool in street clothes, without water or anything to keep him occupied. She sticks out her hand—slender ringless fingers, nails painted turquoise. She could be single, or maybe she doesn't wear her ring to the pool. "Julia. What's interesting about it?"

He wipes his palm on his jeans. "Roger." Her grip is firm. "It says fathers have a greater impact on daughters than mothers. I wouldn't have thought that."

"I'll have to read it. You must have a daughter."

"Yes. Grown, with her own life."

"Sounds like you miss her. I know the feeling. I have a boy

and a girl, both married." They fall silent. A truck on a nearby road beeps, backing up. Zev fans himself with his hand.

"Did you move here with your wife?" Julia asks.

"Not unless she's a cat."

"You're an animal person!" She scrolls through photos on her phone and shows him one of a Chihuahua. "This is Dee-Dee."

"Short for—"

"Desdemona."

He was going to guess Dorothy. He vaguely remembers a character named Desdemona in a Shakespeare play he didn't bother to read in high school.

"Where are you from?" she asks.

"Missouri," Zev says.

"Any family in town?"

Her questions make him uneasy. Rising from the chair, he grabs a leaf skimmer and runs it through the pool.

"Maintenance will do that," she says.

"I like things clean." He sets the skimmer down and scoops water from the pool, splashing it on his face to cool him. It's been decades since he met a woman socially.

"Are you retired?" she asks.

"I'm a locksmith."

"I'll keep that in mind in case I'm ever locked out. Do you enjoy it?"

"Anyone ever tell you that you ask a lot of questions?"

"Hazard of the trade. I used to be a therapist."

Zev's never been in therapy but he has the idea—where he got it he isn't sure—that therapists can tell when you're lying. When he leans the skimmer against a wall, it falls to the ground, clattering. "Have to feed the cat."

"I was just leaving, myself." Throwing on a black-and-gold cover-up, she gathers her things, and they exit via a slate path lined with boulders on either side. Julia in front in flip-flops. They've taken only a few steps when Zev hears the rattle. Glancing down, he sees the snake on the path. It must have been sunning itself, but now it flicks its tongue, its body curled. Julia is about to step on it. Zev grabs her arm and yanks her back, then steadies her, so she doesn't fall.

"What in God's name—" she says.

"Look," he says, and points.

She backs up, putting more distance between her and the rattler, her hand covering her mouth.

"I'm surprised you didn't hear it," he says. "You were just about on top of it."

"I took out my hearing aids. To swim."

The gray-black snake slithers behind a boulder and disappears. They stare at the empty spot where the rattler was, and Zev pictures the snake, doing what it had to do to protect itself. Julia's chest rises and falls quickly, as though she's reliving the incident, too. She looks older than she did at the pool, the lines on her face more pronounced.

"I hate to think how that could have turned out," she says. She raises her eyes to his, and he sees gratitude in them, and uncertainty, whether about him or something else, he doesn't know.

"I could walk you home," he says, knowing he should, though he's hot and tired, and just wants to get back to his apartment.

"If you don't mind. I'm just a few houses down. I'll pay more attention to where I put my feet." They walk to the end of the path, then cross to a block of single-family homes. Julia's is a small ranch house. Her front yard is xeriscaped with cactuses and a mesquite tree, a birdhouse shaped like a castle hanging from a branch. Julia unlocks the door. "I think I'll lie down for a while."

Once she's inside, Zev turns back toward his apartment.

In his kitchen, he fills a glass with water and drinks it down. Sitting at the table, he studies the stains in the butcher block. The refrigerator buzzes. A few small clouds drift by outside, and he remembers how La La used to say clouds were the puff of smoke at the end of a magic trick in which the magician disappeared.

Zev shoves his cart through the supermarket, relieved to be in the air-conditioning. When Colorado's heavy March snow was burying his house, Arizona's high temperatures sounded good, but they don't feel so good now.

He's glad to shop for himself. He hated burdening La La, and she never got what he asked for, buying burritos with peppers instead of chicken, trying to trick him into eating sausage made from soybeans. He doesn't understand the logic behind vegetarianism. If he doesn't eat meat, what will happen to all the cows and pigs? It's not like he's barbecuing a dog. La La says eating a cow is just as bad, a crazy idea that must have come from Dr. Bergman. Even Clem enjoyed a steak now and then, as long as it was grass-fed. Since Zev isn't around to keep an eye on La La, he wishes she and Clem didn't break up. He'd feel better knowing someone is taking care of her, even if that someone is the quack. Taking a bottle of cabernet from a shelf, he wonders if it's the kind of thing Julia drinks, then looks at the price and puts it back.

Longview was filled with university students and professors with young families. Here, especially in the middle of the day, he's surrounded by old people. They don't stare at phones, banging their carts into his, then saying "sorry," when it wouldn't have happened in the first place if they'd just looked where they were going. Maybe Phoenix will suit him, although the lady in front of him is blocking his path, jabbing every package of rib eye with a gnarled finger, as if she has nothing better to do all day.

As he thinks about growing old and useless, the air-conditioning seems to blow colder, his bones feel stiffer and—he imagines—more brittle. When he was under house arrest, the boredom was terrible. He read every magazine that came to the house cover to cover, even the advertisements. Practiced with the extra ankle monitor for hours, until his fingers calloused. After watching several seasons of *This Old House,* his ears rang. It was only when he worked, supporting La La and himself, that he had an appetite at the end of the day and was tired enough to sleep. Backing up his cart, he wheels it around the woman.

That afternoon, he opens a map of Phoenix on the kitchen table, the outer areas of the city flapping over the sides. He checks which neighborhoods are close to highways and researches the prices of homes before going for a drive. Sparse landscaping provides less cover than in Colorado. Retired, many owners are home all the time. Zev scopes out a neighborhood with ten-thousand-square-foot houses and long driveways covered with pavers or colored concrete, doubling back to inspect a place where the lawn is decorated with statuary. A family that can afford a marble fountain is sure to own other valuables. A towering saguaro, the kind people steal from the desert, throws a long shadow across the adobe finish. When an elderly man drives away in the only car in the garage, Zev notes the address and time.

At a discount department store, Zev tosses short-sleeved cotton shirts, twill pants, and a blue newsboy cap—the uniform of older men—into a cart. He adds a frame for the photo of La La, and though he shouldn't spend the money, a cat bed and a plush mouse for Mo, hoping one or the other will coax her from under the dresser. In the hardware section, he selects a crowbar and a wrench. It will take a little more time to gather what he needs for locksmithing.

Mo is curled up on the bed when he returns. She sniffs the plush mouse and goes back to sleep.

Morning sun slices through the living room windows. A film of dust coats the blinds. With a feather duster, Zev beats back a desert he fears will always be settling on everything. Finding the tool inadequate, he wets a sponge and runs it along the slats. The TV is tuned to *Good Morning America*.

At the kitchen table, he inspects the wrench and crowbar while he waits for coffee to brew. When someone knocks at the front door, he grabs the tools and tosses them into a closet. He's not expecting anyone.

"I know you're in there," says Julia, knocking again. "I can hear George Stephanopoulos. I came by to thank you. You saved me from a trip to urgent care yesterday and maybe something a lot worse."

She's too nosy. There's nothing to be gained from a friendship with her and everything to be lost.

"Since you don't have any family here, I thought I could show you around," she says. "Phoenix is a nice city once you get to know it."

He opens the door but doesn't invite her in.

"What have you got in there, Fort Knox? For God's sake, I'm not going to rob you."

"The place is a mess. I've got a lot of unpacking to do."

"There's a film festival in town. I thought you might like to go."

He remembers how she held out a photo of Dee-Dee. Desdemona. A red bandanna knotted around the Chihuahua's neck. Where she found one small enough is a mystery. He pictures Julia's turquoise toenails and the slender hammertoe he had the desire to uncurl. Though she used to be a therapist, now she's just a retired lady looking for company. No need to be afraid of her. "What's playing?"

"It's a romantic comedy. French."

He hasn't been inside a movie theater in years. "I don't speak French."

"You can read, can't you? There are subtitles. I made you something," she says, handing him a loaf pan. "I hope you like cranberries."

He likes the jellied discs on Thanksgiving. He's not sure about putting them in baked goods.

"It's just a small thank-you. I'll pick up the pan when you're done. By the way, that article *was* interesting. I was surprised at how wide-ranging a father's influence can be. So, what do you say, matinee at three?"

"Sure."

"Why don't I drive, since I know the way?"

When she leaves, Zev grabs a broom from the closet. He shouldn't have said yes. He carries the chairs out of the kitchen and sweeps methodically, from one end of the tiny room to the other, reaching the broom beneath the table. He doesn't know which scares him more, that he might hit it off with Julia or that he might not.

He thought he was finished with women. The last time he saw Elissa, she said, "We need milk," and disappeared. La La slept. Zev figured Elissa went out at night to avoid being recognized, her role in La La's near-drowning still talked about everywhere. He waited an hour, then two. Drove to the supermarket, though he hated to leave La La. But he didn't want to wake her and frighten her, either. Elissa's Ford Escort wasn't at the market or the animal shelter.

Imagining she'd been in an accident, he contacted hospitals in Fort Collins and Denver, but she hadn't been brought in. Another hour passed. A little after midnight, he opened their bedroom closet and found a dozen hangers bare and a shoe rack half-empty. Her suitcase was missing from the closet in the den.

Maybe she'd gone to New York to visit her parents until the scandal died down. Yet why wouldn't she say anything? When he called Ruth and Harry in the early hours of the morning, they both got on the line.

"I hope she's okay," her mother said, her voice tight with anxiety. She seemed to be trying to catch her breath.

"She's running from *him*," her father said. "I'm glad."

"Not now," Ruth said.

"Fuck him," said Harry. "He's a criminal."

Three weeks passed without word. Responding to a call, Zev broke off a key in a lock when all it needed was a little lubricant.

At the breakfast table, La La stabbed her toast with a butter knife, refusing to eat, and Zev told her the truth. "For now, it's just the two of us." He took the knife from her hand. "We'll be fine," he said, though he didn't believe it.

Preparing to go out with Julia, he showers again and dresses in his new clothes. He glances at himself in the bathroom mirror. Since his arrest, patches of white have sprung up in his hair. At least La La gave him his last haircut, using a pair of surgical scissors, leaving the bangs full and sweeping them to the side once she was done. A bit long for his taste, but La La assured him they looked better than when he chopped them short. He could see how they highlighted his large, brown eyes. Elissa always said they were his best feature.

He meets Julia out front at two thirty. Her Volvo is clean and well cared for, though far from new. The ham sandwich he ate for lunch churns in his stomach, and he pauses with his hand on the door. Maybe it's not too late to say he's coming down with something.

"Are you getting in?" she says, lowering the passenger window. She looks elegant in a fitted black blouse and gray slacks. Silver hoops dangle from her ears. Nothing worth stealing, still they look graceful against her long neck. He opens the door and slides in.

The label in his shirt pokes the back of his neck. He scratches and then folds his hands stiffly on his lap. "You do this a lot?"

"Go to the movies?"

"Date."

"I said I would show you around." On the way to the theater, she points out a pharmacy, a hospital, and restaurants offering early-bird specials. How old is she? Or does she think he's old?

He's never eaten an early-bird special, but if he's going to take women out, it's not a bad idea to find someplace cheap.

Just when he's sure she's giving him the geriatric tour, she points out a Cuban restaurant. "They have salsa on Friday and Saturday nights. Maybe we'll go sometime."

A vision of her dancing distracts him, and he barely sees the rest of the neighborhood sites.

In the theater, he leans away from her, his ribs pressing into the opposite armrest. She smells like herbal soap, the fragrance lighter than the rose perfume Elissa wore. The movie is slow, but Julia seems engrossed. Zev wonders what she was like as a therapist. How many of her clients' secrets she learned, and whether she held them close or shared them.

After the movie, they drive to a steak house Julia recommends, Zev thinking about the cost, not knowing if he's expected to pay for her. At the restaurant, Zev orders a double Scotch to settle his nerves. Antlers, rifles, and photographs of an African safari hang on the pine walls. Placards read *"Vegetarian" is an Indian word for "bad hunter"* and *Vegetarians eat for free*. La La wouldn't approve, but Zev points them out to Julia, who laughs while shaking her head, having it both ways. She sips her gin and tonic and says how much she enjoyed the movie.

"That makes one of us." Zev lays a napkin on his lap.

"What didn't you like?"

"A woman falling for a homeless man, taking him in, and rehabilitating him? Especially an older woman? Please."

"Especially an older woman?" Julia's ears flush.

Zev tears into a roll, scattering crumbs onto the table. He sweeps the crumbs into a pile and pinches them onto his plate. Julia glares at him, her eyes blue and green with a sprinkling of yellow, like opals. He regrets telling the truth about the movie and tries to explain. "The only thing a homeless guy would make an older woman feel is afraid."

"Is that so?"

"You asked what I thought," he says.

"Maybe an older woman would be confident in her ability to read someone's character. To see the diamond in the rough."

"More like a cubic zirconia."

She examines the menu, though she told Zev on the way over that the porterhouse was the thing to get.

"I didn't mean to insult you," he says.

"No, you just said what was on your mind. Unfortunately, what was on your mind was an ageist, sexist stereotype."

Zev is sure whatever he says will be wrong, so he signals the waiter for another drink, and they order dinner.

Julia sets down the menu. "Do you think your daughter will visit?"

"She's pretty busy. How about your kids?"

"They were here for Easter with my grandkids. They won't be back until Christmas. When they're young, they turn to you for everything. I know some people think that's bad, but I loved it. Now they're grown and I spend six months pining for them, only to have them visit for a long weekend that feels like it's over before it begins."

"My daughter didn't turn to me for everything. I sometimes wish she had. But I know what you mean about them growing up." La La has probably discovered his disappearance by now. His and Mo's. Perhaps she's hurt, which wasn't his intention.

The waiter brings their salads. Zev picks out the red onion

and tomato and coats the rest in Thousand Island dressing. Julia splashes hers with oil and vinegar.

Zev offers her the rolls, but she refuses. "You don't need to worry about your weight," he says.

"What makes you think I'm worried about my weight?"

From her tone, he gathers he's made another misstep, but he doesn't have any idea what it is. "It's just that you're not having bread. And you could have it. You're not fat."

"Thanks for giving me permission. I have celiac disease. I can't eat gluten. And if I were fat, as you say, it wouldn't be any business of yours, would it?"

"I guess not." Zev looks around. Pleasant, easy conversations drift his way. He wipes his mouth with his napkin. "I'm not very good at this."

"You're about average. At least you didn't insist on driving or suggest I have a glass of wine instead of gin and tonic. I've been on dates that made me wish I were gay."

Zev doesn't know what to say to that, so he busies himself once again with the rolls.

A server brings platters of bloody steak, potatoes overflowing with sour cream and chives, and mushrooms and string beans sautéed in butter. They eat, sharing sounds of satisfaction, grunts and sighs. Their plates empty, Julia orders a glass of port, and Zev does the same, trying something new.

"So much of my life I was a mother and a therapist," Julia says. "Those jobs felt important. Now I swim and read, play golf, go out to dinner with a nice man if I'm lucky. Sometimes I ask myself why I'm still here."

"Sounds to me like you earned your retirement."

"What about you? When do you plan to retire?"

Zev sips his port. "As long as people keep getting locked out, I guess I'll keep working."

"Do you play golf or tennis? I could always use a partner."

"Never learned either one. I was always busy working or help-ing my daughter." He refolds his napkin.

"I bet you were a good father."

"I did the best I could. She used to think it wasn't good enough."

"Kids expect you to be perfect. They tell you when you're not. Until they have their own kids. Then all of a sudden you're a parenting guru." She motions for the waiter and asks for dessert menus. Zev doesn't say a word. "What happened to your wife?" Julia says.

"We split when my daughter was pretty young. She never wanted kids. How about your husband?"

"All the things he admired about me when we were dating, my dedication and how I nurtured people who weren't related to me, became sore spots as soon as we were married. He went crazy after we got divorced. Broke into the house just to mess with me. I thought it was a burglar at first, but then I realized he only took things that had sentimental value." She lifts the glass that held the port to her mouth though it's empty. "I had to get a restrain-ing order."

Afraid if he looks at her, he'll betray himself, Zev busies him-self with the check, calculating how many more dinners like this he can afford. "That's awful," he says.

After dinner, they drive to Julia's house. She doesn't have a pool, she says, so she uses the one at his apartment and no one complains. Zev isn't surprised. A nice-looking woman, why would anyone complain? It would be different for someone like him. He escorts her to the door.

Brushing his bangs from his eyes, she says, "How about salsa Friday night? We could stop for an early-bird special first, say five o'clock. My treat this time."

It's a day he plans to work, and he'll probably be tired. "That sounds nice."

He walks back to his apartment beneath a sky full of stars that pulse just for him and a full moon that throws shadows in his honor, surprised that a woman like Julia wants to see him again. Pretty enough to be an actress in a TV commercial, shouting across a tennis net about her worry-free retirement. Perhaps it's because she's lonely. Or, who knows, maybe it's the haircut. He'd like to tell La La but will have to settle for sharing his news with Mo.

14

At Zev's house early Saturday morning, La La searches for something to lead her to Elissa. The police seized the ankle monitors, the train setup, and the screwdriver. Otherwise, the place looks as it always has, if a bit dustier. Her father didn't take much with him. His down coat hangs in the closet—a shiny indentation where his neck rubbed the collar—and his dresser drawers are nearly full.

She leafs through his file cabinets. Zev kept receipts for just about everything: groceries, appliances, paint. He saved the yellowing slips well past their usefulness for returns, as if he were marshaling the proof that whatever else he might have done, he provided for his family. Instructions for two dishwashers, the refrigerator, five vacuum cleaners, and three hot water heaters are filed alphabetically by manufacturer name. But in all of Zev's papers, La La finds no evidence of her mother.

After Elissa disappeared, Zev held on to her belongings for a few months, perhaps hoping she would return. A pair of her mother's cowboy boots stood at attention in the front closet for a

single season, and La La would slip her feet into the stiff leather
and clomp around the dining room. Though her mother's wool
hat slid down over her eyes, La La wore it and felt her way around
the kitchen, touching the cold metal sink and Formica counters
sandy with Borax residue. "Take it off!" Zev would yell, and La
La did, pressing it to her nose to smell Elissa's orange blossom
shampoo.

A mysterious clock having run out one day, her father bagged
all of Elissa's possessions: wool coats and sweaters with stray
brown hairs clinging to the shoulders; corduroy pants, the nap
worn at the knees; bottles of lotion clogged at the nozzle; pill containers that bore her name; the books she had bought, which were
most of their books, and included titles that puzzled La La, such
as *The Second Sex, The Women's Room,* and *The Bell Jar.* Zev got
rid of Elissa's cassette tapes, CDs, and the art she'd chosen, the
empty walls mirroring how La La felt. Using a sewing scissors, he
sliced Elissa's image from every photograph. Of all the things as-
sociated with Elissa, only the barbed rosebushes, the flower box,
and the tulips were spared. He put the bulging garbage bags out
on the curb, crows circling overhead.

He even excluded Elissa's parents from their lives. When
Ruth called on La La's tenth birthday, La La overheard Zev say,
"If she wanted her daughter to know her family, maybe she should
have stuck around."

Sitting in the twice-abandoned living room, La La looks
through photo albums from which Zev excised even the faintest
reflection of her mother in windows and lakes. The albums are
like rotten smiles, filled with holes.

In a cardboard box in the attic, La La finds her old stuffed
animals. She pulls out the lion, stuffing leaking from its seams,

and sets it aside to take home. A plastic storage container yields a Popsicle-stick boat with a gap in its hull, a one-eyed sock puppet, and a homemade candle without a wick, remnants of art projects she made with her father. Another container holds cymbals, a bell, and maracas, their muted percussive sounds as sad as a funeral dirge. Zev gathered the instruments for a music class, he and La La accompanying Elvis Presley and Alabama with more enthusiasm than skill. For years, La La resented her father for keeping her from school. She put it near the top of a long list of ways her father had neglected her. But now she sees how hard he worked to give her experiences other kids had, going so far as to make Popsicle-stick boats with their messy glue and candles with their drippy wax, projects that must have driven him crazy, though he never showed it. Maybe she wasn't as neglected as she thought.

Zev must be settled in his new place, wherever that is. Even Mo will have started to feel at home. She wonders if one or the other is thinking about her.

La La combs the musty room for something with her mother's address—a letter she sent or divorce papers. Coming across a box labeled ELISSA'S COLLEGE TEXTBOOKS, La La imagines a transcript shoved between pages. La La could contact the college and try to get a recent address. When she grasps the box, it's disappointingly light, but she doesn't give up. Even a single book could do the trick. Opening the box, she finds rolled streamers, uninflated balloons, and a folded sign—HAPPY BIRTHDAY LA LA—supplies Zev dug out once a year, the misleading label a remnant from an earlier move. She crushes a roll of brightly colored streamers in her fist.

It takes two weekends to go through the house and brings

La La no closer to Elissa. Outside the kitchen window, a boxer samples new shoots of grass, but to La La the season feels more like an ending than a beginning.

In the spring, Elissa boiled matzo balls for Passover. Once, as steam from the pot coated her face, she told La La about the neurotic animals she worked with: a beagle who howled when left alone, an African parrot who picked out his feathers, a kitten afraid of her own reflection. Later that day, standing in the hall, La La overheard Elissa and Zev arguing in the kitchen about adopting a pet.

"So many are homeless," Elissa said. "I grew up with animals. I miss having a dog or a cat around."

"You don't even like taking care of La La," Zev said.

La La's cheeks tingled. She pressed the side of her face against the wall to cool it.

"It would help me relax," Elissa said.

"Isn't that what your pills are for?"

Her mother sighed. "Fuck it. I don't know why I bother."

La La covered her ears. Though she was thirsty, she returned to her room empty-handed, closing the door behind her.

Without Zev in it, the kitchen seems to have shrunk. The castle drawing still hangs on the refrigerator. Odd that her father never put it away. Though La La has looked at it a thousand times before, this time she thinks she sees writing on the back. Perhaps it's just a trick of the afternoon light. Pinching a corner, she teases the drawing away from the refrigerator, the cellophane tape coming away cleanly. On the back, the name "Elissa" is written above a column of phone numbers, all but the last—which has a different area code—crossed out.

La La sits down, the list in her hand. Zev had Elissa's phone number all these years, and yet he kept it from her. "Why?" she cries out in frustration, though there's no one to hear. He's almost as bad as Elissa. Did her mother and father talk? They must have, or why keep the number? She removes the tape, gingerly. Folds the paper and sticks it into her pocket. At least she finally has a way to reach her mother. Maybe Elissa just needs to hear La La's voice to realize how much she misses her daughter.

That night, La La calls the number, but gets voice mail. "You've reached Elissa and Chloe Roberts. Sorry we can't come to the phone. Leave a message, and we'll get back to you." When she hears the beep, she hangs up. Elizabeth Roberts. No wonder she couldn't find her. And who the hell is Chloe? She paces the length of the kitchen. Did her mother have another child? A child she actually loved? With a man named Roberts?

La La runs a people-finder search on the name "Elizabeth Roberts," and the results include a dozen women the right age, one with an e-mail address at the Mesa Animal Shelter in Arizona. On the shelter's website, La La recognizes Elissa's photo, though her mother has aged and her expression is more business-like and less angry than La La remembers.

The next night she calls again. When she gets the maddening greeting, she's prepared. "This is La La. I know it's been a long time, but I was hoping to speak to you. Dad was arrested. Well, that was a while ago. Now he's a fugitive. Mom"—a word she isn't planning to say, that just comes out—"please call me." She leaves her number and hangs up, then sinks into the overstuffed chair. Her head lists forward. She wanted desperately to find her mother, but now that she has, nothing has changed. Clem is with Naomi, and it's his weekend with the dogs. Mo and Zev are still gone. And La La's alone.

Visiting the *One of a Kind* blog, she leaves a post under the pseudonym orphan1234, with a new Gmail address she signed up for: *You ought to have a* One of a Cruel *blog,* she writes, *because there's so much more cruelty than kindness. Parents abandoning their children. Men abandoning their fiancées.*

As she's getting ready for bed, she gets an e-mail from Clem: *Are you okay? Call me if you want to talk. But stay off the blog, please.*

Two days later, no word from Elissa, La La tries again. "Please, please call me," she says. And then, "It's La La." She hates herself for begging and for leaving her number a second time, knowing her mother might not have bothered to keep it.

15

From his BMW, Zev observes a row of adobe McMansions Friday morning. The sun burns a hole through his windshield, cutting below the brim of his newsboy cap and penetrating his sunglasses. A mud-colored roadrunner dashes across the street with a lizard in its mouth. Bright blue in the cartoons La La used to watch, its actual appearance surprises Zev.

A woodpecker hammers at a saguaro. What magic the bird uses to avoid the cactus's spines, Zev wants to know. Zev, too, needs to find a way to survive in the desert habitat.

At seven forty-five, an Acura pulls out of the garage of a split-level house. Down the street, a woman in a pink bathrobe picks up a newspaper from the end of the driveway. She checks out Zev's car, and he pretends to fiddle with the radio. When she goes inside, Zev drives around the corner and down the block before parking. He returns to the split-level, ignoring the red-and-white security stickers on the window and the sign in the yard, which are sold as a set on Amazon for less than twenty dollars. Holding a clipboard, he rings the bell. He pokes around unsuccessfully for a spare key. Maybe he'll have better luck around back. As he passes a bronze sculpture topped by a cow skull at the edge of the yard, he looks away. He doesn't want to be reminded of death—Claude Thomas's death, or his own death at the hands of police or a frightened homeowner. The backyard bumps up against the foothills.

Pulling a wrench from his bag, he smashes a window. The sound seems to echo louder than it ever has before because the stakes of getting caught are so much higher now that he's wanted for murder. He ties on a bandanna, concealing his face from any cameras inside, and climbs into a playroom. Toy cars park in a plastic garage and line up at the start of a miniature raceway. Beanbag chairs hold the impressions of small bottoms. Zev unlocks the back door and walks toward the front of the house.

Low voices from the kitchen float into the hall, and he stops. How did they miss the window shattering? As he begins to retreat, a salesman offers to buy all cars, *all cars* no matter the condition. The sound is coming from a television. But is someone watching, or did the owner leave it on in his absence? Zev listens for a cup clinking against a saucer, a fork hitting a plate, water running in the sink, anything to let him know he isn't alone, but hears only flat, recorded sounds from a TV speaker. He glances into the room, double-checking that it's empty.

Upstairs in the master bedroom closet, he collects gold and silver bolo ties, embedded with precious and semiprecious stones. Hundred-dollar bills fill the toe of a dusty Oxford. A gold rope chain and a Star of David hang openly on a hook, as if God will protect them.

A landscaping truck rattles to a stop in front of the house. Through a window, Zev sees two members of the crew enter the backyard. They trim acacia trees, their chainsaws tearing through branches. Any minute, one of them might see the shattered window. From a child's bedroom, Zev spots a worker in front, too, spraying weeds that emerge from rock beds. He's trapped.

Flattening himself against a wall, he listens for a sign the workers have noticed the break-in. If they do, they might summon the police. They might not call, too, having their own reasons for avoiding authorities, but it's not a chance he can take. The sour stink of the Colorado jail—a mix of body odor, urine, and fear—fills his nostrils. The chainsaws fall quiet. When Zev peeks outside, two workers are gathered around the broken window. He can't hear what they're saying as they make their way toward the front yard, where he assumes they'll tell the other member of the crew what they found.

Knowing his time is limited, he bolts downstairs and out the back door. He climbs into the foothills, darting around brush, his feet slipping on loose earth and rock, his lungs clamoring for air. He loses his hat, and the sun bakes his head. When he's crested a hill and is no longer visible from the house, he looks back without stopping and trips, scraping his hands. He scrambles to his feet, his side aching. Though no one's chasing him, he runs until his body rebels, then stops to rest. A lizard darts over the rocky earth.

As the sun climbs, heat shrink-wraps his skin, snakes into his lungs until he feels they must be burning. It's deathly quiet. Jetliners streaming contrails pass through a pale sky, too high for their sound to reach him. A buzzard circles overhead, and Zev waves to let it know he's still alive.

When he begins to descend, his knees protest. Eventually, he emerges onto a road. Relieved to be on flat land, he returns the battery to his burner phone and plots a course back to his car, keeping an eye out for the police and avoiding the block of the house he robbed. Dust coats his shoes, but he doesn't stop to wipe them.

As he walks, a creature charges from the brush, huffing and barking, its flesh bristly and gray. He's never seen anything as ugly, the devil himself in the form of a pig. Zev takes off but can't outrun it. The animal gores his calf. He stifles a cry, afraid to draw the attention of homeowners. Swinging his bag, he catches it in the snout, slowing but not stopping it.

He runs down one block and then another, the animal following. Finally, he spots his car. Sweat drips down the side of his face. His knees pulse. As he reaches the door, a tusk pierces his ankle. Pain shoots up his leg. Drawing the wrench from his bag, he slams the creature's head, and it staggers. Zev scrambles into the car and shuts the door, pressing the button for the automatic locks, though it's doubtful the animal could operate the door handles. He drives off, blood dripping from his wounds onto the carpet. Rattlesnakes one day, wild pigs the next. The city's Chamber of Commerce website failed to mention the unfriendly wildlife.

In his apartment, he does his best to clean himself. He doesn't have a first-aid kit, so he improvises, washing the wounds with soap and water and wrapping them with napkins and the duct tape he bought because he knew he'd find a use for it. He stuffs his bloody pants into the kitchen trash.

At the gas station the car dealer recommended, Zev sells for too little what he stole, then drives until he comes to a bar. The place smells of cleanser and stale beer. A stool creaks and wobbles as Zev climbs on. He orders a Scotch from a tall, unshaven bartender with a grin that comes easily, part of the job.

The bartender sets the drink down. "How's your day going?"
People should mind their own business. "I won the lottery."
"Lucky you."

It's one in the afternoon. Zev's injuries throb. Perhaps the
close call with the landscapers and the encounter with the pig
are signs he ought to retire his wrench and crowbar and focus on
locksmithing. The price of getting caught has grown too high.

When the bartender offers a refill on the house, Zev nods.
The guy's increasing his tip at the owner's expense, but why should
Zev care?

Later that afternoon, he hobbles to the pool. Julia's on her
chair, wearing a green one-piece. Watching her, he trips over an
uneven walkway. In the bright sunshine, he sees his new black
swim trunks are a bad choice, accentuating highways of blue
veins that run along his ashen legs. Though he picked up first-aid
supplies and rebandaged his wounds, he still looks battle-scarred
as he limps toward her.

"What happened?" She tilts her head and waits, a technique
he imagines inspired others to talk. When it doesn't work, she
tries again. "How'd you hurt yourself?"

He plays with the tie on his swimsuit, tightening the loops.
"You wouldn't believe it."

"Now I'm really curious."

"I was getting in my car and a pig charged me. Twice."

"Probably a javelina. You may have surprised a female near
her babies. Where were you?"

Zev removes a twenty-ounce soda from a plastic bag and
twists off the cap. "I was in the parking lot."

"Strange. I haven't seen them around here."

He lies on the chair next to hers, cringing as his calf hits the rubber mesh.

"You still up for dancing?" she says.

He can almost feel his hand on the curve of her waist, but the pain in his leg is worsening. "Maybe another time."

Her smile fades, but only momentarily. "How about a movie?"

He hasn't forgotten the trouble he got into over the French film. "An American one?"

"Car chases and explosions. That's what you want to see?"

"Sounds perfect."

She lowers her sunglasses and gives him a dubious look, and he admires her eyes again. Adjusting her sun hat, she says, "There's something I want to ask you."

Zev prepares himself for another prying question. Ripples lap the side of the pool, trapping a yellow foam noodle against blue tiles.

"I'm having a dinner party," she says. "I wonder if you'd like to be my guest."

"A dinner party?" Soda slides down his windpipe, and he coughs.

"You okay?"

He nods, though he's still having trouble breathing.

"Just a few friends. Next week. I'll do all the cooking. You won't have to do a thing." She squeezes sunscreen from a tube and spreads it on her arms and legs though they already glisten.

Is that what people do with their time? When it's so much easier to pop a frozen dinner into the oven? What will he talk about? "I'd rather not."

She rubs lotion on her shoulders. Zev would offer to do her back but doesn't want to seem presumptuous. "You could get to know some new people," she says.

He doesn't want to meet anyone new. He wants to go about life quietly, as he always has. After spending time with Julia, as much as he enjoys it, he always feels like he needs a nap. "I'm giving the cat a bath."

"I haven't even told you when it is."

"Whenever it is, that's when I'm giving her a bath. Besides, crowds are breeding grounds for diseases." He read about it while waiting in line at the supermarket.

"I only invited four people." Julia presses her water bottle to her neck. "Two couples. To tell you the truth, I feel awkward being the only single." She looks toward the pool, her face drawn.

At the edge of the property, a prickly pear blossoms. The ostentatious yellow flower and the spiny cactus make an odd pair. "Okay," he says. "Assuming I don't get a call and have to work. Your friends may hate me, anyway."

She squeezes his arm, and in the rush of her pleasure, he can't remember why he hesitated. "They won't hate you. Your taste in movies, maybe. But not you."

16

Clem drops off the dogs on Friday. As La La walks them, Black stumbles stepping off a curb. The night swirls before La La's eyes; the sky appears beneath her feet before righting itself. Helping Black up, La La notices how the white in his fur has spread from his muzzle throughout his neck and chest.

Back at the house, she calls her mother's number again. She hangs up after four rings, when she's learned it will go to voice mail. Maybe Elissa's taken Chloe to a movie. Bought her popcorn and a large soda. Or maybe Elissa recognizes La La's number now and is avoiding her. Would it kill her to pick up just once? If only to tell La La to stop bothering her? The muscles in La La's neck twitch. She flexes her hand, imagining the weight of a crowbar.

As La La changes into loose jeans, Blue trots by and snatches the yin-yang necklace from the dresser. La La extracts it, wet, from his mouth and drops it into her jewelry box. She slides her feet into men's boots, then drives the Mercedes through a neighborhood of million-dollar homes she found on Zillow. Giant television screens flicker behind floor-to-ceiling windows. Residents move from one lit-up room to the next as La La follows their progress. A raccoon triggers a floodlight, turning a hidden corner of a property into a bright stage.

Nighttime is riskier. Most people are home and on alert. "Might as well call the cops yourself," Zev used to say about working after five. But La La's in the clinic during the day.

Passing a garden inhabited by ceramic frogs and gnomes barely visible in the moonlight, La La's hand aches as if it's broken. The house is dark and there's no security system. As she rings the bell, she wonders in what condition she'll find the animal. A dog begins to bark. Raucously. Unlike the reception she usually gets. "It's okay, boy," she says, but the animal continues to raise an alarm.

Retreating to the sidewalk, La La glances up and down the block. At the far end of the street, a black 4Runner idles. When she recognizes the vehicle, her legs weaken, and she stumbles back to her car. The bounty hunter nearly caught her breaking into the house. La La hadn't even realized she was being followed. The woman must have hoped La La would lead her to Zev. Pain radiates through La La's hand as she grasps the steering wheel. She feels for the animal but can't go inside while being watched.

17

It takes Zev a week to round up the locksmith equipment he needs. On eBay, he finds used key copying and coding machines and sets them up in the trunk of his car. At a locksmith supply shop, he buys blank keys and an assortment of door and window locks and peepholes. He advertises his services on Craigslist. With Roger Cohen's social security number, he opens a bank account.

His first call comes at two in the morning. Returning from a night out, a guy named Jackson discovered his lock was jammed. Zev pulls on clothes and a light jacket. The place is twenty minutes away. Through empty streets, he drives as fast as he can without speeding. A stray dog bites the edge of a fast-food bag but can't pull it through the side of a mesh garbage can. The animal's ribs stick out like iron fence rails. If Zev weren't in a hurry, he would find the dog something to eat in honor of La La.

He looks forward to helping Jackson. When his customers in Colorado thanked him, Zev would say it was nothing, but he didn't mean it. The job proved he was more than a burglar. For years, he thought about working exclusively as a locksmith and would have if the money he made stealing weren't so much better, if he didn't have La La to raise and get through school.

Perhaps Jackson will be so relieved to get back into the house, he'll offer a tip on top of the fee. Zev will decline it, magnanimously, telling him the charge is fair. He'll hand Jackson one of the cards he had printed with ROGER COHEN, SAFETY LOCK AND KEY, and his number in bold.

As Zev pulls over in front of the house, he sees a van, RELIABLE LOCKSMITH glowing on its side, and a guy in a jumpsuit already working on the lock. Hovering behind the locksmith is a man in stylishly torn jeans and black cowboy boots.

"Are you Jackson?" Zev asks, walking up to the door. "I drove twenty minutes to get here."

"I was improving my odds."

Zev turns his head to avoid the alcohol on Jackson's breath. The guy in the jumpsuit doesn't look up.

"Anyway, where's your van?" Jackson says.

"I don't need a fucking van. I should make you pay for my gas."

"I don't think you could make me do anything, old man." When Jackson crosses his arms, his muscles strain against his black T-shirt.

"If you're going to fight, pay me first," the other locksmith says over his shoulder.

Zev can't afford trouble. He just has to accept the night is a waste. It's happened before, more often than he likes to remember. He'll try to get there faster next time.

Driving back the way he came, he doesn't see the hungry dog. Even if he did, he wouldn't look for something to feed it. The expansive feeling he had is gone. Wide awake, he plugs the address of the Mesa Animal Shelter into his GPS, though what he hopes to see in the middle of the night he can't say.

Pulling up to a plain, two-story brick building, he parks beneath a sign showing a cartoon dog and cat dancing. ADOPT DON'T SHOP is stenciled across the building's front window and illuminated by floodlights. He thinks about the animals caged inside. It's hard not to feel sympathy for anything locked up. Yet their chances of seeing Elissa are better than his.

He returns to his apartment, where Mo sleeps on the nightstand. "Fucking drunk customer," he says to her as he undresses, but she doesn't stir. If he doesn't get a few jobs soon, he'll have to return to stealing.

Tomorrow is Julia's dinner party, and the idea of eating with strangers keeps him awake. Maybe he should cancel. He doesn't know what she's making. Probably something exotic, a part of an animal you were better off discarding. If he sees her at the pool, he'll ask and beg off, claiming to be allergic. When at last he drifts into sleep, he's not thinking of food at all, but of Julia, dozing with a magazine on her lap, her mouth open.

Although he lingers at the pool the next day, Julia never stops by, perhaps too busy preparing for company.

Arriving at her house empty-handed, he immediately realizes his mistake. One couple brought tulips and chardonnay; the other, a box of chocolate truffles. He's dressed wrong, too. Wearing black pants, a white button-down shirt, and formal shoes— black lace-ups that he picked up at a thrift store and shined—he looks like a waiter. The other men are in shorts and polo shirts, flip-flops. Julia's tulip-patterned dress looks like something she might throw over a bathing suit.

Dee-Dee runs over and sniffs him, then squats and pees on his shoe. Too late, Zev yanks his foot back, barely restraining the urge to punt the dog across the room. The puddle is so large, the tiny dog must have been waiting all day to empty her bladder.

"I'm so sorry. She's just being submissive," Julia says, and she retrieves wet paper towels from the kitchen. Zev tries not to inhale the sharp smell as he wipes his soaked laces. After washing his hands, he takes the glass of Scotch Julia offers and downs it. The evening is off to a thoroughly bad start.

Introducing him around, Julia says, "This is Roger Cohen, my new neighbor." He would have preferred she said "friend." Zev adds he's a locksmith, something she didn't volunteer, either intentionally or because she forgot.

The house is well kept (not as clean as his apartment, but few homes are), decorated with fresh flowers and watercolors. Sheer drapes hang motionless on the still night. Taking a mushroom stuffed with crabmeat from a tray, Zev surprises himself by liking it.

Paige, a broad-shouldered divorce lawyer with platinum hair, says to Zev, "I have one of your friends on speed dial." Crystal sharks dangle from her ears.

"Same," says her husband, Rick, a real estate agent. With his index finger, he traces the strip of beard on his chin.

"I guess you take whatever work comes your way. You can't pick and choose. Get it? *Pick* and choose," says Cam, a pale CPA with a bulbous nose.

"Funny," Zev says.

Dee-Dee retires to her bed in a corner, but Zev keeps an eye on her.

"I called one of you guys a few months ago," says Lana, Cam's wife, her eyebrows bunching. "Cam locked himself out while I was at a conference. On the phone, the man said it would cost eighty-five dollars, but when he got there, he charged three hundred fifty." The stockbroker wipes her mouth, depositing the napkin on a shelf.

Zev collects the napkin and tosses it into the kitchen trash. "Maybe he couldn't pick the lock, though most can be picked if you know what you're doing." It figures that when he offers an honest service, people suspect him of cheating. He refills his drink from a bottle on the granite island that separates the kitchen from the dining room.

"Show us," Cam says, on his second Scotch, too. "Pick Julia's lock."

He isn't a circus performer.

"You don't have to," Julia says.

"And it would be embarrassing if you couldn't," says Cam.

Zev takes a ballpoint pen from his shirt pocket. He breaks off the clip and bends the edge, improvising a tension wrench. He asks Julia for a bobby pin to use as a pick, and she plucks one from a kitchen drawer.

When she locks him out, he's tempted to leave, and would if he didn't promise to be her date. The night is quiet and cool. Alone, he relaxes. He doesn't much like her friends. Inserting the clip, he turns it, putting a light tension on the cylinder core. He jabs in the bobby pin and draws it out, raising the pins inside the lock one by one. The door pops open.

"Impressive," Paige says. "Dangerous skill in the wrong hands."

"You think I should get a better lock?" Julia asks.

"I'll install it for you," Zev says. "No charge."

While Julia prepares dinner, Zev sits on the couch, nursing his drink. The others discuss financial markets, a topic that doesn't interest him. He's never put a dime in stocks. He rarely has extra money and wouldn't trust a broker not to steal it.

Summoning them to the dining room table, Julia sets out a pot of steamed lobsters, individual bowls of garlic-ginger-basil sauce, homemade coleslaw. She opens the chardonnay. Zev has never eaten lobster in a shell but doesn't ask for help. He already feels that he doesn't belong. It's like getting into a home, he figures. You just have to find the weak points. He copies the others, putting on a bib when they do. A beat behind, he twists off a claw, cracks the shell, and extracts the meat with the pick. All in all, a lot of work, though he has to admit the flesh is good, rich and sweet on its own and spicy with the sauce. But the entire process is too messy. Zev longs for something more than the moist towelettes piled in the center of the table. Something closer to a shower.

"What do you think?" Julia asks.

Zev looks up. "Me?"

"I thought you might not have had lobster this way before."

He colors. The other guests wait for him to answer. "No, no. I've had this before. Yours is good, though."

"I don't know why I thought that," Julia says. "Of course you've had it." She busies herself refilling wineglasses. They're on their second bottle.

Zev pokes around in a claw that's empty. How soon can he leave without being impolite?

"You must get calls at all hours," says Rick. He caresses his club soda in two large hands.

"I'm glad any time a call comes in."

"I feel the same way," Paige says. "And I've gotten my share in the middle of the night. Husband pulls up with a truck, thinking he'll decide how the property gets divided, or enters the property in violation of a restraining order."

"Men are so entitled," Julia says.

Zev wonders if it's the alcohol or how she really feels.

"It doesn't matter how we treat you," Cam says, lifting his glass. "You women find us irresistible." Zev cringes. "Do I offend you?" The CPA's words run together.

Lana puts her hand on Cam's arm.

"I always tell my clients to change the locks after the property settlement is finalized," Paige says. "You should give me some of your cards. I could send you some business."

"I'll take some, too," Rick says.

Zev hasn't brought any. "Give me your address, and I'll send you some."

Paige hands Zev her business card. "Send a bunch, and I'll give some to Rick if he's good. Do you have a website?"

"It's being redone at the moment," Zev says, making a mental note to create one when he can afford to.

As she serves the chocolate truffles for dessert, Julia says, "Roger just moved here from Missouri." The table falls silent, as if no one has ever heard of the state, which is just as well, since Zev knows little about it. The conversation turns to the Diamond-backs' chances for the season, but Zev doesn't follow sports.

18

La La watches from the audience as her classmates don their gray hoods. She should have told Nat she had to work. One of only a handful of students from their class not graduating, La La feels naked wearing street clothes on what should have been the happiest day of her life. In a year she'll receive her diploma with people she hardly knows. The graduates return down the aisle, their faces stretched into impossibly wide grins, except for Nat, who looks distracted. La La scans the room for Tank but doesn't see him.

After the ceremony and photographs, she meets Nat at a Moroccan restaurant to celebrate. They sit at low tables on cushions. Next to scenes of Marrakesh, five-fingered hamsas wave from blue walls. Bells jingle on the server's costume as she brings them bottles of Casablanca beer. Nat has been hired at a clinic in Atlanta, the city where she grew up, and leaves in a week. Tank is staying behind, Nat says.

"What happened?" La La asks, though she can guess.

"He was using again. Selling, too, I'm pretty sure. He says

he'll join me in a few months in Atlanta, but I don't want him to. Not unless he gets clean."

La La sips her beer. "Sorry."

"It's been going on for a few months. I had enough."

"Your family must be happy you're moving back."

"When I planned it, I thought Tank would be a buffer. My father's afraid of him." Nat picks at a scab on the back of her arm, a souvenir from a frightened cat.

The server returns with a dish of roasted and salted chickpeas and takes their orders.

La La raises her bottle. "Congratulations!"

"Somehow I don't feel like celebrating." Beads of blood have sprung up on Nat's arm.

"What happened to your philosophy of staying a thousand miles away from family?"

"My parents are getting older."

"You're lucky to have them."

"I don't know about that," Nat says. "I think mountain gorillas have the right idea. When they reach a certain age, they leave their families and don't come back."

La La licks salt off a chickpea. "If you're dreading it, why do it? Why not stay with the people who appreciate you? Like your friends."

"I want to spend time with them while they still know who I am, before I have to change their diapers." Their food—lamb for Nat and vegetarian stew for La La—arrives. Nat rips a hunk of meat off the bone with her teeth.

"I guess it's the right thing to do," La La says, mashing an overcooked carrot with the back of her fork.

"Atlanta isn't exactly Marrakesh. You can visit. And we'll talk on the phone."

"Just don't disappear on me." She couldn't handle losing another person.

Nat puts a hand on La La's arm. "That's not how I operate." Nat's skin is warm, her hand, solid. It's almost enough to make La La believe her.

That night, still smarting from the graduation, her mother continuing to ignore her, and Nat about to move to Atlanta, La La cruises to a community thirty-five miles south. She makes sure she's not followed, slowing down on the highway to see if anyone fails to pass her, then exiting and driving east before taking a series of turns, until she comes full circle. No one duplicates her unlikely path.

If Nat were really her friend, she wouldn't desert La La. Not to go back to a family Nat doesn't even like. But that's the way it is. People always abandon her.

Driving toward a large Tudor house, La La senses something unusual inside. A compassionate presence, unlike anything she's encountered before. Curious, she pulls up in front and detects young animals in distress. The house is dark. She parks a block away and jimmies the back door. Four blue eyes and two charcoal faces greet her. The Siamese kittens wail, and La La scratches beneath their chins. At least they have each other.

She crosses bamboo floors, her flashlight illuminating black-and-white fine art photographs: a turbulent ocean, dancers, the Joshua tree. They could be worth something, but La La wouldn't know. She's an ordinary burglar, not an art thief, unexceptional in every way except when it comes to understanding animals. A good reason not to jeopardize her veterinary career with senseless crimes. The thought has barely taken shape when a photograph of a family wearing wet suits, sun glinting off their surfboards, chases it away.

Retro furniture—a slim leather couch, a wavy coffee table, and a round king-size bed—fills the master bedroom. La La's feet sink into an olive shag rug. She gathers jewelry and watches, the family so wealthy they haven't bothered to hide them or even to put them away. La La ducks into a child's room to see if there's anything worth taking.

A rumpled cheetah-patterned blanket drapes off the bed. On a series of posters, a blue-footed booby nods to its mate, a sea lion sunbathes, and a whale spouts. The kittens slip their paws beneath the base of a closet door and cry. Perhaps their mother is trapped inside.

"Are you going to kill me?" a boy of about twelve asks, aiming a flashlight at La La when she opens the door. The kittens crawl into his lap.

La La is about to run when she sees a copy of *Caring for Your Cat,* the book that came with Mo, in the boy's hand. She shuts off her flashlight and orders the boy to do the same. No reason to give him a better view of her than he's already had. "I'm not going to hurt you," La La whispers. "Are your parents home?"

"They won't be back for a few hours."

La La sets down her duffel. Her eyes having adjusted to the dark, she grabs one of the kittens by the scruff, and holds him to her chest. She takes the kitten's pulse and feels his abdomen.

"He's scared of my dad, but not of you," the boy says.

"How do you know?"

"When he sees my dad, his heart does a dance and mine does, too."

"What else can you tell me about them?" La La says.

"They're very cold, and that makes my fingers turn blue. But when I turn up the heat, my dad says I'm costing him a fortune."

La La has never met anyone like herself before, though Dr. Bergman said there were others. "Did you tell your parents about your feelings?"

"My father said I have an overactive imagination. My mother said it's best to keep certain thoughts to myself." The kitten kneads the boy's belly. "They miss their mother."

About four weeks old, the kittens are too young to have been weaned. La La switches cats with the boy. She examines the kitten's eyes and ears and warms him against her chest.

"My father won't return them. He says it's too late to get his money back."

"Someone else would just buy them," La La says.

"I don't want them to feel sad."

"Cradle them to keep them warm. For the next few weeks, bottle-feed them with kitten formula. You can find a recipe online. Mash up their solid food with water." She shows him how to pick them up by the scruff.

"You mean be their mother?"

"Something like that."

"Doesn't their mother have to be a cat?"

"You'd be surprised. The kittens will be fine as long as someone gives them what they need. That someone could be a cat or it could be a boy."

"How come you believe me about the kittens?" the boy says.

The Siamese paws her chin. "Let's just say I know someone like you."

"You?"

La La sets the second kitten on the boy's lap. "Take them to a vet to get them checked out. But don't mention me."

"Because you're not supposed to be here?"

"Right."

"Are you going to take our stuff?"

She picks up the duffel and slings it over her shoulder.

"Do you steal because you're poor?"

"Not exactly."

The kittens have fallen asleep. The smaller one whistles through his nose. "To give away, like Robin Hood?" he says.

"Not that either."

"You could get into trouble," he says.

"Yes."

"I'll say I slept through it."

"Good thinking."

19

The morning after the dinner party, Zev mails business cards to Julia's friend Paige. At a hardware store, he buys pick-resistant bolt locks, more secure than the ones he carries for customer installations, for Julia's front and back entrances.

Dee-Dee yaps as if he's a serial killer when he knocks on Julia's door. As she opens it, the dog rushes for Zev's shoe, but Julia intercepts her. Zev holds up the locks.

"That was fast," Julia says. She wears a short white robe over her bathing suit, her legs aging and trim.

"I'd hate for you to get robbed because I took my time." He sets his toolbox down.

"Want to come in for a cup of coffee first?"

"I'd just as soon get this done. I'll bring the new keys out to the pool when I'm finished."

Julia hesitates, and he can tell she's uncertain about leaving him alone in her house. "Sure," she says, though she sounds anything but. It's something women do, act polite when they should protect themselves. Zev has seen it more times than he can count.

Women who answered the door and let him use the phone when he lied about being stranded, giving him a chance to observe the layout and contents of their homes. They would have been better off being honest, telling him it wasn't safe to open the door to a stranger. Julia closes Dee-Dee in the bedroom, so Zev can work in peace.

After she leaves, Zev takes his time. He bought a set of locks for the front and back doors that work on the same key. He removes the lock plate and the worn cylinder in front, unscrewing the dead bolt and pulling it out. He measures the backset to make sure the new lock will fit. He repeats the process for the back door.

Although he kept the new keys to test them, now he has another idea. He walks to his car and opens the trunk. He looks around for Julia, and when he doesn't see her, he grinds a third key and tucks it into his pocket. He tells himself she might be locked out sometime, that he'll never use it without permission, that Julia isn't someone he'll rob even if he becomes desperate.

Sitting on a lounge chair, Zev waits for Julia to finish her laps. She swims the crawl, barely disturbing the water, flipping like a pro at the end of the lane. In the pool and elsewhere, there's an elegance about her. Watching her is hypnotic.

She climbs out and shakes water from her ears, wraps a towel around her waist. When she's settled on a chair, he hands her the keys. "I don't want you to think this is bulletproof," he says. "A burglar can still kick in the door."

"You're full of good news," she says. She fishes in her canvas bag for a keychain and slips one of the new keys onto the ring. "What can I do to be safer?"

"Having Dee-Dee helps. I wouldn't rob the place if I heard

her barking. Not that I would, anyway, of course. Rob your place. Or *any* place." He scrambles out of the chair and grabs hold of the pool skimmer.

Julia gives him a long look, or maybe it's his imagination.

Wishing he hadn't brought up the topic of security, Zev scoops a flailing bee from the water. When he shakes it onto the concrete, it doesn't move.

Back at his apartment, he gets a call from a woman named Sheila Brandt who just bought a home and wants all the locks changed.

"Lucky for you, I just had a cancellation," Zev says. "I'll be right over."

According to Zillow, the house is worth a million five. Zev wonders how the Brandts became wealthy enough to afford it. There's no path he can take, legitimate or otherwise, that would allow him to buy such a house. Even as a veterinarian, La La won't be able to afford it. He doubts the homeowner is worthier than La La, which just goes to show the randomness of good fortune. The woman didn't ask for a quote. As he drives to the property, Zev doubles what he is planning to charge.

From the driveway, he sees large colorful shade sails flapping in the backyard. Stone Buddhas, sitting and reclining, flank an enormous front door. They have some religious significance, but Zev doesn't know what it is. Jews aren't supposed to make images of God, though he's seen some in Passover seder books, illustrations of an old man with a white beard blowing the Red Sea apart for Moses. Always easier to escape with God's help.

Sheila greets him at the door, wearing sky-blue silk pants, a white tank top, and a ring with a yellow diamond wider than her finger. The marble floors and granite-topped table in the entryway inspire a moment of regret. He'll earn a fraction of what he could have made robbing the home. "You're smart to replace these," he says. "You never know who had access to the house." He could just rekey the locks, changing pins and springs at a fraction of the cost, but he doesn't tell her that.

She rests her hands on her hips, her arms as thin as curtain rods. "How long is this going to take? I have a yoga class at two."

"It takes what it takes." The house has three entrances, one in front, one in the garage, and a sliding glass door in the back.

Running her right hand over her left bicep, she pulls her arm toward her, stretching.

From his trunk, Zev withdraws two bolt locks, a sliding door lock, and his tool kit. "They might as well have put up a sign that says, 'Pick Me,'" he says, after he removes the front lock.

Sheila gazes at the hunks of metal, her face blank. "That bad?"

"Worse. You're lucky you called me." He tosses the old lock in a box, saving it for parts.

As she watches him work, he overtightens a cylinder and has to loosen it. It makes him nervous when customers look over his shoulder. He decides to order a khaki shirt embroidered with his business name, Safety Lock and Key. People are suckers for a uniform. Puts them at ease. Hot air blows in through the open door and is quickly tamed by the frigid air-conditioning.

He installs the garage lock, which he's rekeyed to work on the same key as the front. Then finishes up with the sliding door in the back. "How many keys do you want?" he asks, after he puts away his tools.

She counts on her slender fingers. "One for me, one for my husband, one for the housekeeper, and two extras."

A housekeeper, naturally. Zev looks through the front door again. He asked Sheila to lock up any pets before he arrived, but evidence of a dog is everywhere. Reddish fur collects under the granite-topped table. A front window is covered with noseprints. That's what you get when you hire a maid.

Zev duplicates the keys, making one more than she requested and leaving it in the trunk of the car, an insurance policy of sorts. He tests the others and slips them into an envelope. "Here you go."

"And I'll make my class." She pays him and adds a generous tip.

He needs more customers like her. "I know you're in a hurry, but you should consider window locks. They'll give you an extra layer of security."

"I'll talk to my husband about it."

His advice would carry more weight if she knew his background, but of course she wouldn't hire him then.

When Zev gets home, he tags the keys for Julia's and Sheila Brandt's homes. On Julia's he writes *Aunt Jenny's studio,* and on Sheila's, *Mom's house.* In a small notebook he keeps a record: *Aunt Jenny = Julia, Mom = Sheila Brandt.* He deposits the keys in a zippered pouch he tapes to the inside of Mo's carrier, the notebook in a plastic bag that he buries in a fresh sack of the cat's litter.

At four thirty, wearing a ball cap and sunglasses, he parks across the street from the Mesa Animal Shelter. He just wants to see her. Half an hour later, Elissa comes out of the building, leading a medium-size brindle mutt with the blocky head of a pit bull to her car. The auburn hair Zev loved has turned a harsh metallic gray. She walks with a stoop, as if looking for something she lost. "Come on, girl," she says gently, when the animal sticks its nose in another dog's pile. As Elissa focuses on her pet, the lines around her mouth relax. She opens a car door and buckles the dog into a canine seat belt. Observing the care she takes, the kindness she shows the animal, Zev has a desire to ram her with his car.

Three days go by before Zev gets another call. Taking garbage to the chute, a tenant locked himself out. The building is around the corner from Zev's, the halls nicked and streaked from one too many moves, concrete exposed where floor tiles are missing.

The man sits cross-legged outside his door in wrinkled jeans, getting up when he sees Zev. "Thought I had the key in my pocket. Super said he couldn't come by until tomorrow."

Zev eyes the lock. He could pick it in less than a minute, but if he does, he can't charge much. Though he feels bad for the guy, he has to feed himself. He goes through a series of metal picks, all the wrong ones. He works on it for twenty minutes before opening it. "You're lucky I was able to do that without destroying the lock."

"I appreciate it," the tenant says, one foot in the apartment.

Zev taps a pick against his chin. "I could install a lock with a keypad. I have one in my vehicle. You'd never be locked out again."

The guy regards Zev skeptically. "You sure my landlord would be okay with that?"

Zev isn't sure. "You think he wants you bothering the super?"

"I might forget the combination."

"It comes with a key, too."

"I guess I'll just stick with what I have."

"I'll take ten percent off the new lock," Zev says.

The tenant looks back into his apartment. "What do I owe you?"

Zev struggles to think of a way to convince the guy. With business slow, he's been eating toast for breakfast, macaroni for lunch, and skipping dinner altogether. He and Julia are supposed to go to a restaurant that night, but he can't afford it. "This lock isn't very secure."

"Look, I appreciate you coming out so fast, but I'm not going to buy a new lock. And I have things to do. So—"

"Suit yourself." He writes out a hefty bill.

The tenant disappears into the apartment and comes back with a checkbook.

Zev could call the bank to see if there's enough money in the account to cover the check, but he doesn't want to insult the guy. He knows where the tenant lives. He'll get paid one way or another.

Back at his apartment, Zev clips a leash to Mo's collar. La La always said the cat would live longer if she exercised. The trip to Phoenix aged Mo, who sleeps most of the day and misses the litter box half the time. Then Zev gets on his hands and knees to scrub the bathroom floor and the sides of the plastic box. She's all he has left of his former life.

After years of keeping her in, it will be strange to take her out, and he worries how she'll manage in the heat. The cat bites at the leash. She refuses to walk, and Zev drags her along the floor, but when she yowls, he stops. "You'll like it," he says. "Birds out there, other cats. Wouldn't you like to meet another cat? Don't you get lonely in here?" He tries to lead her out, but she won't budge. Imagining what La La would do, he lays a trail of treats through the front door. Mo eats until she comes to the threshold and stops. Zev lifts her, intending to carry her out, but she claws his cheek and jumps from his hands. "Ow!"

In the end, they compromise. Zev leads her on a circuit of the small apartment: through the kitchen, across the living room, down the hall, to the window in the bedroom, and back to the kitchen, where she lies down. After he unclips the leash, she returns to the bed.

"I thought you don't like to cook?" Julia says, when Zev calls to suggest they have dinner at his place.

"I'm turning over a new leaf."

At the supermarket, he buys marked-down shoulder steaks, two Idaho potatoes, and premade salad. He can't serve Julia a microwaved TV dinner, though he'd like to. He returns to the discount department store where he bought a single place setting and repeats the purchase, adding a plastic salad bowl and two steak knives.

When Julia comes to the door in a sleeveless blue dress and a silver necklace, Zev admires the way the dress falls without a single crease. In khaki shorts and a T-shirt, he's the one who's opted for casual this time. If there's a proper way to dress around her, he hasn't figured it out. Hugging him, she presses a bakery box and a chilled bottle of wine into his back. She's warm from the brief walk over, and her mild, clean sweat mingles with the scent of her herbal shampoo. There's something miraculously solid about her. When she isn't around, Zev sometimes wonders if he's imagined her. Afraid he's becoming aroused, he extracts himself.

He takes the bakery box into the kitchen and opens it. Inside is a fruit torte. How did she know he would forget dessert?

Compared to her tastefully decorated home, his apartment must look like a dump. The cheap furniture and clichéd posters, the sofa whose springs collapsed long ago and that smells like dirty socks no matter how much fabric freshener he sprays on it. Discovering his poverty, she's bound to lose interest.

"I have extra throw pillows that would look great on your couch and a lamp I'm not using that would brighten up the room," she says, joining him in the kitchen. "You'd be doing me a favor if you took them. They're just taking up space in my storage unit."

He isn't a charity case. Or at least he wasn't until he attempted to make an honest living. "Sorry if my place doesn't live up to your standards."

"That's not what I said." She turns away, and Zev knows it's what she meant. "Corkscrew?" she asks, rummaging through the mostly empty kitchen drawers.

"Let me get that." Zev opens the wine with a penknife, expertly he thinks, until Julia picks cork from the mouth of the bottle before pouring the wine into two water glasses he sets out.

Mo massages her face against Julia's calf. Julia looks from the cat to Zev's cheek. "Looks like she won that round." Crouching, she runs her hand along Mo's back. "You must be the assailant."

"She was my daughter's cat. I made her leave Mo with me when she went to college. That way, I knew my daughter would always come home. If not for me, then for Mo." He spreads oil in a frying pan as the butcher at the market instructed.

"Funny name for a female cat."

"Her name is Mother. My daughter named her right after my ex disappeared."

"Sorry."

"It was a long time ago."

"Some losses you never get over," Julia says.

"Me or my daughter?"

"You tell me."

Another line she would have used with clients. After salting the steaks, Zev lays them in the pan. He shakes the salad into the plastic bowl. "Let's talk about something else," he says, plunking a bottle of store-brand dressing on the table.

"Next time I'll bring some of my homemade Thousand Island."

He should focus on the promise of "next time," but he can't. "What's wrong with this?"

"When you have all day to cook, it's easy to be a snob. I didn't mean anything by it." Julia sits at the table. "How's locksmithing?"

"Slow." Zev flips the steaks.

"It's hard to start over in a new place." When Mo hops into Julia's lap, Julia gets the cat's motor going, rubbing her chin.

"She likes you."

"It's mutual. How old is she?"

"Around eighteen. I don't know what I'll do if I lose her."

"*When* you lose her."

She's right, but there's no need to remind him. He refills their glasses. "We might as well eat." As Julia lowers the cat to the floor, Zev serves them in silence.

Her jaw works overtime on the tough meat, and she slides a piece of wilted lettuce to the edge of her plate. He remembers their first meal, at the steak house. The tender porterhouse, the perfectly cooked vegetables. He'd like to take her there again. Erase the memory of this night.

"Paige said to thank you for the cards," Julia says. "She's been giving them out, so don't be surprised if a bunch of divorcées call you. I think you already helped one of her husband's clients, a woman named Sheila."

"That was a good job. Nice woman. Tell your friends thank you."

"They're happy to have an honest person to send over."

Grease congeals into gray blobs on his plate. "How about some of that torte you brought?" he says. "Just give me a minute to wash these plates."

"You have only two plates?"

Zev squeezes soap onto a sponge. "I left everything back in Missouri. I wanted a fresh start. I picked up this cheap stuff while I look for a set I like." Keeping his eyes on the dishes, he doesn't see how his explanation is received. He half expects Julia to offer him a set of old plates.

After dessert, Zev gets out the broom. Julia and Mo bat the cork between them on the floor, while Zev sweeps around them and straightens the chairs.

When he's finished cleaning up, they stroll through the neighborhood. It's finally cooled down for the evening. She takes his hand, her fingers as soft as the polishing cloths he left behind in Colorado. Unlike his hands, which are calloused from working with metal and raw from cleaning. Blue-collar hands, unpleasant to hold. He waits for her to pull away, but she doesn't.

Reaching a park, she tells him she sometimes spends hours on a bench just to hear the kids shriek, nostalgic for an earlier time in her life.

"I miss my daughter, too," he says, careful, as always, not to mention La La's name or to give away anything from his prior life that could tie Roger Cohen to Zev Fine.

In front of her house, Julia invites him in for a drink. He wonders if she means sex. More likely she's just being polite. In either case, he doesn't trust his body not to betray him, failing to perform, if sex is what she wants, or getting aroused, if a drink is all she has in mind. It's been so long. "Maybe another time."

"Of course," she says, spots coloring her cheeks.

It wasn't his intention to embarrass her. "Why not?" he says. "It's early."

As soon as she opens the door, the dog straddles his tennis shoe. "Dee-Dee!" Julia snatches the Chihuahua, but not before a stream of urine hits his sneaker. "I'm so sorry! She'll get used to you eventually."

He takes off the sneaker, runs water over it in the kitchen sink, then sets it outside to dry. When he returns, Julia pours two glasses of port. Standing in his socks, Zev wishes for a stronger drink. They sit on the couch, and Julia slips off her shoes and tucks her legs beneath her. She leans over and presses her mouth to his, and he tastes lipstick, burnt meat, and the floury torte. To discourage his erection, he thinks of the javelina and of jail. He wonders when she'll realize she can do better.

She seems content to kiss. Zev is relieved, unsure whether he would know what to do anymore in the bedroom. How to satisfy her. Surely things have changed over the years.

It's past eleven when he gets home. Sitting on his bed, he searches the Internet on his phone for Louise Fine in Colorado and is relieved not to find any recent burglaries linked to La La.

•   •   •

Over the next few weeks, Zev's phone begins to ring. There's poetic justice in lawyers, on whom he spent a fortune, helping him get back on his feet. New customers learn about him through word of mouth, too. They schedule daytime appointments, in advance, hiring him to rekey entire houses, to install window locks and security cameras. He hooks up electronic home safety devices that can be monitored on smartphones.

Mindful of the professionals who refer him, Zev is prompt and begins to bill fairly. There's still the matter of the extra keys. He cuts one at each job, hoping never to have to use them, and he hasn't yet. So what's the harm?

When he worked as a burglar, he ground his teeth while he slept, and the slightest noise woke him. Now, he sleeps soundly. If he'd made this change decades before, would he still be with Elissa? Though it doesn't answer his question, he parks outside the shelter regularly to watch her come and go. Maybe he hopes she'll recognize him, despite his aged appearance, the cap, and the glasses.

He and Julia visit the Phoenix Art Museum. As they stand before a Picasso, Zev scoffs.

"Cubists look at a subject from a variety of perspectives," Julia says.

It makes so much sense, Zev feels as if he's been hit on the head with one of the compositional blocks. "That's what I do when I pick locks."

Julia nods, but he doesn't know if she's humoring him.

Whenever they go to the movies, Zev has Julia select the film. "What did you think?" he says, as soon as the credits roll.

He waits to share his view, which is always remarkably close to hers.

At restaurants, they try different cocktails—the Snowball, the Basilico, the Red Velvet Shortcake—taking a taxi home if both drink too much to drive. It isn't unusual for them to end up in Julia's bed.

As they linger naked one evening, king-size sheets at their feet, Dee-Dee hops onto the bed. Zev expects to be showered, but the dog licks his toes, instead.

"I told you. She just needed time." Julia carries Dee-Dee out of the room. "We could use a little privacy," she says to the dog, closing the door.

Zev circles Julia's navel with a finger he scrubbed and anointed with lotion earlier that day. He traces a triangle connecting her belly and hipbones. Goose bumps rise on her flesh, which is a mix of suppleness and stretch marks. He's still astonished she will have him. He doesn't discount the role loneliness plays. He understands it as only another aging, single person can. But there are other men she could choose, wealthier, more attractive men who can cook a steak without turning it to leather. The knowledge makes him tender and attentive, sacrificing his own pleasure to hers.

On a Sunday, Julia drives them to Mount Lemmon, where it's twenty degrees cooler. They walk on trails surrounded by evergreens that remind Zev of Colorado, pine needles under their feet. "I never liked nature much," Zev says. "Too messy." They're out of range of his cell phone, but Zev doesn't worry about missing a job, confident there will be others in its place.

"There are worse things than messy," Julia says, brushing a needle from his hair.

It depends what you mean by messy, Zev thinks.

On the way home, they stop at a restaurant that has fondue. Though the fad is over, Zev has never tried it. He's enjoying it, until cheese drips onto his shirt. With his napkin, he wipes furiously at the stain, until Julia grabs his hand. She orders a glass of sparkling water and dips her napkin in, then dabs at his shirt.

"You're amazing!" Zev says, as the oil comes out.

"That's what makes me amazing? Getting a stain out of your shirt? Not the sex or managing to teach you salsa? If I didn't know what a freak you are about cleaning, I'd think you were a real chauvinist."

"But you do know." Zev laughs, never so happy to be understood, and soon Julia is laughing, too, until tears roll down their cheeks.

"You're going to make me pee," she says, her chest quaking.

Later in the week, they attend a classical concert. Zev worked the night before and falls asleep as soon as the lights dim.

When Julia nudges his arm, he wakes. "You're snoring," she whispers.

It takes a minute to figure out where he is and with whom, but when he does, he clutches her hand and kisses each finger. How strange that just when he thought he'd lost everything—La La and the hope that Elissa would return to him—just when he resigned himself to a life of seclusion in Arizona, he met Julia and discovered there was love in front of him, not only behind. Even Elissa is back in his life, though she doesn't know it.

After the concert, they go out for a drink, and Zev confides he's worried about Mo. She's sleeping more and losing weight.

"Animals slow down as they age," says Julia. "But why don't you take her to the vet?"

Zev makes an appointment with the doctor Mo sees for her arthritis, and the next week he brings the cat in. The clinic always reminds Zev of La La. In the waiting room, a young veterinarian returns a rabbit to its owners, the doctor's eyes fixed on the animal even as he addresses the humans.

The vet does a geriatric cat exam, but doesn't find anything new. She draws blood and tells Zev she'll call with the results in a few days.

In his apartment, Zev releases Mo from the carrier. Later, when Julia knocks, he invites her in and offers to make tea. He's bought a full set of dishes and a kettle since she was over for dinner. As they wait for the water to boil, Zev gets a call and takes it in the bedroom.

It's a developer wanting him to install locks in an entire building. He's still on the phone when the kettle whistles, but he lets Julia get it. With the money from the job, he can hire another locksmith to handle emergency calls at night. After he hangs up, he looks out the window and imagines a fleet of Safety Lock and Key vans. He pictures himself living in a house like Julia's or one that's nicer, with her. He's been given a second chance, one more than most people get.

20

It's a Friday night in early June, and another endless weekend stretches before La La. She has no plans. As she sets a plate on the kitchen table, it clatters, echoing through the house. She longs for the dogs' company but won't see them until Monday.

The kitchen walls, gray-white, appear soiled. She means to hang photographs in the new place but never has the energy. And which images would she choose? Ones of Zev, who's gone? Surely not of Clem, though she has those pictures and sometimes looks at them.

As she spreads peanut butter on wheat bread, she considers calling Elissa, but whether her mother is home or out with Chloe, she won't pick up. La La bites into the sandwich, which has the texture of wet cement. If she were still with Clem, they'd be having a real dinner, salad and pasta with greens. Or they'd be splitting a bottle of wine in a restaurant, perhaps the place where they got engaged. La La fiddles with the engagement ring in her pocket.

If only she had the kind of mother she could confide in about how much she misses Clem. As it is, all she has for Elissa are questions. Why did she leave? Why didn't she take La La with her? Having abandoned her, Elissa could at least provide some answers.

La La pulls up a map of Mesa, Arizona, on her phone. It's a little over eight hundred miles away. If she drives through the night, she can arrive soon after the shelter opens. Animal shelters are busy on weekends, and her mother will likely be working. She'll be forced to see La La and answer her questions.

She tosses two peaches, the jar of peanut butter, and a spoon into a canvas bag. Sitting in her car, she enters the shelter address into the GPS app on her phone.

Perhaps Elissa has a good reason for avoiding her calls, although La La can't fathom what it might be. La La imagines everything will change as soon as Elissa sees her. Her mother will realize what a mistake it was to leave her. She'll fold La La into her arms and apologize for all the years she's been away. Leaning back, she'll take La La's face into her hands and caress her cheeks. If there's another way for the meeting to go, La La doesn't dwell on it. She lowers her foot onto the gas pedal. Pulling a peach from the canvas bag, she discovers she's too nervous to eat.

Traffic moves, though the roads are full. La La doesn't bother to check whether she's being followed. She hopes the bounty hunter tails her. The woman will waste a weekend and several tankfuls of gas only to find La La visiting her mother. Time and fuel the agent might otherwise spend looking for Zev. It would serve her right for refusing to believe La La doesn't know where her father is.

La La wills time to speed up, the night to pass. She selects one radio station after another, music and talk, all of it heightening her impatience, until she turns the radio off altogether. The endless hum of the road beneath her tires is like a lullaby, but the hope that Elissa will welcome her keeps La La going, that and the six-pack of Mountain Dew she picks up at a gas station.

In the early hours of the morning, calm settles over the landscape. The road spools out, fingerlike trees beside it. The day seems to harbor a promise. When La La graduates, perhaps she'll find a job in Mesa. Her mother could pull strings at the shelter, arrange a position for her there, so they can see each other every day. Under a pink sky, La La eats the two peaches, juices dripping down her chin.

Zev parks a few buildings away from the shelter, knowing he might have missed Elissa's arrival. Mo made several messes that morning, delaying him, and he considered not coming at all, but he hoped Elissa would be late, too. He has a strange feeling his timing is right. And he has nothing else to do, Julia having gone to visit her son for the weekend.

While he waits, he listens to a radio host interview a locksmith. He'd love to get a gig like that, which would be great advertising. Then again, being on the radio might not be the best idea for someone like him. As the segment ends, a woman in a car just like La La's pulls into the shelter parking lot. It *is* La La. Fear prickles his scalp. He ducks down in his seat. His first thought is that she's looking for him, but then he realizes she's probably there for her mother and is unlikely to spot him in the unfamiliar car down the block. He sits up again. How did La La find Elissa? And why the hell did she bother when he told her not to? The woman's not worth La La's time. Not worth his time, either. Yet here he is. He wants more than anything to say hello to La La, but it's too risky.

A woman pulls in after La La. When she gets out of her car, Zev can't help but notice she's well-endowed. If she isn't a waitress at Hooters, she should be. A brown ponytail brushes her back.

Worried about how it will go when La La meets her mother, he decides to wait. He craves another look at his daughter in any case.

Just as La La predicted, would-be adopters crowd the shelter, their cars nearly filling the lot. In a corner of the building, a flap covers an opening, reminding La La of the book drop at the library where Zev occasionally took her when she was a child. CATS ONLY reads a sign next to it. Four feet away is a drop for dogs. La La has heard about these night boxes for people too embarrassed to surrender pets during the day. What lie explains the pet's sudden disappearance to family and friends? An illness? A bout of aggression? The poor thing ran away? La La's done many things, but she's never quit on an animal.

She hurries to the entrance, anticipation making up for her lack of sleep. Sweat trickles down her back. Once inside, La La clutches the edge of the counter. Trembling, she says, "I'm here to see Elissa Roberts."

"Do you have an appointment?" the clerk asks. His cap reads WAG MORE—BARK LESS, and if she isn't mistaken, he sniffs, trying to catch her scent.

"I'm her daughter," she mumbles.

"What's that?"

"Her daughter!"

His eyes widen. He picks up the phone and dials. "Your daughter's here?" After a pause, he says, "One flight up at the end of the hall."

La La finds the office. When she enters, Elissa says, "Please shut the door." It's her mother, though a different woman than the one La La knew. Not just the gray hair or cheeks that fold like fabric, which she recognizes from the website photo. Elissa's voice is flatter, too. Only a hint of the brittle edge remains. But perhaps it's because her mother's at work. La La waits for Elissa to say more, but she doesn't. Her mother barely looks at her. A dog that is part pit bull lies on a bed in the corner of the room, panting nervously. La La's breathing speeds up to match the animal's. She understands at once that she will not get what she came for, neither answers nor love nor a future with her mother. Yet she has to try. "I miss you."

"I'm sorry," Elissa says, as she straightens a paper on the desk.

"Why did you leave?"

"It's complicated."

"I'm not in a hurry." Though her mother hasn't invited her to, La La sits in a chair opposite the desk.

"I didn't want to be married to a thief."

"Maybe I didn't want to be a thief's daughter. Did you ever think about that? You should have taken me."

"I wasn't meant to be a mother."

"But you have a daughter now. Your telephone message—"

"Come here, Chloe," Elissa says.

The pit bull raises her head. A dog. Of course. It makes so much sense. As Chloe waddles over to Elissa, La La feels pain in her knee. Perhaps the dog has the beginnings of arthritis.

Her mother caresses Chloe's head and feeds her a treat from

a giant ceramic bowl on the desk. For a moment, it's as if La La isn't in the room at all. Is that what La La herself is like, ignoring people as she cares for pets? Even if it's true, it's not La La's fault. What animals feel is amplified inside her, creating a din that crowds out people's emotions. What excuse could her mother have? Unless—is it possible?—her mother has the same connection to animals that La La does. Considered in that light, so much of her childhood and her mother's inability to love her take on a more reasonable cast. They're alike! How can La La hold it against her?

Her mother whispers something to Chloe, and the dog lays her head on Elissa's lap.

"Do you feel their pain, too?" La La says. Sunshine floods the room, the air a wavy living thing filled with spinning dust motes. La La imagines the talks she'll have with Elissa, comparing their talents. Perhaps her mother will teach her additional techniques, learned over a lifetime, for tuning in to a creature's discomfort. How close they'll become! She can forgive everything now that she understands.

"Whose pain?" Elissa doesn't look up.

"All of them: dogs, cats, birds, squirrels. I'm the way I am because of you, right?"

"I don't know what you're talking about."

La La kneels in front of Chloe and manipulates her leg. "She's hurting. Can't you feel it? Probably early arthritis."

Elissa tightens her hold on Chloe. "How can you tell?"

"The same way you can. Because you can sense what animals feel."

"I can't—"

"That's why you were so cruel."

The phone rings. "I was unhappy," Elissa says, over the phone's insistent cries. "I felt trapped."

"Dad got arrested, and I had to take a leave from veterinary school. I left you messages."

"You're in veterinary school?" For the first time, her mother looks at her with respect, and something, La La likes to imagine, like regret.

"I was—I took a leave."

"Yes, that's what you said."

"Why didn't you call me back?"

"After all these years, I didn't know what to say."

"You could have said anything. I just wanted to hear your voice." The distance between La La and her mother feels as vast as the mileage La La drove to get there. "Mo's still alive," La La says. "Or I think she is. Zev took her when he went on the run."

"Mo?"

"The cat you left."

Elissa's expression softens. "I knew you'd give her a good home."

So, she *was* a gift from Elissa. Mo, her first friend after Zev isolated her, her first patient. The animal that led her to Dr. Bergman, who helped La La understand who she was.

Elissa gathers papers from her desk and stands.

"Can't we just talk?" La La pleads.

"I'm no good at this. I wish I was. But I'm not. I'm sorry." Elissa leashes Chloe and steps from the office, shutting the door behind her.

La La rises, her eyes hot. A familiar absence all that's left of her mother. She lifts the bowl of treats above her head and lets it fall to the linoleum floor, shards of ceramic mingling with Milk-Bones. Tearing a framed poster that says *Kindness Is the Best*

Training from the wall, she spears it on a corner of the desk, glass showering her hands.

As she stumbles through the hall, tears pool in her eyes. In the stairway, she gropes for the banister and makes her way down. What can she do but return home, as much an orphan as when she left.

Zev sees his daughter lurch from the building, tear slicks on her cheeks, shoulders heaving. What did Elissa say? He'd like to throttle her. No good can come of La La knowing where he is, yet he can't bear to do nothing. Shoving the car door open, he runs toward her, calling her name. Shock registers in her eyes. When he embraces her, she hangs on, burying her face in his neck. Her suffering causes him anguish, but he relishes having her in his arms. He wasn't sure he would ever hold her again.

"She was the same," La La wails. "She couldn't wait to get away from me."

"I'm here," he says, and strokes her back, trying not to think of the soup of fluids dampening his shirt. "It's all right."

A dog at her side, Elissa exits the building, tripping on a landing she must walk every day. Unlike the other times Zev's seen her, she looks uncertain of her direction and hesitates before continuing.

La La's back is to her mother. "Why did you marry her?" she cries.

"I love her," Zev says, though what he feels is closer to obsession. "I wish I didn't." His eyes meet Elissa's. He shakes his head, warning her not to come closer. Odd that he should feel anything for Elissa, given how she treated him and La La and with a woman like Julia in his life. But Elissa married him, knowing who he was, and stayed with him at least for a while. Julia doesn't even know his real name.

Over La La's shoulder, Zev sees the ponytailed woman exit the shelter. He's blocking the sidewalk, but the woman can go around. Before he knows what's happening, the woman skirts Elissa and points a gun at him and La La. From beneath her T-shirt, she extracts a silver shield that hangs around her neck.

Elissa pulls Chloe to her. She backs up to the shelter door.

"Step to the side, Louise," shouts the bounty hunter. After turning to look, La La obeys. "Zev Fine, turn around and put your hands behind your back." The agent handcuffs him. "On the ground," she says, and he drops. She checks him for weapons, handling him roughly, taking the lockpicks and pen from his pockets.

The sidewalk presses against his cheek, warm as an oven. He investigates the handcuffs with his fingers, but she's smart enough to have used a hinged pair with a virtually unpickable Yale tumbler lock. And he hasn't got a tool.

Zev shouts an address at La La, adding: "Get Mo. And don't forget to take her litter."

A week later, back in Colorado, La La visits Zev in the Longview County Jail. It's as grim as she feared it would be. The cement floor is cracked, and they're surrounded by windowless cinder-block walls. Zev's hair is unwashed. The torn zipper on his jump-suit doesn't close all the way, but Zev is so out of it he doesn't seem to notice. He's lost weight and his cheekbones protrude. The deputy tells her she has half an hour.

"I got Mo," she says. Zev nods. La La wishes she had something to hold, the copies of *Scientific American* and *National Geographic* she brought for him that jail officials wouldn't let her bring inside. Anything to distract her. As it is, she doesn't know what to do with her hands and sets them on the orange plastic table between them that bears scratches, but nothing else. "I brought your clothes back to my house." He'll figure out she took the other things, too, the important ones. Or at least she hopes he will. The keys and notebook are safe—she buried them next to a mountain path—but she can't mention that in the jail where conversations might be recorded. She wonders if he'll want them when he gets out. "A woman stopped by while I was packing your things."

Zev looks up. "What did she say?"

"She asked if you were okay. I said you had some health problems and were coming to live with me."

"That's terrible. She'll think I'm old."

La La looks around. "Better than the alternative." Quiet falls over the room. La La tells Zev about Nat moving back to Atlanta.

"O'Bannon was here," Zev says without elaborating. La La had her own conversation with the lawyer, so she knows he's trying to negotiate a deal.

Her father, who was always so full of energy, barely moves. Not even when she tells him she'll be returning to school in the fall. He should be happy for her after nearly robbing her of her career. "At least look at me," she says. When he does, she regrets asking, because his expression is blank, the affection she's used to seeing gone.

She traces a scratch on the table with her finger and wonders why she bothered coming at all. Her visit doesn't seem to make any difference to him. His choices are what led to his being here, she reminds herself. She tries not to think of her role in his capture because then she'll just be angry at herself, and what good would that do?

"I miss Julia," he says.

"The woman who stopped by?"

"I even miss Dee-Dee."

Why is he talking about strangers when he can't seem to muster even a bit of care for her? La La studies the two rows of identical plastic tables and chairs and the beat-up vending machine. She leans back in her chair until it's about to tip.

"Stop that," Zev says.

She brings the chair forward. "I haven't heard from Mom."

Zev examines the sleeve of his jumpsuit, touching the frayed edge. "You shouldn't have gone to see her."

"Why didn't you tell me you knew where she was?"

"So you could surprise her? Look where that got me." The effort to talk seems to exhaust him. His shoulders drop, and he renews his survey of the floor.

"How was I supposed to know you were spying on her?"

"You didn't know. But it was possible, right? That I would try to see her, too?" Zev rests his head in his hands. "I can't stop going over it in my mind. The minute I saw that woman, I should have known she was a bounty hunter. That she was carrying. You can tell if you really look. She didn't see me in the car. There was still a chance to get away. But I wanted to see you. I'll pay for that mistake for the rest of my life." He tugs at his hair and moans.

"O'Bannon will work something out," she says, but he doesn't stop moaning. She turns from him, the smell of his acrid sweat following her.

"Was it worth it?" he says after a while. "To see her."

"I'm sorry."

"That's not what I asked."

With fifteen minutes left in the visit, La La takes off.

Though La La's given up trying to reach her mother, she can't help thinking about her, and when she does it spoils the taste of her food and distracts her in the clinic. "You said you'd be here half an hour ago," she snaps at Clem when he brings the dogs over. "You're making a mess!" she chastises Blue when he sloshes water out of the bowl. "I know how to tie a surgical knot," she barks at Dr. Bergman when he gives her routine instructions. He regards her with compassion, and it makes her want to scream. She doesn't want his pity.

She imagines returning to the shelter and harming Elissa. It would be easy. The receptionist would let her through now that he knows she's Elissa's daughter. She could use a crowbar or a wrench. If she didn't want to be discovered, she could follow Elissa home and attack her there. Why shouldn't she? Certainly her mother deserves it. Perhaps she'll steal Chloe, the one thing Elissa loves. La La relishes the thought of Elissa's distress at finding the dog gone.

Burgling a house in the evening, La La concentrates on what belongs to the mother—clothes, purses, jewelry, scarves. She doesn't bother selling them, dumping them in a trash can miles away. Coming home, she sees the stuffed lion on her dresser and crams it in the back of a drawer.

Gone is her dream of reconciling with Elissa, a dull emptiness in its place. She has neither words nor tears for her disappointment, which keeps her in bed long into the morning. Any boss other than Dr. Bergman would fire her. When she manages to crawl out from under the covers, her torso feels as heavy as stone.

Only Mo's return gives La La comfort. She missed the cat's contented purr and the way Mo kneaded her thighs. It took only a few warnings for the dogs to understand Mo is family. Now the cat brushes against them, marking them with her scent, and they lick her ears. La La feels a reluctant gratitude toward Elissa for the gift of the cat.

Two weeks after her first trip to the jail, La La returns.

"I wondered if you were ever coming back," Zev says, as he's brought into the visitor's room.

"I'm working," La La says, but she knows Dr. Bergman would give her time off if she asked. She was in no hurry to return to the bleak facility with its stale air and long list of rules. She can't stand seeing Zev there.

"Don't forget me." Her father has a deep cut on his palm and another on his chin. The injury on his hand, he tells her, required a dozen stitches. "Psychotic prisoner. Couldn't get his meds but had no trouble getting ahold of a knife. Place is so goddamned crowded, you can't tell where the threats are coming from." He steadies his hand on the table. The injury oozes yellow pus, but Zev says the wait for further medical attention is long. He hasn't even been able to get Tylenol for the pain.

"I'll tell O'Bannon," La La says. "Maybe he can help."

"I hate to pay him for something like this."

"It will hardly make a difference with what we owe. And you're going to need your hands when you get out." Zev gives her a look, to which she says, "To make me a mocha latte. And to do whatever legitimate work you decide to do."

"Exactly right."

Zev's wearing a different jumpsuit. Bright orange like the earlier one but the sleeves fall well above his wrists, which are frighteningly thin and covered with small red bites, from bedbugs or some other vermin living in the jail. He scratches the bites and worries the cut on his chin.

"You'll get that one infected, too," La La says.

"What does it matter?"

"It matters to me."

"I can't always tell," Zev says.

La La looks toward the door. "I'm working at Dr. Bergman's clinic until I start school."

"He always took better care of you than I did."

"You took good care of me."

"Not really."

La La reads graffiti etched into the plastic table, a series of numbers and letters that might be a code and were made with a blade. "Clem is seeing a woman named Naomi."

"That's too bad."

"You never liked him," La La says.

"I won't like anyone who takes you away from me."

"I guess you don't have to worry about that now." She starts to tilt her chair back but stops herself.

"You'll meet someone else," Zev says. "Even I met someone."

"You want to talk about it?"

"No." He closes his eyes. "She must wonder why I haven't called. Why I didn't stop by before I left."

La La imagines he's picturing her, this woman named Julia. The life that he shared with her. She studies her empty ring finger. "I didn't think you believed in relationships."

"I didn't think so either. She surprised me."

"Maybe you can write to her."

Zev waves his uninjured hand around the room. "From here?"

"Maybe not."

His fingers return to his chin, but La La doesn't say anything. She hopes he figures out a way to protect himself. If anyone can improvise a weapon it's him.

"Not much to do in here but wait," Zev says. "And remember. Things I never told you about, that I thought I forgot." He pauses and scratches his wrist. "My mother wasn't as bad as your mother," he says, "but she was weak. I'll never understand why my father treated me the way he did. The only thing I want to remember, if you want to know the truth, the only good thing left in my life, is you." His lips tremble, and he continues. "It seems unfair, doesn't it? Some people born into love and others . . . it makes me angry at God. But what good does that do? He forgot about me a long time ago."

La La thinks about her childhood dog, Tiny, how he arrived at their home battered. And how Black's original owners neglected him. If there is a God, he doesn't take care of animals, either. "Do you want other visitors?" La La says. "To help pass the time? Dr. Bergman might come if I asked him."

"The fewer people see me this way the better."

When "Lawyers, Guns and Money" starts up on her phone a week later, La La wonders if Zev has escaped. She answers and sets the brush she's been using to groom Mo beside her on the couch.

"He's going to plead guilty to felony burglary," O'Bannon

says, and La La doesn't know whether to feel disappointed or relieved—perhaps a little of both. "He doesn't want you to worry about him anymore or to interfere with your life," the lawyer continues. "He tasted normal life in Arizona, and he wants you to have it."

La La knows how hard it will be for Zev to plead guilty and accept a prison sentence. Yet he's considered not only that he might be convicted of murder, but also what would happen to her if he decided to fight the charges. The choices she'd once again have to make with O'Bannon billing for all the hours he'd spend on a trial. If Zev had stolen her life when she was a child, now he was giving it back.

She feels a burden lift, even as she mourns for her father. With her free hand, she massages Mo's ear.

O'Bannon tells her he convinced the DA to drop the murder charge in exchange for the plea. The lawyer argued the family's action in discontinuing life support was the actual cause of death. He warned the DA that defense experts would introduce doubt about whether the burglary caused the stroke. There were also the matters of the cops' handling of Zev's phone, which had been sloppy and potentially destroyed fingerprints belonging to a third party, and the alibi witness, who was admittedly weak. Together it had been enough. "The prosecutor will recommend a sentence of six years, to be served in a state prison. I've added the additional fees to Zev's balance."

21

A month later, as La La exits the clinic on a warm July day, her phone buzzes with a text. It's Clem. *Black's sick*, he writes.

She dials his number. "What's wrong?"

"He's losing his balance, and he won't eat."

La La settles behind the wheel of the Mercedes. It isn't unusual for older dogs to get a condition called vestibular syndrome, which could cause his symptoms. It looks scarier than it is. "I'll be over as soon as I feed Mo."

Walking into Clem's apartment at a little after seven o'clock that night, she's overcome with dizziness and has to clutch the door to stay on her feet.

Clem grabs her elbow. "Easy there."

When Black rises to greet her, his head angles to the side and he sways and falls face-first into the carpet. Blue hovers over him. "When did this start?" La La says.

Clem keeps his eyes on the dog. "Last night. Scary, isn't it?"

"Why didn't you call!"

"I took him to the emergency vet, okay?"

"*I'm* his emergency vet," La La says.

"You're not even a veterinary student right now."

The words sting, but he's right.

"I didn't take him to just anyone," Clem says. "Naomi knew the doctor."

"Now your girlfriend is making decisions for our dogs? That's great." Kneeling next to Black, La La strokes his muzzle.

"She cares about him."

"Like I said, great. What did the vet say?"

"That he probably has an ear infection. She prescribed antibiotics. Naomi said she had a dog with a similar problem, and he was fine in a few days."

"I really don't want to hear what Naomi said." Taking out her otoscope, La La examines Black's ears. She doesn't see signs of infection, but she might not if the problem is in the middle or inner ear. "Let me see the antibiotics."

Clem retrieves a bottle from the kitchen.

La La's head throbs. But perhaps she just has a stress headache. "We should get an MRI."

"What's going on?" Sitting on the couch, Clem grabs a throw pillow.

La La studies the bottle. "His symptoms can also be caused by a brain tumor. I just want to be cautious. Let's see what the test results show." Her hand on Black's head, La La dials the emergency vet. The doctor who treated Black isn't in, so La La asks another vet to order an MRI.

The vet sighs. "Vestibular syndrome is often caused by an ear infection and clears up with antibiotics."

"I'm a fourth-year veterinary student," La La says, trying to keep the irritation out of her voice.

"Then you know I'm right. Why do you want the test?"

"I'm afraid it's a tumor." Black tries to stand again and falls.

"Unlikely. And the test costs a fortune."

"I know."

"And he'll have to be under complete anesthesia."

"Look, I know all that. We want the test."

"Suit yourself. We'll make the appointment." The vet hangs up.

Clem hugs the pillow to his chest. "I'll call you in the morning and tell you how he's doing, okay?"

"I was thinking I'd take him home with me. I want to watch him." La La looks at the photo of Clem and the dogs. A picture of Clem and Naomi has joined it. They're standing next to a table, arms around each other's waists. If La La's not mistaken, they're in the restaurant where she and Clem got engaged. Pale and plain, Naomi has enormous green eyes similar to La La's but that seem more content.

"Why don't you stay here and we'll both watch him?"

"I didn't think you wanted me around."

"I didn't. But now that your dad's case is over, I guess it would be all right." He sets the pillow aside.

"How do you know what's going on with my dad?" La La says.

"Nat called."

"And she just happened to mention my dad pleaded guilty?"

"She thought it might matter to me."

"Does it?" La La sits perfectly still, holding on to a fragile hope.

"It doesn't change anything, if that's what you're asking."

"It's none of Nat's business."

Clem joins her on the floor. "She knows I care about you. You know that too, right?" His voice is kind, the way it was before La La wrecked everything.

"I'll take Black," she says.

"Why don't you take Blue, too?"

As Clem loads Black into the Mercedes, the dog moans, and La La flinches. A tumor could be pressing on a nerve, causing Black pain. Driving away, streetlights appear as halos, and roads seem to waver. Her palms sweat. A drive that normally takes fifteen minutes stretches to forty-five.

They take Black for the MRI. Clem puts the charges on his credit card, the total exceeding three thousand dollars.

"I'll pay you back," La La says.

"Oh, yeah. How will you do that?"

"Once I'm a veterinarian."

"I don't want the money any sooner."

The radiologist sees what La La feared he would, a tumor pressing against Black's brain stem. They schedule an appointment with an oncologist. The next morning, La La tells Kali she needs more time off.

"You just took a day." The senior vet tech doesn't look up from the pills she's counting.

"It's a family emergency," La La says, her voice breaking.

Kali returns the pills to a large bottle. "Treatment Room One," she says. Following La La into the room, Kali closes the door and motions for La La to sit. The woman hands her a box of tissues. "What's going on?"

"My dog has a brain tumor."

The vet tech's firm demeanor falls away. She clears her throat. "I'll get the doctor."

When Dr. Bergman comes in, he sits in a chair next to La La and doesn't say a thing. She's grateful he doesn't try to comfort her, saying Black's a fighter or that she's given him a good life. Instead, when she's ready to talk, he listens. She tells him what they know and what they don't. "Take as much time as you need," he says. "We'll advance you vacation. And let me know how it's going. Or if there's anything I can do."

The doctor's always been there for her. When she was young, he taught her about animals and about school subjects beyond Zev's grasp. He gave her this job though she had disappointed him. And it isn't just him. La La considers everyone who's helped her: the mysterious black dog who called her back from the depths of the lake; Tiny and Mo; her friend Nat; Black and Blue. She and Clem loved each other for a while. Perhaps even her father did the best he could. Though she's always felt scarred by her mother's absence, now La La wonders if that's right.

The next day, she and Clem see the oncologist. He says they can't operate because of the tumor's position. Chemotherapy isn't an option. The blood-brain barrier would keep the drugs from reaching the mass. La La doesn't know Black's age, but after examining him, the doctor determines he's too old for radiation therapy. To reduce inflammation around the tumor, he prescribes prednisone. He gives them tramadol for Black's pain.

Her empathic abilities give La La greater diagnostic skills than other veterinarians, but she has no special talent when it comes to treatment. In the face of Black's illness, she's helpless.

"Are you going to leave me, too?" she asks one night a week later as she runs a washcloth across Black's forehead. "I'm not sure I could take it if you did. I'm not sure Blue could either." Blue's been dropping gifts at Black's paws all night—a pen, puzzle pieces, a bread roll—but Black doesn't even raise his head to sniff them. Eventually, Blue gives up and lies next to Black, licking his head. Mo, too, seems worried, sniffing Black's head and rubbing against it.

The dogs have always watched out for each other. Like the time Blue chased a stick thrown for another dog and was about to enter a busy road. Black corralled him, blocking his way and barking, until Blue saw the army of cars approaching. And there was the night La La dropped the bottle of Black's antibiotics, and Blue took off with it. Recovering it, La La examined the pills. The pharmacist had filled the prescription incorrectly. Black was allergic to the medication in the bottle.

After she and Clem broke up, Black took care of La La during the weeks he was with her. He always knew what kind of day she had and whether he should lean into her when she got home, comforting her, or bring his leash because what she needed were exercise, the smell of earth, and the luminous green of growing things. Accompanying her on a trail, he was friendly to passersby if she was in a social mood, and growled when she preferred to be left alone. He seemed as aware of her feelings as she was of his. At least he did before he got sick.

Clem comes over after work to help. Stretching out on the floor, he presses his chest to the dog's back. Black's eyes stay closed and he groans. His balance is so bad they have to carry him outside to relieve himself. To tempt him to eat, La La prepares food she wouldn't allow herself—chicken soup with rice—but Black refuses it.

La La doesn't invite Clem to stay over, but one night he says he just needs to rest his eyes, and before she knows it, he's snoring on the couch. It's late. Through an open window, La La hears coyotes celebrating a kill and the mechanical slide of an automatic garage door. She covers Clem with an afghan threaded with dog hair, and clears a path from the couch to the bathroom, collecting squeaky toys and sharp-edged bones and depositing them in the toy basket.

The next night, Clem arrives with an overnight bag. Though he should have asked, when La La sees the bag, she imagines it means he's forgiven her and perhaps something more. "Naomi's okay with this?"

"I didn't tell her," he says.

"You can get into trouble hiding things," she says, and shrugs.

"I suppose you can." He sets his bag on the couch. He's been reading about canine chiropractic, he tells her. He doesn't think it will cure Black, but it might relieve some of the effects of the tumor and calm him.

As Clem presses his fingers into Black's spine, La La's muscles relax, and she remembers how he used to adjust her, the tension of veterinary school evaporating. She wonders if he'll ever work on her again.

She hunts for an extra set of car keys Blue stole. When she finds them behind a couch cushion, she returns them to a bowl on the table and waits for Blue to make off with them again. Caught up with Black, they've been neglecting their Jesse James. Moments later, keys dangling from his mouth, Blue disappears into the bedroom. She may have to dig them up in the backyard, but she doesn't mind if it keeps Blue occupied.

La La puts on Johnny Cash, and Clem sings along, his voice

rough-edged and deep. Mo conducts with her tail, while La La places sheets on the couch. When Clem finishes the treatment, the dog falls asleep, his legs twitching as he runs in his dream, his balance uncompromised. The adjustment has relaxed La La, too, who doesn't have the energy to make it to her bed, lowering her head onto her arms at the kitchen table.

In the morning, Clem showers and walks Blue, while La La stays behind with Black. When Clem returns, he asks for the engagement ring.

What La La wouldn't give to travel back to a time before she decided to steal for Zev. Since that's impossible, she considers pretending she lost it, so Clem can't give it to Naomi over a glass of wine, while telling her the story of his grandparents. She retrieves the silk drawstring bag from her jewelry box. She could say she sold it to pay Zev's attorney fees. Taking the ring from the bag, she puts it on. But there are some things you can't steal, and a relationship is one of them. She puts the ring back.

When she holds out the bag, Clem grasps it, but she doesn't let go. Not right away. Not until he tugs three times and says, "La La."

"I guess you want to give it to Naomi."

"I don't know about that." He shoves the bag into his pocket.

Maybe there's hope after all. "Anything new on the blog?" she says.

"I haven't been checking it. We've been pretty busy with other things, haven't we?"

La La pulls out her phone. "Look at last night's post." She reads the account of a stray dog that was hit by a car in Manhattan. A team of vets operated on him for free, saving his life. The surgery lasted for four hours and one of the vets missed his plane to Paris. He was supposed to start his honeymoon. "Maybe it's a sign. That Black is going to be okay."

Clem pulls organic oatmeal and a package of Medjool dates from his overnight bag. "A sign, huh?" He boils water and pours in the oatmeal. It's La La's favorite but, like Black, she has difficulty swallowing. When it's ready, she forces down a few spoonfuls, scraping the rest into the trash when Clem isn't looking.

22

Eyes half closed, La La goes through the motions in the veterinary clinic, her thoughts with Black. Feeling dizzy, she wobbles in her clogs. She cuts a terrier's claw too short, hitting the quick. Pain shoots through La La's index finger. The animal squeals, and blood drips from the nail. The owner of the terrier, an elderly woman whose hands form permanent fists, demands that Dr. Bergman fire La La.

"It happens," Dr. Bergman says, as La La checks the clock on the wall to see when she can return to Black.

"Not to my dog." The woman stomps from the room, her pet tucked under her arm like a football.

In surgery, La La hands Dr. Bergman tissue forceps instead of bone forceps and is slow to suction. He dismisses her from the procedure, finishing the sutures himself.

At the end of the day, he sits her down in his office. A thank-you card from a grateful pet owner stands on his desk. La La can no longer imagine herself in practice. She can only picture the time she has left with Black. She waits for the doctor to fire her.

Dr. Bergman rubs his forehead. "How's Black?"

La La describes the dog's condition.

"Listen carefully," Dr. Bergman says. "The good guardians rarely tell me they put their animals down too soon. Often, they tell me they waited too long. This is something you can do for Black."

"I can't."

"Take time off, spend it with him, make some decisions."

She slips out of the clinic without saying good-bye.

She wants only for Black to go on living. His tail still bats the floor when she enters a room. His pulse slows when she strokes his head. But he's shrinking. His flesh strains to cover his bones, which cling loosely to one another and can't support him. He sleeps much of the time and is confused when awake.

"The doctor's right, don't you think? Maybe it's time to put him down," Clem says that night.

Steadying herself against the back of the couch, La La makes her way to Black. His breath comes in noisy, rattling gasps. Touching him, she feels the outline of his skeleton. She's lost weight, too. Her pants drape from her hips; her shirts inflate like balloons when the wind catches them. She's lethargic and her head constantly aches.

Clem stands over them, kneading his neck. "He's suffering," he says, but La La already knows that. Nevertheless, she clings to memories of Black when he was well. The dog used to thank her for every meal by licking her palm. On walks, he would pause if she or Clem or Blue fell behind. Once, he guarded an injured jay—snarling when Blue tried to mouth the bird—until Clem returned with a box.

When they visited the shelter, Black would comfort dogs

who had been abused, approaching with sidelong glances and patience until the animals relaxed. They were scampering in the yard by the time he left. He slept next to La La during the weeks she had him, snoring almost as loudly as Clem had.

What, La La wonders, will happen to Blue without his friend? Who will bite his neck in play, follow him across fields, and lead him home?

Devoting themselves to Black, La La and Clem are a couple again. As if she never deceived him. Until Naomi calls. Then Clem steps outside, and La La counts the minutes, wishing she could hear their conversation, wanting to know if Naomi makes him laugh, if he is himself or someone else with her.

Clem runs a washcloth around the dog's ears and feet to cool him, hooks him up to IV saline so he doesn't dehydrate. These are things La La should do, but as Black deteriorates, she grows sicker, too. She's convinced that what she feels is more than empathy this time. That, like Black, she has cancer. Afraid to confirm the diagnosis, she avoids doctors. They wouldn't believe how she got it, anyway. No one would, not even Nat, certainly not Clem, who says she must have the flu. Because her illness is following the course of Black's, she's afraid if she euthanizes him, she'll die.

23

Three days pass. Black's legs become paralyzed. La La's legs stiffen, too, and she moves with difficulty. Sitting on the floor, she massages his limbs. His headache is worse. The tumor must be growing larger.

Clem begs. "It's wrong. No creature would want to live this way."

La La ups his pain medications, gabapentin and tramadol, until the doctor says they can't increase them any more.

"You've got him so drugged all he does is sleep," Clem says.

"But he's alive." La La's speech is slurred.

"Barely."

Unaware, Black soils his bed and himself. As La La struggles to clean the mess, Clem takes the bucket from her.

Later, when Clem leashes Blue, Black attempts to join them but can't rise. At night, Black cries, awake. La La stays up with him, struggling to hum tunes that used to soothe him, "This Old Man," and "The Farmer in the Dell," until she collapses, her head on his fur.

The next day, Clem cooks bone broth and scrambled eggs for Black. Blue must think it's a holiday, but Black won't touch the food. La La brushes Black's fur, but he doesn't open his eyes. She tells him stories, her words running together. "Remember when we went to the shelter and you were the only one the Doberman would let near and then he cried when you were leaving? I wanted to bring him home, but Clem said two were as many as we could handle." The dog blinks and La La imagines he's remembering.

Black whimpers through another warm night. La La curls on the floor next to him, her head throbbing, dozing only as dawn lightens the curtains. When she wakes, the dog is gone. The couch is empty, except for folded sheets. She checks the kitchen and bedroom, Blue following her, but she doesn't find them. Looking outside, she sees Clem loading Black into his car.

Through an open window she screams, "What are you doing?"

When Black is settled, Clem says, "It's time."

"Were you just going to drive off?"

"Could you not shout?"

"I'm coming." La La approaches the car in the T-shirt and underwear she wore to sleep.

"I took him outside and he passed out," Clem says.

La La looks at Black, lying in the back seat. Although awake now, he stares straight ahead, the knowledge in his eyes gone. "You were just going to go? Without asking me?"

"I was going to wake you and give you a choice, to come or not. But I'm taking him. I love him, too. I can't watch him suffer."

"You think I like it?"

"I think you're afraid the world will be too empty without him. But you have Mo and Blue and all the other animals who need you, and Nat and Dr. Bergman, and I'm here, too."

"I'm scared."

"I know."

"You don't know." She climbs into the passenger seat, her thighs sticking to the vinyl, the temperature already in the eighties.

Clem slides behind the wheel. "Aren't you going to put clothes on?"

"I'm scared if we euthanize him, I'll die."

"It doesn't work that way."

"It does with me." She pauses, winded. "You know I've always experienced what animals feel. Now that Black is dying, something new has happened. I think I'm dying, too."

"You're not dying. Look at Black. I'm not an animal empath, but I can see there's nothing left to him. But you're still here, every bit of you, as sick as you feel."

La La observes the dog she has always known as Black and senses nothing but a weakly beating heart, pain radiating from his head, and the tumor that thrives. Everything that made Black himself is gone, especially the love he offered so freely to her and Clem and Blue.

While La La dresses, Clem loads Blue, and then they drive to Dr. Bergman's clinic.

"You're doing the right thing," the doctor says, squeezing La La's shoulder. He arranges Black on soft, worn blankets. After giving them a chance to say good-bye, Dr. Bergman administers the two shots that take Black's life. When the dog is gone, La La presses her face to his body and hangs on to his fur. Blue sniffs him and howls, the sound nearly rending a hole in the clinic. Kali clips some fur, deposits it in a plastic bag, and hands it to La La. She tells them they can pick up his ashes later in the week, but La La can't bring herself to leave. The staff tend to other patients. La La breathes in Black's smell, the most beautiful she has ever known, and soon to vanish.

Clem presses his forehead to Black's. "My boy."

A post-op dog cries, but La La can't tell what surgery he had. When a cat yowls, La La can only guess why. Her chest throbs with the ache of losing Black, but as to the rest of the animals in the hospital, her body is silent, as silent as it's been since before she was rescued from the lake. When the black dog summoned her back from the depths, he changed her, allowing her to experience what he and other animals felt. Now that Black's gone, her empathic ability seems to be gone, too. Which leads her to wonder, *Was it Black himself on the lake that day?* But it can't be. Seventeen years have passed. He'd be too old, wouldn't he? And maybe it doesn't matter whether the dog she saved was the one who saved her. She couldn't have loved Black any more than she did whether he rescued her or not.

Not feeling the animals' pain brings a measure of relief. La La stretches her arms without constraint, trying her new independence, and breathes easily. But with the freedom comes emptiness. Who is she without her connection to animals? How will she treat them? And don't the animals need someone like her? She remembers the boy, sitting in the closet, kittens on his lap. Perhaps it's his turn. Once upon a time, Dr. Bergman said there were others, too.

In the waiting room, La La sees worry on owners' faces, and hope, and grief. She used to miss all of that. A woman touches her heart, perhaps having seen Clem carry Black in.

On the ride home, she can't feel Blue's sadness, though it shows in the downward tilt of his muzzle and the tuck of his tail. It's strange to be shut out. Clem's lips are pinched, his cheeks, pale. She wonders how he can drive.

"Are you okay?" she asks.

"No," he says, a tear spilling over and running down his cheek.

La La's cancer symptoms have disappeared.

La La returns to work the next day because if she doesn't keep busy, she'll think of nothing but Black. Without her empathic abilities, she must rely on a physical examination of each patient and observations—hers and the owner's—to understand the animal's condition. At times it's like trying to make out an unfamiliar room in the dark.

Owners comfort their pets in the waiting room, holding them, offering them treats. They lean in to hear Dr. Bergman's every word and ask for reassurance, even when they must know the doctor can't give it. Love is a perilous thing. In the clinic it causes more pain than joy, though of course there are reprieves. Relief softens an owner's body, relaxes her face. It's all new to La La, and exhausting.

That night, for the first time in weeks, Clem doesn't come over. The next night is the same. She has no right to expect otherwise, yet it's too much on top of losing Black. She and Clem worked so well together, nursing Black, La La hoped Clem would see they were meant to be a pair. That he would forget Naomi and forgive the past.

She wanders through the house, Black's presence nowhere and everywhere, in his blanket, freshly laundered, his collar and leash, in a photograph of the dogs wrestling the day she and Clem brought them home. Clem is in the picture, too. Isn't it time he stopped judging her?

Though Blue stays at her side, it's not enough. Not knowing what else to do, she closes her fist around a crowbar. She hasn't pulled a job since Black fell ill. It's Wednesday, a bad night for a burglary. Even if people go out, they don't stay out. But she needs something to fill the emptiness Black and Clem have left, even if that something is a watch or a necklace. Her fingers caress a wrench before she drops it into her duffel.

La La knocks at the entrance to a dark split-level home, then knocks some more. She waits but doesn't hear anything. She tries again, wanting to be sure the home is empty, and is about to walk around back, when a woman speaks from behind the door. "Yes?" she says, hesitantly. When La La remains silent, the woman calls out, her voice tight, "Who is it?"

I'm lost, La La had intended to say if someone came to the entrance. She'd memorized an address a block away to give the homeowner. But the fear in the woman's voice rattles La La.

"I think I have the wrong house," La La stammers, and she hurries back to her car. Driving away, she thinks of Dr. Bergman's daughter, afraid to sleep at night or to live alone since her apartment was robbed. She pictures Dr. Bergman, stricken when he told her. Like the owner of the parrot when she described what it meant to have her mother's necklace and the memories that accompanied it stolen. La La didn't understand their anguish at the time, didn't appreciate the terror she had caused, but she does now.

Her face prickles with shame. Staring through the windshield at the empty street, she thinks about loss, what she's experienced and what she's inflicted on others. She turns toward home.

An owl calls to its mate, but the night is silent in reply. Whether the bird suffers, La La can't say.

Back in her house, she opens a heavyweight garbage bag and tosses in crowbar, wrench, lockpicks, the box of veterinary gloves, the baseball cap and glasses, the infinity scarf and duffel bag. Everything she needs to commit a crime. She drives to a dumpster two miles away and discards the garbage bag, believing her separation from that life is complete.

The next day she trades the Mercedes for a Honda.

24

Fall semester begins, and La La returns to school. Mourning Black, she is sometimes forgetful and always tired, but she's also glad to be back. She develops an interest in cancer treatment, not only because the disease took Black, but also because it's the number-one killer of dogs. Later in the year, she'll apply for post-graduate work in veterinary oncology.

The shorter days keep La La home in the evenings, but it's okay because she wants to catch up on all the studying she missed. Watching a video on her tablet about how to perform a biopsy, she's startled by banging at the door.

"Police!"

Mo's ears shoot back, and she flattens herself on the couch. Blue dashes from the room. It's eight o'clock at night, and La La wears sweatpants and a long-sleeved T-shirt. She drops the tablet on the chair without bothering to switch it off and peers through a window. Two officers stand at the door. "Yes?" she says, as she opens it.

"We have a warrant to search the place," the older one says.

Below thick lids, his eyes scan La La, the room, and the blaring iPad. His partner hardly seems old enough for the work. His cheeks flush, and he blinks too often.

La La asks to see the warrant. Items the police can look for include a crowbar, other burglar's tools, and a long list of possessions she's taken from homes, including the engraved yin-yang pendant. Her heart begins an unsteady beat as she hands the document back.

"Take a seat," the officer says.

La La sinks into the overstuffed chair, pulls the iPad out from under her, and tosses it toward the coffee table, missing. It thumps onto the floor. She can't remember if when she changed from her scrubs, she put the yin-yang necklace away or left it on the dresser. Either way, the police will find it. It's the only thing connecting her to the burglaries, but it's probably enough, the date engraved on the back identifying it as the stolen one. She'd worn it so often under her clothes, she'd begun to think of it as hers and neglected to dispose of it with everything else. Her knee bounces, and she quiets it with her hand.

The officers search the front closet. They enter the bedroom, and she hears them open and close drawers. They talk to one another, but she can't make out what they're saying. In the kitchen, they dig into cabinets, rustle items in the refrigerator and freezer. Blue returns and squeezes next to her on the chair. Though he's too big for that, she's glad to have him near.

The police take their time. Thinking about her visits to Zev in the state prison, La La wonders if the women's prison is as dull and depressing. Whether the guards are as short-tempered. She supposes Clem will care for Blue if she's sent away, but who will watch Mo? The cat is too old to keep getting shuffled from home to home.

The officers return to the living room, their hands empty. How is it possible they missed the pendant?

"That'll be all," the older one says, though he seems reluctant to leave, surveying the room one last time.

She doesn't move until they're out of the house. Then she locks and chains the door. Through the window, she watches their car pull away.

The pendant isn't on the dresser. It's not in her jewelry box, either. On a hunch, she grabs a flashlight and shines it through a back window. A fresh mound of earth rises next to the fence. A trail of dirt leads through the dog door into the bedroom.

La La kneels in front of Blue and scratches his ears. "Good boy," she says.

After digging up the necklace, she drives to a lake she's never been to before. Making sure no one's watching, she throws the pendant as far as she can into the water.

The next day, she calls O'Bannon and tells him about the police visit.

"Let me see if I can get more information from my contacts in the precinct," he says. A few hours later, he calls back. "An informant gave the police a tip. Seems this guy has been notoriously unreliable in the past, and they don't put much stock in anything he says. He identified you as the perpetrator of a few burglaries to reduce the charges against him in a drug case. They may want to interview you, but I wouldn't recommend you talk to them. Bottom line is, they don't have enough on you."

Tank.

25

Nat has flown in from Atlanta and stands with La La on the veterinary school lawn after her graduation ceremony. Clem has brought Blue. Naomi discovered he'd been lying about who La La was to him and about staying at her place and broke up with him. Clem and La La haven't gotten back together. "I need a break from women," Clem said, when La La suggested it. They're friends and sometimes take Blue hiking or watch weekend marathons of *Grey's Anatomy.* Clem's busy with his blog, too. Ever since he changed the name to *Small Kindnesses,* posts pop up throughout the day and thousands of people have begun following him.

O'Bannon shows up at the graduation, too. La La sent him an invitation, thinking he would be too busy to come. But here he is, handing her a gift, an envelope full of cash. After she looks inside, he takes it back. "I'll put it toward your balance," he says.

Taking her friend's arm, Nat says, "How does it feel to be a vet, La La?"

"Actually, I've started calling myself Louise. Doctor Fine in the clinic." La La smiles.

Dr. Bergman walks toward her, a gift in one hand that's coming unwrapped, a glass of champagne in the other that spills a little with each step. "I couldn't be prouder," he says, crushing the gift—a six-pack of apple juice, like the kind they drank from when he tutored her—against her chest as he draws her into a hug.

Zev applied for permission to attend the ceremony, but the request was denied. La La has promised him pictures. She didn't bother inviting Elissa. Stepping back from Dr. Bergman, La La takes in everyone who's come to celebrate with her. She'll thank each of her guests before the day is over. Glancing at Blue, she wonders whether he's lonely without Black. Or maybe that's just how she feels. Black's identification tag hangs from a chain around her neck. She squeezes it between finger and thumb, thinking of all the animals who have been part of her life. Family, she realizes, is more than who you're born to. Her own can encompass every person and every animal whose life she touches. The thought startles her, then makes her laugh. She rubs Blue's ear and it doesn't take an animal empath to feel his affection as he leans up against her.

Epilogue

Sometimes, when Zev's watching a movie on the TV in the common room, he thinks about Julia. As the screen fills with fiery cars and half-naked women, he imagines her reaction and laughs, then aches, missing her. He can't see a Chihuahua in a dog food commercial without involuntarily protecting his feet. He's indebted to Julia for showing him how rich his life could be.

Ever since the prison put him in charge of cleaning assignments, the place smells of bleach rather than urine, and he's earned extra laundry privileges that allow him to keep his jumpsuit clean. Next spring, he'll work in the garden. He's been looking through catalogs and has picked out seeds for cucumbers and tomatoes and a variety of roses that, if you can believe it, are called Elizabeth Roses. So far, the prison's proven safer than the jail, with more guards and fewer mentally ill prisoners mixed in with the general population, or at least fewer that have come at Zev.

La La visits when she can. She's changed since Black died, though he can't put his finger on how.

His first day in the old, run-down prison, he knew he could pick his cell lock, which is ancient and unsophisticated. But to escape, he would have to get past closed-circuit television, a barbed-wire fence, and an alarm, so he's chosen instead to advise the corrections authority on strengthening the locks and getting rid of items prisoners might turn into picks.

He'll do his time and consult on prison security when he's released. He's too old to be climbing through windows. Tired of risking his life for a candelabra or a watch. He's ready to live a normal life. Maybe one day he'll be a grandfather. It's a long shot, but who knows. He'd like to be around for that. Anyway, that's the plan, which he's been telling La La, the warden, and anyone else who will listen. He's pretty sure he's convinced them.

Acknowledgments

My deepest gratitude to my editor, Deb Futter, and assistant editor, Randi Kramer, whose suggestions helped me strengthen and refine the book. Thanks, as well, to the entire Celadon team, who treat with such great care every book entrusted to them.

For believing in the book when it was just an idea and a few dozen rough pages, I'm indebted to my agent, Victoria Sanders, and her amazing team: Bernadette Baker-Baughman and Jessica Spivey.

I couldn't have written the book without the editorial help and advice I received from Erika Krouse and Will Allison. Early feedback from Deborah Jayne, Sarah Schantz, Hilary Zaid, Melissa Scholes Young, Joy Allen, Carrie Esposito, and Heidi Pate was invaluable. Amelia Tanttila was a trusted sounding board.

Professionals in several fields gave so generously of their time and knowledge. LeeAnn Toolan, DVM, read the manuscript and guided me with regard to veterinary medicine. Katie Thomas, DVM, answered my questions about veterinary education. Donald J. Andrews, JD, and novelist Jeanne Winer, JD, assisted me with criminal law and procedure. Stephen Devries, MD FACC, and Linda Keyes, MD, advised me with regard to the human medical issues. Sky Mignery helped me find answers to questions about emergency responses. Any mistakes in these areas are entirely my own.

To my sisters, Beth, Victoria, and Miriam, thank you for your friendship and love. To the animals who have traveled alongside me—Tilly, Chance, Molly, Flora, Arie, and Rosie—my life is immensely richer because of you. We found each other thanks to the dedicated people who staff humane societies.

I don't know where I would be without the custodian of my heart, my husband, Steve. We just celebrated our tenth anniversary, and, as he likes to say, "No one said it wouldn't last."

CELADON
BOOKS
NEW YORK

Founded in 2017, Celadon Books, a division of
Macmillan Publishers, publishes a highly curated list
of twenty to twenty-five new titles a year. The list of
both fiction and nonfiction is eclectic and focuses
on publishing commercial and literary books and
discovering and nurturing talent.